Five Alarm Love

Five Alarm Love

Yukon Valley, Alaska Hospital Novel

Jillian David

TULE

Dedication

To my Gordy.

Chapter One

EMT LOUISE WRIGHT and her work partner, paramedic Maverick Steen, sipped on coffee Monday morning in the Three Bears Alaska grocery, convenience, hardware, and clothing store. As the only source of supplies for hundreds of miles, this place had it all.

The most critical item? Freshly brewed coffee.

The morning's steaming drink cut the late August chill. Fall began early in Yukon Valley, Alaska, with cool mornings and warmish days. It was supposed to be sunny and in the sixties today. She'd likely ditch her light EMS jacket by afternoon.

Mav chatted with their friend Tulimak Sampson, who worked the deli counter today. The two exchanged player statistics and debated the chances of the Seahawks going to the Super Bowl. Same conversation every year. Pretty much, same result.

She leaned against the cured meats display. Tuli rested his forearms on the counter while he talked. His short-sleeved Three Bears uniform strained over the thick muscles of his arms. He had let his dark hair grow longer over the summer, and now a wave of it covered one black eyebrow until he pushed it back off his forehead, revealing a twinkle in his brown eyes. His light tan skin, courtesy of an Athabascan heritage, had a much healthier color than last spring when he had nearly lost his leg—and his life. He caught her staring and winked.

Warmth in her chest grew. It was certainly due to her coffee.

Tuli was her closest childhood friend. He had always been there as she went through school and life. From his central location at the deli, he eventually heard everything about every person in Yukon Valley. He was never bashful about talking with anyone ... and helping to spread rumors. Surprising how he had never said a word about her breakup with Ryan West last fall.

Truth be told, there was nothing left for Tuli or anyone else to say, because Ryan had broadcast his side of the story to anyone who would listen, both in person and online.

Didn't matter if Ryan's side of the story was true. Lou's personal life had been on display, whether she liked it or not. Now the greater Yukon Valley area population knew how she was a frozen fish in bed and didn't provide Ryan enough support in their relationship.

Lou's need for privacy was no match for Ryan's big mouth.

"You and Doc getting along?" Tuli asked, as he wiped down the deli counter.

Speaking of a big mouth...

Mav's broad grin made his answer redundant. "Best thing that's ever happened to me."

"What about us?" Tuli pressed his hand to his sternum.

"We've been friends for years."

"That's different." He laughed and glanced at his phone.

The lock screen was a picture of Lee hugging one of Mav's sled dogs.

Dr. Lee Tipton was a new doctor at Yukon Valley Hospital. She had only been here since January but already had made an impact in Mav's life and in the community. She had spoiled the plans of a speculator who wanted access to a vein of gold and other rare earth minerals on Athabascan corporation land as well as private citizens' properties. Now the town and village worked together to manage the access rights, respecting the land and the people.

Along the way, Mav had fallen totally in love with her, and from all appearances, the feeling was mutual.

Lee and Mav were perfect together. A great team. Lucky.

Lou stared at her drink, thoughts muddy, like the milk in the coffee. Up until last fall, she had also been heading in the general direction of a committed relationship. However, uncertainty about her future and a sense of something just not being right had been enough to make her take a step back. Thank God. Ryan went from cuddly guy to growling brown bear in the blink of an eye.

Disagreeing with someone—anyone—had taken all of her courage. She never rocked any proverbial boat, always went along with the flow. Never made waves.

Breaking up with Ryan? Talk about a big wave.

Next thing she knew, her privacy was gone, thanks to Ryan and his inability to shut the hell up.

Everywhere she went, Lou sensed the stares and the

whispers. Sure, she might be imagining things, but the damage was done. She had been intensely private before. Nowadays, she walked around every day feeling exposed and hated every minute of it.

That failed relationship with Ryan had gotten her thinking about her promise to Tuli those many years ago. A promise between children, but one she had never forgotten.

Tuli. Her always-present option for having a family. For being a mom and dad together.

But dating? No thanks. She had no stomach for that part of the process.

Her chest wall pinched, and she rubbed at it.

Promises didn't matter. Not now. Until she knew more about her future, there would be no other people in it, and that included Tuli.

She sighed and took another sip of coffee and stayed quiet while the guys talked, as per usual.

Mav leaned a hip against the register countertop. "So, Lee and I are getting along great. But did you hear the latest about Dr. Garrett and Dee?"

Tuli whipped out his ubiquitous cell phone, thumbs poised to type and likely post to his The Real Alaska page. "No! Tell me."

Lou leaned forward.

Mav said, "They're getting married next month!"

She was startled into making a comment. "Oh, congratulations to them."

Tuli looked up from the phone, narrowed his eyes at Mav. "That's right around the corner. They're moving along quickly."

"Dude," her work partner growled.

"What? It's an observation."

Reason number 491 why Lou kept her personal life and innermost thoughts and feelings locked down tight—Tuli's *observations*, which he shared out loud and online with reckless abandon. There wasn't a thought in his head that didn't shoot directly out of his mouth.

Mav nodded. "I think they realized how much time they had lost over the years and decided not to delay being together any longer." If he tipped his head toward Lou, she pretended not to notice. "They're adults. Their timeframe works for them. They are going into this with their hearts and their eyes wide open."

With a wise nod, Tuli said, "Makes sense." His gaze slid past Lou, then a broad smile creased his face. "The biggest question is, am I invited? And can I use the wedding for The Real Alaska online content?"

"The invitation list isn't up to me, but I imagine everyone in town will be there. Most folks seem to ignore RSVPs and just show up for these things." He pointed a finger. "You'd better clear any social media plans with Dee first. You do not want to get on her bad side. I tried to argue for downgrading my suit to hiking pants and a flannel shirt. That conversation went about as well as you'd expect."

"I bet." Tuli grinned. "Boy, oh boy, I can't wait to see you in a penguin suit."

Lou smiled as well. The town loved a good wedding event, and this one might take the focus off of her social failure. At least it would give people something else to talk about until their collective memory ran out.

"Hey, at least I won't have to scramble for a date." Mav stopped, clamping his mouth firmly shut. The silence was punctuated only by the tiny squeak of a grocery cart wheel coming from somewhere near the front register.

Lou's face burned as she studied the contents of her coffee mug.

"My bad," Mav began.

Tuli cleared his throat. "Say, Lou, any interest—"

Her phone buzzed with a notification, and she glanced at the screen. She froze. Time stopped. The email she had been waiting for popped up.

Her heart thudded, and she held up a hand. "Excuse me for a minute."

"Everything okay?" Mav asked.

"Yes," she murmured as she walked out of the deli and over to fishing supplies on the far side of the store.

No customers in sight. Ducking behind a rack of waders, she set her coffee cup on the floor and opened the email. As the message from Gensight loaded, she wiped her palms on her EMS uniform pants leg.

Since last fall, when she and Ryan had seriously discussed starting a family, she had wanted this information to help make those kinds of life decisions.

Too bad the decision was moot. No more Ryan.

Actually, no. Not too bad. Good riddance to him and close call for her.

Now Lou really wanted to know the answer. The information could impact everything in the rest of her life.

Dating or no dating.

Kids or no kids.

Career or family.

She glanced toward the deli.

A past promise turned into a future partnership. Or nothing.

She swallowed against a dry, hard lump in her throat and tried to slow her racing pulse.

Like riding a boat up the braided and twisting Yukon River, this email represented a fork in her path. So many possibilities, only she had no control over the result.

Maybe she didn't have the genetic factor her brother Gordy had.

Maybe she had plenty of choices available to her for when it came time to start a family.

What if her plan B was still an option?

After a deep breath, she opened the email, which contained a few unsatisfying boilerplate lines of text informing her that the test results were not in the email but in the attached document.

Muttering, Lou clicked on the PDF and waited for the download. Yukon Valley had internet coverage supplied through a few cell towers, and Three Bears had Wi-Fi, but internet speeds weren't quick by any stretch of the imagination. The status bar slowly filled in. *Come on. Come on.*

The report popped up, and she enlarged it and scrolled up and down, squinting at the small type. So many words. There. She found the section labeled RESULTS.

Chapter Two

"WHAT WAS THAT all about?" Tuli asked in a low voice.

He craned his neck to watch Lou walk away.

"No idea."

"She been acting okay? Is it something at home? Are things all right?" He and Lou had been friends for years, yet he didn't know the answers to these questions.

Despite having known her since they were babies, Tuli had never seen her look that ... stunned? Scared? Terrified? It was hard to describe the stark, ashen expression on her face, but it drove the wind right out of him. Tuli would fight whatever demon made her feel that way.

Friends helping friends, right?

"As far as I know, she's fine and family is fine." Mav took a sip of coffee. "You know Lou. She keeps her thoughts and opinions to herself."

"Yeah, but you two are partners." Tuli paused and typed her name into the search bar on his phone.

Nothing. No news. No mention of her on any social media sites, which kind of made sense. As far as he knew, she didn't do any social media.

"For most of the shifts, we work together. But we do

rotate our schedules."

Tuli huffed. "You are like her work husband."

Mav scowled. "Man, that's weird. She's more like my little sister."

"Okay, your work *sibling*."

"That's better."

Tuli tapped the counter. "So?"

"Nothing. She's been her usual quiet self."

"Don't you ask how she's doing?"

Mav ran a hand through his unruly hair. "Dude. Yes. At the beginning of every shift, I say, 'How's it going?' and she says, 'Just fine, thanks,' and I say, 'That's great.' Then we get to work. That's it. I don't ask probing questions. It's not my job. I might be in charge of Yukon Valley EMS, but I'm not everyone's counselor and confidante unless they expressly ask for that service."

Tuli peered out toward sporting goods but didn't see the top of Lou's head. "You could try harder."

Mav set down the coffee cup on the counter. "Or you could try harder."

"First of all, you're leaving a wet ring on my glass." He brandished the cleaning cloth at Mav until he removed the offending beverage. "Second of all"—Tuli wiped away the ring and prints—"it's complicated." Only he knew why.

Tuli didn't have enough to offer someone like Lou. Not yet anyway. He had to raise his stock price in the present to make up for what he lacked from his past. He wanted to be enough to provide what she needed.

However, accomplishing that task required that Lou tell

him—or anyone—what she needed. He slung the cloth over his shoulder.

"Since when do you hide details about your personal life?" Mav snorted and shook his head. "Never mind. My opinion? It took you long enough to start looking in her direction."

"Huh." His friend was wrong about the hiding part and the looking in Lou's direction part, but damned if Tuli would mention it. "I had a lot of things I needed to focus on lately."

"Like getting your best angle for the website?"

"It's a social media page, and yes, angles are an important part of content creation. What's more important is the content creator, aka, me." He smiled and fake-batted his eyes. "But no, I meant the accident last spring."

"That's fair. It did slow you down for a few months."

His friend had no idea the extent of the injury. No one did. Tuli needed to be whole before he moved in Lou's direction. He needed to make up for the broken pieces.

So, for now, Tuli pretended, like he always did. "It took a while to get back on track after the injury. I know that I look like a specimen now, but it took a lot of work to get this ripped." He needed to compensate with muscle and money for what he no longer had. What he never had.

"You're such a humble guy."

Tuli fake buffed his nails on his aproned chest. "I'm told humility is my greatest quality. Makes me more photogenic."

Mav groaned. "Man, you're pretty wrapped up in this Real Alaska page stuff."

"Up to a hundred thousand followers and growing."

"Is that good?"

"Heck yeah, it's good." He stared at the ceiling for a second. "Not as good as sports figure or music star numbers, but good enough to become monetized." The increase in followers had been a recent development, thanks to his spring video documenting the arrest of that crooked speculator. That one video bounced Tuli from ten thousand up near fifty thousand, and his account continued growing in the months since then.

"Huh?"

"Now that I have a large audience, brands pay me to mention their stuff in a post, and I get bonuses for clips that perform well."

"What if you don't like the brand? Or their stuff?"

"Then I don't have to post about it or accept their money."

"Mr. Big Time. You must be rolling in money."

"Not yet but hopefully soon. I want to make this my primary income stream or at least heavily supplement the fire chief job. I'm leveraging the account to bring attention to this area and our home." He also wanted to prove his value and erase his past.

Mav upended the cup with one last sip, walked around, and threw the cup in the trash can behind the deli counter. "Well, your site really helped me and my sister, getting the word out about our lodge. All of your followers amplifying the information made a difference. Did I tell you that we're nearly booked for every available weekend through the end of the year?"

"That's great."

"I should pay you for more posts like that."

"For friends and family, I'll boost for free. It was fun to get back at that nasty speculator who tried to sue you out of house and home. Justice was delicious."

"That was pretty awesome. Then Lee pretty much KO'd the guy by using the medical record against him, which was also satisfying."

"Yep."

Mav peered down the aisle and Tuli followed suit. "No Lou yet. Must be working on something."

"Hope everything's okay."

His friend crossed his arms. "I'm sure it is." He paused. "So, now that you're healed up from your accident, you're getting money out of your page, and you're living the dream here at the deli, what's holding you back from talking with Lou?"

Eighteen years ago

TULIMAK SAMPSON DASHED out the back door of the Yukon Valley Elementary school to recess. Freedom!

Man, he hated math, but he sure was going to add up a high score in kickball today.

He couldn't wait. The cool September breeze coming off of the nearby Yukon River pushed him to run faster and warm up before kickball domination happened. He didn't even need a jacket today. Fewer layers meant he would play even better.

The shouts and happy chatter of his third-grade class-mates followed him as he headed for the field. The grass was still mostly green. Ground was dry. Good. He'd be quicker around the plastic-lid bases. Conditions would never be as perfect as this fall day.

It was time to steal bases and take names. He stood in the middle of the field, waiting for the other kids to gather in front of him so they could pick teams.

Off to the side of the field, several third-grade girls clumped together like gossiping aunties. He strained to hear what they were saying. One blonde girl, Zelda, pointed at him, and he puffed out his chest.

For as much as Tuli liked kickball, he *loved* being no-ticed. Loved being the topic of excited conversations. Grandma Ruth always shook her head and made a *tsk* noise when he discussed his current popularity and his future plans to harness that star power. One day, people would listen to what he said.

People would forget all about how he didn't have parents attending the school holiday program or watching his baseball games.

They would forget that he was poor.

No. Tuli was going to be famous and popular.

But for now? Kickball!

Another giggle came from the clump of girls. He couldn't hear the whispered words, only the *esses* of their hissed conversation.

Whatever. He could put together a team without them. He didn't need to know what they were saying about him.

He glanced over again. What *were* they saying?

Grandma kept quiet about how Tuli had come to live with her, but Yukon Valley was a small community. People knew about his parents' issues with drugs and alcohol. There hadn't been enough time for everyone to forget.

Tuli sure hadn't forgotten. He rubbed his wrist, reliving the memory of the fracture thanks to his dad's alcohol and anger, only a few years ago. Right before his dad died.

He shook his head and stood straight, hands on his hips. Grandma always told him to project the image of the person he wanted people to see. She said that if people were talking, he should assume they were saying good things. If he heard bad things, then he should act like their words were water and he was a duck. The words would slide right off his back.

Image was everything.

Attitude was everything, even if he didn't feel confident on the inside.

Time was wasting, people. Recess was only forty-five minutes long.

"Come on, guys. Let's go."

The older kids would be out soon and probably try to take over the game. The third graders needed to mark their territory right now.

As they divvied up the teams, Tuli checked the side of the field. His classmate, Louise Wright, who never got in trouble for talking out in class because she barely spoke a word, stood at the periphery of the group of girls. Her long, dark hair hid her pretty face. The girls' conversation drifted over to him, even as the kickball teams were being decided.

"Let's play house. We need two parents and some kids. I'll be the mom, obviously," the ringleader, Zelda, said, tossing her golden hair over a shoulder. Both of her parents were teachers at the school, and she acted like she owned the place. "We need a house. Here."

Lou followed the other girls as they arranged themselves under the jungle gym with assigned family roles.

Just then, another class exited the back door, with about ten students running toward the playground. Tuli squinted in the fall sunlight. Actually, those kids didn't all run. Some of them rolled in wheelchairs or used crutches. They were the special kids, and they always had extra teachers and aides helping them.

One skinny boy staggered as he stepped from cement onto the turf. Everyone knew Gordy Wright, Lou's older brother. Tuli didn't know what sort of problem he had, but he wasn't able to talk. Sometimes he pointed at a picture board to show what he wanted. That was kind of cool. Gordy always smiled and waved at people too.

Gordy paused and scanned the playground, his face lighting up in a lopsided smile when he appeared to spot Lou. He walked in his halting gait, arms spread for balance, hands flapping, in Lou's direction.

When he reached Lou, he rested his arms over her shoulders and let out a high-pitched, barking laugh that turned heads. Tuli smiled. Gordy wasn't much for words, but he sure was a happy guy. Lou patted his back as he leaned against her shoulder.

Zelda pointed toward the swings. "Gordy, go back over there with your friends."

Lou froze, and her eyes narrowed. But she didn't let go of him.

"Gordy can play house and be one of the kids," Lou offered.

That might have been the most Tuli had heard her say since school started last month.

"No. He's older than us, so he can't be one of the kids," Zelda said, closing her eyes dramatically as she made her logical proclamation. "He should go somewhere else. We're busy here."

Other girls echoed the complaint, scowling at Lou and her brother.

Even from here, Tuli spied the downturn of Gordy's mouth and his watery eyes. Hey, Tuli understood all about not being included. Lou's small, tight smile seemed to freeze in place, and her face turned red. But she kept a hand on Gordy's arm as he turned to leave.

Tuli looked from the two teams in front of him, then studied the clump of girls. Dang it. He had been looking forward to kickball all day.

"Go on. Shoo," Zelda's voice rose as she waggled her fingers.

Tuli's hands rolled into fists. "Hang on, guys. Let me go get Gordy and Lou."

Frustrated groans from his kickball teammates rumbled around him, but Tuli ignored them as he walked over to the gaggle of girls and Gordy. "Anyone wanna play kickball?"

Gordy smiled and waved, then gave a whoop and stuck two fingers in his mouth.

Lou patted her brother's arm, a faint smile on her face. "I don't think Gordy can play with his hip surgery."

"He can't do sports at all. He can't catch or walk right," one of Zelda's friends sneered.

"Yeah." Zelda crossed her arms and hiked up her nose to the sky. "If you're not gonna play family, then you two need to get out of the house."

Tuli glared. He didn't like mean kids. He knew how much it stunk to be left out. He knew how it felt to be different from other people. It wasn't Gordy's fault. The kid had medical problems and just wanted to hang out with his sister and her friends.

The kickball teams took to the field, the kids hollering at Tuli to join them. He took a half step toward the field. Then he stopped. Dang. When he looked back, Lou was murmuring to Gordy. They stood together but separate from the girls, who had all turned their backs and ignored them.

Tuli wasn't the smartest kid in school, but he knew when people were getting treated badly. *Project the image of the person you want people to see.* Loudly, Tuli said, "Forget playing house. That's dumb second-grader stuff. We're going on an adventure today. Lou, you wanna go with me?"

"With Gordy?"

"Yup. It's going to be awesome."

One of Zelda's followers stomped a foot. "I want to go on an adventure."

Another classmate nodded while Zelda hissed and pulled the girl back to her side.

Tuli grinned. "Sorry, secret club only." He squirmed in front of the snooty expressions.

It was hard standing there while his classmates judged him. But he didn't need Grandma's reminder to do the right thing.

He knew. "Yeah. We're gonna have the best adventure today. Way better than … this dumb house stuff." He copied Zelda's stuck-up expression and waggled his own fingers in the direction of the jungle gym-fake house setup. "Cool kids only."

Gordy laughed out loud, drawing a smile from Lou in response.

Tuli liked making people smile.

He really liked seeing Lou smile.

He racked his brain for something that would impress his classmates. "How about, let's play fire station? We're going to help with a big fire emergency. Gordy, for obvious reasons, you get to be the siren. Can you handle that?"

The kid obliged with an ear-blistering happy squeal and turned in an unsteady circle while flapping his hands.

Tuli winced and raised his voice over Gordy. "Lou, you and I are the firefighting team." He planted his fists on his hips. "We'll go find people to rescue, probably with the jaws of life and fire hoses. Gordy will make sure everybody knows that we're coming."

The brightness in Lou's eyes made Tuli feel kind of weird inside. Not bad weird, but in a good way. Funny in his tummy, like when a snow machine went up and over a short, steep hill.

He pointed at the trees on one side of the schoolyard and off they went, identifying the disaster and putting out the fire, complete with siren sound effects that did not stop for a second. After a few minutes of directing Lou and Gordy in spraying a fake hose with fake water at a pretend barn fire, they stopped near the slides. "That was hard work. Good job, team."

Lou murmured, "Thank you," as she hovered near her brother. Thankfully, Gordy had gotten tired of being a human fire truck siren. Wow, for a kid that couldn't talk, he had volume in all the sounds he did make.

One of Gordy's aides walked up to them. "All right, buddy, we're going back in. It's time to do stretches and have snacks."

Gordy waved and then headed back into the building.

Tuli and Lou stood next to the slide. The breeze was light and cool on his sweaty skin, a relief after running around. Hey, fake firefighting was hard work. He peered across the field to the game, in full swing, complete with shouts and cheers. He did a fake kick and scuffed his toe into the grass.

"You missed your game," Lou said. "Sorry."

"Sorry you missed playing house. Although we could play house now if you want."

"I thought you liked being a firefighter."

"I do. I'm gonna be a firefighter when I grow up. But after I fight fires all day, I will want to go home to my family." A family very different than the one he had. Grandma Ruth loved him, but it wasn't the same as having parents around.

His future would be different. It would be perfect. Two parents who never fought. A couple of kids they loved and didn't hurt ...

Lou nodded and stuck her hands in her pockets, her hair swinging forward to hide her face.

Tuli asked, "What do you want to be when you're older?"

Her face lit up, brown eyes sparkling as she glanced at him. "Help people like at the hospital. And I want to be a mother, like my mom."

"Me too!"

"You're going to be a mom?" she asked with a little smile.

"Naw, but I'll be a good dad. I'm gonna play kickball with my kids, take them to *neehoot'on*."

"Ooh, potlatch. I love the food there. Yum," she said.

He nodded. "I'll have adventures with my children. Also, I'm going to be famous!"

"Famous in Yukon Valley?" Was she really laughing at his dream?

"You'll see."

"Okay."

He scuffed his toe in the silty dirt and grass. "Say, Lou ..."

"Yes?"

"Can we be best friends?"

"You already have friends," she said.

"This would be different friends. Friends that play firefighter and friends that are going to grow up to be a mom and dad."

"I would like that." When Lou smiled, it was like seeing purple shooting star flowers pop through the last bit of snow after a long winter.

Something shifted inside of Tuli. It felt like when he rode in Grandma Ruth's old truck and she changed gears. He shoved his hands in his pockets. "Maybe one day we'll grow up to be a mom and dad together. That would be cool."

Lou stared at the ground, but her smile remained. "What if we're a mom and dad with other people?"

He paused. That made sense, but he didn't like it. "How about if we get old, and we're not mom and dad with other people, we can be a mom and dad together?"

Her face brightened up in a quick smile. "Deal."

Tuli met her hand with his and pumped the handshake twice. "Now it's official."

"It's going to be awhile before we're old."

"True." Tuli looked back over his shoulder at his friends, who waved and shouted at him. "We should go play kickball first." He grabbed Lou's arm, and they ran over to join the game.

Chapter Three

*P*ATHOGENIC BALANCED *SCL8A7* gene translocation *affecting chromosome 14.* What did that mean?

Lou frowned at the page until she saw the next section, INTERPRETATION.

"SCL8A7 gene duplication is linked to Bledsoe Syndrome as well as other related syndromes, which are known to cause epilepsy and developmental delays."

A whooshing in her brain fuzzed out the sound around her. She read it again.

Bledsoe Syndrome. Just like Gordy.

Lou studied the text in the document. "This test result demonstrates translocation of the duplicate SCL8A7 gene onto a long arm of one copy of chromosome 14 with a reciprocal deletion on the other copy of chromosome 14. In balanced gene translocations, the patient will not express phenotypic abnormalities…"

Her pulse thudded as she struggled to process the dense medical language. She paused to look up the term *phenotypic*.

Phenotypic meant how the gene made someone look or function. How the gene affected someone. She reread the note until she understood. The end result was that she wouldn't have any symptoms, and she wouldn't look different. Lou knew that. She didn't have any medical issues or physical abnormalities that she knew of.

Why couldn't the specialist instead say, *Looks and acts normal?* Did they think everyone reading these reports had a PhD in science? She blew a stray piece of hair back from her face and kept reading.

"Due to the duplicated gene found on one copy of chromosome 14 and the absence of the same gene on the other copy of chromosome 14, it is likely that 100% of offspring would have phenotypic abnormalities." Her ears rang. She blinked to clear her vision.

Phenotypic abnormalities.

Her children would function and look different.

"There is a 50% chance that offspring would have Bledsoe Syndrome due to the presence of duplicated SCL8A7 genetic material on one copy of chromosome 14. There is a 50% chance that offspring would have other abnormalities due to the deletion of SCL8A7 genetic material on the other copy of chromosome 14."

The fourteenth chromosome. Gordy had the SCL8A7 gene duplication on chromosome 14. The gene for Bledsoe Syndrome had only recently been discovered. She had seen Gordy's updated genetic report. Updated, because genetic science was constantly evolving, and the tests from fifteen years ago hadn't detected any abnormal chromosomes.

That was then. The time when her future held unlimited possibilities.

She stared at the screen.

Other abnormalities. Lou was no genetics doctor, but she

understood that *other abnormalities* could include a range of symptoms—anything from minor health issues to devastating symptoms.

Her choices for having a child were 50 percent chance of other abnormalities or 50 percent chance of Bledsoe Syndrome.

But 100 percent not-normal genetic material.

She took a deep breath and read it again.

A balanced gene translocation. She concentrated on the words that kept blurring in front of her. Gordy had one normal chromosome 14 and an extra copy of the SCL8A7 gene on the other chromosome 14. That net extra genetic material caused the syndrome.

Lou didn't have net extra genetic material because it was missing in the other chromosome. Mother Nature's dumb luck or by design? Who knew?

Balanced translocation. Nothing about Lou felt balanced right now as the ground under her feet tilted.

All of a sudden, her future crystallized like water hitting a freezing pane of glass.

Lou pressed a hand to her mouth. Even though Gordy was four years older than Lou, many of her earliest memories were of him and his care. Gordy having seizures. Recovering from surgeries on various joints. How many times had she gone with Mom or Dad when Gordy needed to be rushed to the ER? Visiting him in the hospital. The whole family traveling to Fairbanks for neurologist appointments. Bottles of medications lined up on the kitchen counter with paper charts of when to give each drug. Physical therapy sessions.

She remembered how they cheered when he finally reached his delayed milestones. That time he walked all the way up their gravel driveway after getting off the small school bus when she was four years old and he was eight. His big, beautiful smile. His big, beautiful laugh.

They shared silence together, sitting in front of the living room fireplace, watching *Sesame Street*. Not talking, because he couldn't. They simply existed in the same space.

Yet Gordy had been a litmus test for her friends and relationships.

Not everyone passed the test.

Then there was Tuli. Always Tuli. From the time they were in kindergarten together, he'd included Gordy. Even when it was obvious that Tuli didn't understand what was wrong with Gordy, he'd just accepted her brother and showed everyone around them how to accept him.

Tuli. An invisible fist tightened inside of her as more memories buffeted her like wind-driven ice.

Tuli and Lou playing firefighter. Playing house. Talking about her dream of being a mom and his dream of being a dad. Joking about how they could be parents together.

Her chest ached like it was being crushed by a glacier. When she swallowed, dry silt choked her.

Truth be told, she had been waiting to see if he remembered their childhood promises.

It didn't matter now.

This one email took her up a different tributary on the river of her life. It took her away from hope and onto a different path.

What if…

What if she had a child? What if she took the chance?

Lou loved her brother. But his life had been difficult and had become more so as his condition progressed. The medical challenges continued to grow for him. He wasn't going to get better.

She loved him, but she couldn't knowingly bring another Gordy into this world.

Of course, there were other options for being a parent, like adoption or egg donation. But that wasn't what she had envisioned for herself. A partner might not want that, either.

Her dreams had crumbled to ash in her email inbox.

Swiping the pads of her fingers to dry her eyes, she took a few big breaths and did a full body shake to try to dislodge the grief. How would she go through the rest of her day acting like nothing was wrong? Her stomach knotted. Oh God, she had to watch her friends get married. Deirdre and Calvin would likely be followed by Mav and Lee. There were discussions about starting families. She had to be happy for them, knowing that would never be her future.

Later. She'd deal with all of this later. Unpackage the whole mess later.

After pacing between the fishing nets and the hunting vests, she took several more deep gulps of air and got a grip on herself. Lou had to help people today. She had a job to do. She would focus on that concrete task.

Maybe this was the kick in the pants she needed to start work on attaining her paramedic license. If she couldn't heal herself, at least she could learn to better heal other people.

No relationship plan B.

Time to move forward with her career. Lou nodded to herself.

Life decision made.

She rubbed her aching chest.

After dropping her cold coffee off at a trash can behind the rod and reel counter, she strolled back to the deli, hands in her pockets, trying to act casual. The guys were debating defensive line statistics.

Both men paused.

"You okay?" Tuli asked. "You look like you saw a ghost."

Mav studied her until sweat prickled her chest.

She rolled her hands into fists inside of her pockets until they shook. No way would she break in front of them. Not here. Not now. Not ever.

"Just fine." She steadied her shaky voice. "Mav, I think we need to go get that patient from the hospital for the discharge transport home."

Tuli's mouth dropped half open, and he took a breath.

Please don't say a word.

Mav paused for another two seconds, frowned, then nodded too enthusiastically. "Sure, Lou. We'll go do that run."

Tuli stammered, "L-let me know if—"

"If what?" Lou snapped.

Both guys' eyebrows shot up.

There was nothing he could do. Nothing anyone could do. No future. She needed to reconcile herself to that fact.

Lou helped finish the conversation. "Have a good day." She turned on her heel and headed toward the rig, Mav trailing behind her.

Chapter Four

F ALL IN YUKON Valley had been drier than normal, and Tuli had been using The Real Alaska page to promote fire safety awareness.

Thick, sharp smoke from the far end of town scented the air. The fire's glow was visible against the early evening sky this first Saturday of September. Tuli shook his head. Public service announcements only went so far when burn piles and teenagers were involved. Dispatch called it in as a structure fire, possibly started by high schoolers. Great.

Tuli catalogued protocols and mourned the fact that he couldn't livestream this moment as he ran into the station to gear up. Video from a true callout to a fire emergency would get millions of views and reinforce his message about fire safety.

Maybe he could do a clip afterward in his turnout gear. Viewers liked to see first responders dressed for action. He could frame the shot with smoke behind him. Tuli was still considering camera angles when he got out of his truck.

Only one other vehicle was parked outside the station. Damn it. A small fire department in rural Alaska meant that most firefighters worked other jobs. Heck, even as the fire chief, he even worked part-time at Three Bears. A small crew and infrequent callouts meant that people had to drop everything to help when they could. Labor Day weekend also meant vacations for many people in town, including several members of his already-sparse team.

He would have to make do with whatever help was available.

Tuli raced into the station and opened the locker, struggling to balance as he donned his turnout gear. Foot placement took extra concentration for that stupid right leg, but he'd damn well make it work. How could a leg be both numb and painful? He dropped a fist on his quad, as if willing it to work.

"Ready to go, Chief?" the new hire, Hunter Wright, piped up as he buckled his hat over his dark hair. All swagger and a cleft chin, that guy. Lou's first cousin on her dad's side, Hunter had leveraged his connections to get hired on at the fire department. Tuli mentally grimaced. On the one hand, Tuli needed the help, and it was his job as fire chief to train the guy.

On the other hand … Geez.

Hunter was only a year younger than Tuli, but his fitness and confidence made Tuli look like a scrawny, stammering nerd. And that was saying something, because Tuli was a specimen. A hundred thousand followers weren't wrong.

He glanced over at Hunter. Did the noob actually flex, or was it Tuli's imagination?

Or something else? Hunter was strong as an ox and had two perfectly functional legs. #Jealous. Which might be the real issue.

He managed to keep from glaring. Barely. Hunter's buddy-buddy attitude played well with bystanders, swooning ladies, and groups of fawning preschoolers, but right beneath that Hey-bro demeanor was an undercurrent of razor-sharp competitiveness.

Heck, this guy had been Ryan West's wingman for years. Ryan and Lou had been dating until last fall. Then suddenly, they weren't dating. Ryan had a big mouth when it came to Lou, and there were a couple times Tuli had considered filling that mouth with some knuckles. Good riddance.

"Pull the rig out," Tuli said.

Hunter jumped up into the driver's seat like gravity wasn't a problem, but Tuli took precious seconds to manually lift his damned right leg so he could get his foot into the boot. Hip flexion hadn't completely returned, along with full sensation. All due to the femoral nerve damage from the snow machine accident last spring.

That accident might not have been an accident. One second Tuli was on the machine, and the next he was impaled by a backward-facing branch whittled sharp and set at the perfect height. Lieutenant Kate and the state trooper investigation team hadn't been able to conclude that it was intentional.

Sure felt intentional as Tuli was bleeding out in the snow.

Now he was left with loss of function that he hid from the world. Funny how he had never wanted to post clips from those early rehab visits. Now his recovery clips were fifteen seconds of nothing-to-see-here and a big smile as he worked out on gym equipment.

He hoped that his physical function would catch up with his attitude.

All Tuli had wanted to do since childhood was become a firefighter. He had been so focused on his goal of returning to work and retaining his position as town's fire chief that he bluffed his way through the doctor's appointment to get clearance for active duty.

Tuli grabbed the handle of the passenger door and stepped up, relying on the upper body strength he had built up over the past several months to compensate. He had banked on not having to test the leg quite so soon. Maybe he wouldn't have to bend and lift much.

"Let's go," he motioned.

"Think EMS will be there?" Hunter flipped on the siren and turned onto the two-lane state highway.

"Sure. How come?" Tuli knew why but dreaded the answer.

Somehow, the bro flexed in full turnout gear while driving. If Tuli wasn't baseline irritated by the dude's attitude, he would have been impressed.

Hunter grinned. "Hanging out with my cousin, showing her my firefighting skills."

"Really?"

"No. You figured out my endgame." Somehow, he turned up the wattage even more on his broad smile. "I want to rescue someone cute and be a hero. Get on TV."

It took all of Tuli's willpower not to tell the guy to cram it up his fire hydrant. As chief, Tuli had to maintain control and some level of professionalism.

As a normal dude in normal society, he wanted to drop a ladder on Hunter. But he had to tread cautiously with Lou's cousin.

Tuli wasn't confident that Hunter had her best interests at heart.

Heck, who was he kidding? Hunter had *Hunter's* best interests at heart.

Who had Lou's best interests?

Did Tuli want to steer her toward a guy who did? A guy who would be right for her and who could provide what she needed? Tuli's palms sweated in the gloves. At one point he had been ready to try to be that guy.

That was then.

Instead of responding to Hunter's dumb comment, he held up a hand to shut the guy up while working the satellite phone. No radio, because so much of their work was in remote locations. Dispatch relayed additional details.

"Damn it." He put the phone back in the holder.

"What?" Hunter asked, peering through the windshield as the few vehicles pulled over on the highway to let them pass.

"Single dwelling. Two family members not yet accounted for."

For all his swagger, trainee Hunter knew when to shut his mouth, grip the wheel, and press the accelerator. He also seemed to know where to go without directions. Made sense. After all, he'd lived in Yukon Valley much of his life up until he'd left for Seattle for the past several years. He'd just returned a year ago and lived at his dad's place in the village.

Tuli knew everyone's history. #Smalltown.

They turned off the highway onto a gravel-and-dirt road that led to the dwelling. The Beck family had been in Yukon Valley for three generations. They worked hard and were solid folks. Now they needed Tuli's help.

The fire engine bumped and bounced under him as it climbed the hill to the property. Smoke billowed up from what he assumed was the structure. Or what was left of it. In the side mirror of the firetruck, additional flashing lights spun behind him. Likely EMS and state trooper vehicles.

His chest tightened as they crested the low hill. He hadn't seen Lou since their strange interaction at Three Bears earlier this week. Some casual probing comments to her friends and family when they came into the store hadn't revealed any hint of what was going on with Lou. Even know-it-all Hunter had no clue.

Tuli had almost asked her out last week. Almost felt like he had finally compensated for his injury to where he was whole enough. Almost believed that he could bring enough to the table to be the quality guy Lou deserved. All his life, he had worked to be good enough before moving forward with that childhood promise to Lou.

But he hadn't made his move.

Time was ticking if he wanted to ask her to Calvin and Deirdre's wedding. There had been no opportunity. Besides that day in the deli. Or besides picking up the phone, which was not his style. Tuli wanted the ask to be casual and friendly, worked into a natural conversation or social setting.

To leave an escape route if it didn't go well.

He scanned the scene in front of him—people running around, emergency vehicle lights. EMS. Lou might be here. Hey, nothing like fighting fires and creating social opportunities at the same time.

The sudden dip in his gut had nothing to do with the uneven gravel as they rumbled to a stop.

Time to focus on the work at hand. Hunter whistled low as they both took stock of the situation and jumped out of the truck. Or eased down with upper body strength, in Tuli's case. The night was illuminated by flames leaping from a one-story home. The entire structure would soon be engulfed.

He stumbled on the last step and glanced around. No one had seen. Hunter unrolled the hose and turned on the water, bracing as the stream surged out to hit the flames. Hissing clouds of billowing steam added to the mess in front of them.

Natalie Beck yelled and reached out as her husband, Wayne, held her back. "My daughter and dad are in there!"

Tuli's heart pounded. Priorities changed when the job went from structure salvage to saving humans. He glanced behind the rig. No other red lights and engines headed this way yet. He could still hope that some of the local fire fighters were in the area and willing to answer the call.

"Get them out of there! Please," Wayne pleaded.

One arm had the flannel sleeve burned off. Pink, raw skin glistened on his arm and hand that he cradled.

Hunter met Tuli's gaze, turned off the water, set his

respirator, and snapped his face shield down. Tuli did the same. They grabbed axes and Tuli led them up to the house, where they easily broke down the partially charred front door and turned on their flashlights.

Just like in training and drills, they communicated with hand signals and brief radio exchanges as a roaring wave of flame reached for them and the thick smoke dropped visibility. Most of the fire appeared to be centered in the kitchen and dining room area. The side wall of the house was gone.

"Hallway." Tuli indicated, and they headed toward the smoke-filled back of the house.

Hunter ran into one bedroom, and Tuli checked the other one across from it. Empty.

His heart pounded.

The hallway ended with two more doors, presumably another bedroom and the bathroom.

He kicked in the bathroom door. A semi-conscious, coughing man with soot covering his face looked up from where he sat in the empty tub, the whites of his eyes stark in the dim light. In his arms was a child who looked to be around eight or nine years old. She didn't move.

Tuli's mouth went dry as he stowed his axe.

Hunter said over the com, "I've got him. Grab her. Let's go."

For a split second, Tuli bristled as the new hire took charge. But he didn't argue the plan or the logic. His partially numb leg wasn't ready for Tuli to support himself and a full-grown adult yet. Hunter looped the man's arm around his shoulder and heaved with his legs, settling the man into a fireman's carry. Then he trundled him out of the bathroom. Tuli scooped up the limp girl and followed. *Please let her be alive*. He clutched her to his chest, trying to protect her from more smoke inhalation and flames.

His right leg protested the extra weight. As he reached the living room, he stumbled against the end of a couch that had caught fire. Damn it.

Shifting the girl into a position over his left shoulder, he grabbed the couch with his gloved hand. Hunter disappeared out the front door with the man.

One victim evacuated. One to go.

His leg shook beneath him. Sweat beaded his brow. Numbness and pain swirled together when he put weight on his foot. *Come on. Work.*

It was about ten feet to the front door.

Flames licked at the ceiling above him and roared behind him. The girl coughed once, then went still.

One step.

Another.

He could see ghostlike flashes of emergency lights throwing shadows across the flickering flame- and smoke-filled room.

On his third step, the right leg buckled, and he landed hard on his knees, the girl tumbling onto the floor.

No. Damn it.

Heat buffeted him, even through his layered gear.

He staggered to his feet and bent to pick her up. The right leg didn't hold, and he went down hard on his hip.

Timbers creaked behind him.

He glanced up and around.

The ceiling above the hallway cracked and collapsed.

Chapter Five

LOU WHIPPED HER head up at a loud snap of wood in the burning structure. Her hands were full, bandaging Wayne Beck's burned arm, but she glanced over at Mav, who met her eyes with a jaw-clenched stare of his own.

"Hunter and Tuli are in there," he said.

Her heart twisted. No emergency call was ever routine in first responders' line of work.

Tuli was Tuli.

Hunter was a relative.

"I have to help!" Wayne tried to get up from where he sat on the back of the rig.

She rested her hand on his shoulder to keep him still. "Let the firefighters do their work." Her heart squeezed as Wayne's wife, Natalie, stood at his side, tears running down her soot-covered face.

Lieutenant Kate and another trooper hovered nearby, and the trooper offered a blanket to the Becks.

Flashing lights competed with the brightness of the flames leaping out of the structure.

Lou couldn't breathe. How long had Tuli and Hunter been in there? She taped the bandage in place and walked over to the other two ambulances. Luckily, the call had come in at shift change when she and Mav were wrapping up a run to the ER. Mav and another EMS team member, Moose, took one rig to the fire. Paramedic Hilda took another rig, with one of the ER nurses, Amberlyn, who was also a former EMT. Lou had driven the recently repaired backup ambulance to the scene.

As Mav and Hilda were the trained paramedics, they would treat the most critical patients. Lou, an EMT, was assigned the less severe injuries. Even more reason for her to get her paramedic license. She studied how Hilda and Mav double-checked their airway kits and lined up meds.

"Look!" Natalie yelled and pointed.

A firefighter slowly emerged from the smoke-filled front door with a man draped over his shoulders. Was that Tuli or Hunter?

The shiny yellow helmet indicated it was Hunter.

Where was Tuli in his beat-up red fire chief's hat?

"I'll take this one," Hilda said, scraping her orange curls off her face. She and Amberlyn, along with the trooper and Lou, pushed a gurney across dirt and gravel to meet the patient. Even as Hunter lowered the man to the bed, Hilda and Amberlyn began working with a flurry of efficient movements and murmured communication. Lou helped them pull the gurney to the rig, then eased Wayne and Natalie back a few feet as Wayne Sr. received care.

The older man coughed and wheezed. His facial hair had been singed off and his lips were red and burned. With that presentation, there was a high risk of swelling in the airway and sudden airway compromise.

After securing Wayne Sr. in the ambulance, Hilda prepared for rapid-sequence intubation. Amberlyn set the IV and hovered next to Hilda with labeled syringes of meds ready to push.

Lou turned back toward the house and approached Hunter. "What's going on?" The words ended on a quaver.

Hunter's face floated behind the respirator and mask. His voice was muffled as he yelled, "Tuli's still in the house with the girl. I'm going back in."

Another whoosh of flame burst into the night with a strange engine-like rumble as he raced into the building.

Tuli was in there.

Now Hunter as well.

Lou could only watch and wait, along with everyone else.

Off to her side in the back of their rig, Hilda and Amberlyn gave medications to sedate the agitated Wayne Sr. and then medically paralyze him. Hilda quickly secured his airway.

Natalie and Wayne clung to each other as their house burned. Another siren pierced the night as a second fire truck trundled up the dirt road in the distance.

Hurry.

What if Tuli was hurt? Trapped inside the building? His leg hadn't healed. She had seen the limp and shuffle that he tried to hide. His shoulders had broadened over the past several months. Mav had mentioned the long hours he spent in the fire hall, working out in their makeshift gym, trying to overcome his injury. Even not functioning at full capacity, Tuli was still risking his life to save someone.

Damn it. Lou had avoided him for the past several days, going so far as refusing Mav's offer of Three Bears' coffee. She couldn't face Tuli and his open, welcoming smile. She couldn't face that hopeful expression that he gave only her. She couldn't face him with the knowledge that her life and her future were taking her down a path that didn't involve him.

Sure, they were great friends. Always had been.

Right about now, friendship felt like a consolation prize.

She blinked back tears from the smoke-filled air. A consolation prize that included a live, healthy Tuli would be better than the alternative.

Hurry.

Someone shouted again.

A figure appeared from the smoke with a child in his arms. Bright-yellow helmet. Hunter.

Her heart stuttered.

Where was Tuli?

Mav and Moose raced over with their gurney to receive the girl. Immediately, they began treating her. Wayne and Natalie met them as they dragged the gurney and patient to the back of the ambulance.

Hilda and Amberlyn shut the doors on their rig and peeled off into the night, lights flashing and siren blaring, headed to the hospital with Wayne Sr.

Where was Tuli?

Chapter Six

*G*ET HER OUT *of here.*

Tuli gripped the back of the unconscious girl's pajama shirt, prepared to drag her out while he crawled. Next to him, she rested, unmoving. His leg quivered, but he shoved it under him and pushed against the knee to make it work.

It held, but not when he added the child's weight.

Damn it. Tuli bunched his arms and legs underneath him. Time to crawl, then.

Appearing from the smoke at the front door, Hunter swept his flashlight beam through the haze. He knelt down with ease. "I'll take her. Can you get out on your own?" His expression was unreadable behind his respirator mask and helmet visor.

"Yes. Go." Tuli waved.

Hunter ran out with the girl. Over the roaring inferno, Tuli made out shouts of bystanders and medics. He fisted his hands on the floor. *Please Lord, don't let that child die because of my pride.*

More ominous creaks sounded above him.

Please don't let me *die because of my pride.*

Tuli's gear was good, but fireproof material didn't matter

if the entire structure buried him alive. Waves of heat buffeted him like a scorching, clawing wind.

Gripping a charred coffee table with a gloved hand, he pulled and then pushed to lever himself into a standing position. He reached down and fisted the material over his right leg, yanking the leg forward. Staggering the last few steps to the entrance, he exited the house, even as nasty pops in the deteriorating ceiling urged him to move faster.

From the porch, he looked back. The entire ceiling came down with a loud moaning, roaring crack of flame and timber. Flames chased him. Too close.

He stumbled to the front rail and hung on for a few precious seconds, shaking out his leg. Faces appeared through the smoke, and Hunter turned the fire hose again, sweeping a wet steam across Tuli.

People were watching. Tuli gritted his teeth as he navigated the single step to ground level and then concentrated on slow, steady, non-limping progress across uneven dirt and gravel to reach the engine. His thigh burned and quivered beneath him.

Two sets of ambulance crews worked on the victims. One vehicle sped off, sirens blaring.

He spied Lou's wide-eyed expression as she hovered near the open back door of a third ambulance.

"How are they?" he shouted.

Mav briefly lifted his head from the care he was providing and, with a neutral expression, waved a so-so sign.

Tuli's work was done. He hid his hobble as he joined Hunter, who aimed the hose at the house. The pressure of a thousand gallons per minute was less than the flow through a typical city water line, but it still took muscle for one person to control the nozzle.

"I'm behind you," Tuli said, bracing as he added his strength to Hunter's. He couldn't rely on his legs for stability, but his arms were plenty strong. Together, they battled the flames.

The second fire truck arrived with off-duty firefighters. Hey, everyone kept their duty phones on around here, just in case. Good timing, since Tuli's truck had run out of water. Three thousand gallons in a pumper truck and no main water line out here meant that in rural Alaska, when the truck's tank was empty, that was it. No more water.

He took off his respirator and lifted his visor, then directed the second team to hook up and keep dousing the fire. Their efforts finally knocked down the flames to the steaming, charred black remnants of what was once a home.

Their tank emptied in under five minutes as well.

Thankfully, they had extinguished most of the flames. Not much more to be done, other than ensure no secondary fires.

Hunter, his helmet now dangling from his right hand, rubbed at a smudge of ash over his cheek. "Looks like we got it."

Tuli nodded. "Good job, everyone," he said to the team.

Hunter opened his mouth like he wanted to say something, but then clamped it shut.

The two additional firefighters stowed equipment, while Hunter headed out to check other property structures.

Tuli removed his helmet, laying it on the back of the truck. He turned toward the remaining two ambulances.

Man, he hoped everyone would be all right. At least he had done his part to get the victims out of the house.

Sort of. He rubbed his leg, which was somehow both irritated and numb.

Tonight, he had been lucky, not good.

Keeping a hand on the side of the truck while he walked the length of it, he concentrated on every step. Poker-hot nerve pain shot down his leg with each stride, but at least the leg held him.

Mav was treating the girl. Tuli racked his brain until he recalled her name. Anna. Around eight years of age. She coughed and moaned behind the oxygen mask, and the top of her hair was singed, but she otherwise seemed alert and responsive. Tuli would bet money that her grandfather had borne the brunt of heat, flame, and smoke exposure to protect her.

Natalie and Wayne hovered near their daughter, their worry for her suffering written starkly on their faces. Tuli's heart clenched. What would it be to love a child that much? Swallowing against a hard lump, he pushed those thoughts away and focused on his job.

"Need any help?" he asked. As a firefighter, Tuli had basic medic skills and could assist with medical emergencies as part of his scope of work.

Mav shook his head, paused, and shot him a strange look. Then he said, "Thanks, man. We have it under control right now. You take it easy."

As Tuli headed back to the truck, he stopped at Lou's ambulance. Maybe he could find out what was going on with her lately.

"Hi, Lou."

"Tuli." She smoothed the navy EMS uniform material over her trim figure, but her warm brown gaze didn't meet his. Her long, dark hair was pulled back in a ponytail that emphasized the smooth skin of her neck.

He'd missed seeing her this week. Missed her quiet, calm, and shy smile that brightened his day. He had missed the gentle ribbing she sometimes aimed in his direction. There was always a sense of history mixed with future possibilities with Lou that got him in the feels.

Lou's brows drew together as she studied him. She had always been way too perceptive. "Everything okay?"

Tuli bore most of his weight on the left leg. "I'm good. How are you doing?" His right leg quivered. Hopefully, it wasn't noticeable.

"You sure you're good, boss?" Hunter walked over, moving easily in sixty pounds of turnout gear and holding his helmet and respirator in his arms. "Because you had some issues back there."

Gritting his teeth, Tuli said, "I had things under control."

"That was under control? Your leg gave out on you, man. You should get that checked out. There's a medic right here."

"Tuli?" Lou said, extending a hand to him.

The sour taste of shame coated his tongue, and new

sweat irritated his back. He wanted to lash out at Hunter. Deny weakness.

He wanted to appear strong, adept, and whole in front of Lou. Like someone who was worthy of her time.

He bluffed in the only way he knew how. "Naw, that was just a bad step on burnt flooring. Freak accident." He smacked his gloved hand against his leg, ignoring how the impact felt both dull and hot at the same time. "Leg's fine."

"Huh. Bad time to put the wrong foot forward." Hunter's smile slid over to Lou, but when it landed back on Tuli, it had turned into a sneer. "Hey, glad I could be there to save some lives and help a buddy out." Only *buddy* sounded like he said *loser*. Nothing about Hunter's perfect jaw and hero swagger looked like a buddy to Tuli.

"Good you were there," Tuli managed to say through a clamped jaw. He'd give credit where it was due, even if the guy irritated the piss out of him.

Lou's raised-brow expression shifted from concern to pity.

Tuli's pride deflated like a stuck balloon.

Damn it.

"How did the rest of the homestead look?" Tuli asked, steering the conversation away from his physical weaknesses.

Hunter looked toward the smoldering ruins. "Nothing else caught on fire. No evidence of foul play."

Tuli snorted. "Your job isn't evaluating for arson. The state trooper fire investigation team takes care of that."

He threw up a gloved hand. "Just giving my two cents that I didn't see any obvious materials, cans of accelerant, or anything like that."

"That's really specific."

Hunter's voice came out like a whip. "Sue me for going the extra mile." He opened his mouth, closed it, and then huffed. "Forget it." After another beat, Hunter turned on the charm. "Hi, Louise. Fancy meeting you here. Need help with your gear?"

Lou ducked her head, but not before Tuli spied a shy smile. He grimaced. They might be cousins, but, nevertheless, a tight twinge of jealousy twisted in Tuli's chest.

She zipped up her kit. "I'm okay, thanks," she murmured, even as Hunter grabbed it and lifted it into the back of the ambulance with an abundance of chest puffing and assistance theater, in Tuli's opinion.

"No problem," Hunter said. "You work hard. I can do my part to care for the carers."

Okay, that was the biggest line of BS Tuli had ever heard.

Also, he was mad because he hadn't come up with it himself.

She paused, looked around, and finally said, "Um, you too."

Hard to tell in the low light, but if he knew Lou, she was blushing at the attention. Didn't matter that Hunter was her first cousin. Tuli knew how much she disliked being in any spotlight.

Hated being noticed. Probably hated when people realized she was pretty.

Hell, she *was* pretty—

He peered at her smooth skin, high cheekbones, and faint smile.

Tuli rocked back on his heels.

No, Lou wasn't pretty. She was beautiful.

Tuli wanted to lean into her space as she loaded her equipment. Damn it, he had no claim to Lou. Not like that, anyway.

Was that a true feeling or jealousy talking? Not having two working legs had done a number on Tuli's already shaky self-confidence, more than he cared to admit.

"Tell Uncle Steve that I'll call about a day to go fishing soon," Hunter said, clearly trying to claim all of her attention.

Lou pulled the ambulance keys out of her pocket. "How has it been, being back in Yukon Valley?"

"Those years away were tough." He made a face like he had eaten a tart salmonberry. "Dad's glad I'm in town, so I guess that's something. Sounds like your dad and mom are happy I'm back too." He took a few steps toward the driver's side door and leaned against the rig. "For many reasons, it's so nice being home and helping people."

None of what he said sounded remotely sincere.

If Tuli rolled his eyes any harder, he'd be looking at his own butt.

If Hunter would kindly go away, Tuli could talk with Lou in private. He opened his mouth to tell the guy to check that the hose was properly stowed.

Hunter said, "I'd love to catch up sometime. Hear what's been going on with the village and in town."

On the one hand, they were cousins, so of course they had some catching up to do. They were family.

On the other hand, warm, slimy shame that Hunter had managed to do the thing Tuli hadn't been able to washed over him. Cousin or no cousin, Hunter had platonically asked Lou out. Of course, not for a date. But still, her time was a commodity that Tuli cherished. She didn't need to waste it on Hunter. A rumble formed in the back of Tuli's throat.

Lou's eyes went wide, and she looked around, catching Tuli's gaze. Oh crap. He knew that expression. She had read the room, so to speak, and had taken up her usual position as the peacemaker.

She stammered, "Um … I'm not really up to, uh, my schedule is not good…"

Tuli connected the dots. Figured out the hesitation. The bozo she had dated last year was Hunter's BFF. Hell of a conflict of interest, if you asked him. Didn't matter that Lou's and Hunter's dads were brothers.

Hunter rested a gloved hand on the side of the ambulance.

He intoned, "This is the part where you let me know your schedule." She opened her mouth, but no sound came out, and Hunter continued, louder, "Or I could always call 911 and have dispatch broadcast my request to the local EMS team." He laughed but seemed unaware that literally no one around him was laughing with him.

Lou ducked her head, but Tuli caught how her hand was shaking as she opened the ambulance door.

Stop it, man. She hates making a scene. Hates being the center of any attention. Nearly twenty years of friendship had taught Tuli that much.

"Yo, Hunter, we have some work to do," he said, rolling his hands into hard fists to provide an outlet for his anger.

How had this tool disrupted Tuli's plans to ask Lou out?

"In a sec, boss." Hunter ignored the chain of command and leaned down toward Lou, his physically imposing size obvious next to her slight frame. "How about something fun, like hanging out as friends? Not just cousins. We were friends before all that junk with Ryan, right?"

Lou murmured, "Sort of. We're related, at least."

"Friends. Cousins. Like old times." This guy with zero situational awareness wasn't taking no for an answer.

Lou didn't have an argumentative bone in her body. "I guess…"

Hunter looked around, waggling his eyebrows at Tuli and grinning like he'd bagged the season's biggest caribou. Also, the guy bared way too many teeth. "Good. We'll catch up later this week, Louise."

"It's Lou," Tuli ground out.

With a shrug, Hunter pushed off and walked over to the other firefighters and law enforcement personnel, slapping them on their backs and laughing too loudly.

Tuli fought to keep his jaw from dropping.

This idiot. Yukking it up in front of him. With Lou.

Tuli could have stepped in and diverted the attention.

Instead, he, Tuli, social media influencer, total specimen,

and Yukon Valley fire chief, had stood there like a limp fire hose.

Lou looked up with a forehead-wrinkling, perplexed, and sheepish expression.

Recovering from the blow to his ego, he focused on her. "You okay with that, Lou? I mean, he's family and all, but..." Didn't take a rocket scientist to know how much Hunter's friendship with Ryan must have felt like a betrayal.

For a split second, he had wanted to cram his fist through Hunter's face. Tuli wasn't a violent guy, but for the right reason, he would make an exception.

Lou shrugged. "Maybe it'll be fun catching up again. Old times and all." Every word fell like a dagger into his chest. "It's okay."

"If it's not, you can always call me. I'll come up with an excuse for you to leave."

That relieved smile lit up the night. He could survive for weeks on a genuine smile from Lou. "I know," she said.

He wanted to say more.

What else was there? He'd been outmaneuvered by the Brad Pitt of the Yukon Valley Fire Department. The guy was her first cousin, but somehow, he'd still scooped Tuli right in front of him.

It was Tuli's own fault. His own insecurities held him back, and he knew it.

Problem was, he couldn't snap his fingers and make his family history go away. He couldn't blink his eyes and have two normal legs and a million dollars. And Tuli needed all of those things sorted out before he felt that he could be the man that a quality person like Lou deserved.

When he didn't say anything more, Lou shook her head, got in the ambulance and, with a small wave, drove off.

He turned back to his truck, stumbling on the gravel.

Chapter Seven

THE FOLLOWING DAY, Lou sat on the banks of the Yukon River, her fishing line in the water next to Hunter's, counting down the minutes before this meetup was over. The early September afternoon warmth still lingered, with temperatures in the sixties, but at least mosquito season had ended. No way would she be in short sleeves without DEET if the bugs were swarming.

Hunter stood up tall to recast his line with a dramatic flip of his arm and a big exhale, then sat back down with a satisfied nod.

She suppressed a sigh, then glanced over to make sure he hadn't noticed.

Objectively, her cousin Hunter was a nice enough guy who'd been a star football player when he was a grade behind her in high school. He might be related to her and a bit of a mess, but he was a persistent mess who, for some reason, wanted to catch up. She hated having to say no to anyone. Hated conflict.

This situation was extra icky. Hunter was also Ryan's friend and had returned to town last year, right in time for the end of her relationship. Which, fine, that didn't make Hunter the culprit, but he did carry some blame for the damage to her reputation, at least by association with her ex. How much did he know about her failed relationship details? Seemed like the whole town knew way too much after Ryan got finished blabbing. At least Ryan had left for work in Fairbanks, and she didn't have to see him around town.

To think she had once liked him. Before she figured out what a jerk he was.

Stop it. Not all men were like her ex.

An image of a certain guy with a shock of dark, thick hair and a playful smirk came to mind. She chuckled to herself. Then there were guys like Tuli who couldn't navigate their way through a basic social situation, but that didn't make them bad.

"You're smiling. Great day, huh?" Hunter said.

Lou's face warmed. "Mm-hmm."

"I should bring your dad out here to cast a line or two. Spend some time with him. Pal around more."

Okay, weird. First of all, Lou was acutely aware that she wasn't the son her dad had always wanted, and neither was Gordy. Hey, life happened.

But Hunter's persistent noodling in to try to be the complete package of a son her dad never had? Weird, considering he lived with his father, her Uncle Keith.

He touched her wrist and pointed out an eagle swooping to snag a fish snack from the river. The action was—she struggled for a good word—friendly. Friendly was nice, right?

"I'm glad we're out here, Louise," he said. "It's been a while since we talked."

Before Ryan.

And she preferred being called Lou. She'd mentioned it how many times before? She gave a mental shrug. Not worth the conflict to bring it up again.

Maybe her issue was that she hadn't been prepared for her flaky, absentee cousin to suddenly take an interest in her life and their family.

She continued to struggle with the concept of family and legacy and what it all meant, especially given that she still was processing the genetic test result and how it would affect her life. At some point, she'd have to inform not only her parents, but Hunter too.

His future could be impacted by shared genes.

She stared at his familiar, friendly face and opened her mouth to say something. Then closed it.

She wasn't prepared to tell him this yet.

Lou glanced at his model-like face. There was a hint of familiarity in his features, like echoes of Gordy. Or what Gordy might have looked like in a different life. She surreptitiously rubbed her damp palms on her cargo pants, then pushed her long hair behind her shoulders.

"This park is one of my favorite spots from childhood. Dad and I came out here a lot," she said honestly.

She withheld sharing the memories about also hanging out here with Tuli or bringing Gordy to the accessible fishing platform on a regular basis. Seemed too heavy and complicated to insert those topics into the conversation.

They fell silent again. Around them, high delicate chirps of what sounded like a bluebird or sparrow meshed with the sound of rushing water. There was a sudden rustling in the brush, and Hunter spun around.

"What's that?" he asked, putting a hand on his bear spray canister and another on the pistol at his hip.

Reasonable response. While this park just outside of town didn't tend to have a lot of bear activity, those fur-covered grouches could pop up anytime. Which made Hunter's choice of activity—a picnic and catching fish—seem odd. Lou patted her own bear spray canister and shrugged. She hadn't wanted to upset his plans, but safety was a concern.

Welcome to Alaska, where survival was linked to preparation, common sense, and sometimes luck. Looked like they were aiming for luck today.

Lou calmed her heart rate and listened for a few seconds to the odd crunching sound, followed by a cartoonish, croaking voice saying quickly, *"Around, around, around. Yuk, yuk, yuk."* More rustling followed.

She pointed to the tottering and awkward brown-and-white hen-like bird strutting out of the undergrowth. It acted like it owned the land and that natural predators didn't exist.

"Willow ptarmigan. Even before we saw it, I could tell by the call." Lou laughed. "I thought you had lessons at the village, growing up."

He pulled his head back like she'd slapped him. *Uh-oh.* Lou rushed to add in a lighter tone, "That's the male. I think he wants to challenge you."

"He's like ten inches tall, and he sounds like a fast-forwarded *Lilo and Stitch* episode." Hunter pulled his head back as the bird croaked at him. "Shoo."

The ptarmigan finally gave up posturing and stumbled its way back into the brush to challenge other birds before flying south for the winter.

Hunter stared at her. "How'd you know that? About the bird."

"Elders taught me how to spot local birds when I was young. You had those lessons, too, right?"

"Um, sometimes I was doing other things." His gaze dropped.

Sure, his dad had personal issues, and it sounded like he sometimes wasn't nice to be around. Uncle Keith always laughed at family gatherings, asked Lou how she was doing, and playfully tugged on her hair. She also knew that Uncle Keith kept to himself and there was some darkness that seeped through his smiling expression from time to time.

Of all people, Lou understood far too well that outward appearances didn't necessarily match inner turmoil.

Something about Hunter's comments, or the intensity behind them, felt off. Didn't fit, like gifted handmade caribou boots that she was determined to wear, despite them pinching a little too tightly. Lou gritted her teeth and maintained dogged optimism that they were having a nice time, and she was reconnecting with her cousin. They were family, after all.

"I should spend more time with the village elders," he said.

"No reason why you can't. You and your dad are part of the Koyukon village." Not Hunter's mom. Aunt Patty had left for the lower forty-eight years ago. No one ever mentioned her, and Lou wasn't about to step into that topic. "You can spend time learning more about traditions."

"Still wouldn't be enough for Dad." A hard muscle popped in his jaw.

"I'm sorry?" She vaguely remembered his parents divorcing back in grade school. Uncle Keith lived nearby, but she rarely saw him.

"Never mind." He flicked a piece of grass off the blanket. "Yes, you're right. I should talk with the elders. Actually, Dad is thinking about putting his name in as an elder when there's an opening."

Lou knew changing the subject when she saw it. She also knew that Uncle Keith, while a decent guy, was not a good candidate for local leadership. "Um, that's great that he wants to be more involved in the tribe," she managed to say.

"Something like that."

"Pardon?"

"Just grumbling." Hunter made a face. "He's tough to be around."

"Don't you live with him?" Maybe it was a difficult situation, the two of them under one roof.

"Temporarily. I'm saving up to get a place outside of town before winter."

No need to pry. She didn't need to know about his family drama. Lou had her own fish to fry. "That'll be nice."

Inhaling and leaning back on her arms, she lifted her face to the sun and took in the beauty of the world in front of her. Mountains reached high in the distance and lower hills rose closer to the banks. The Yukon River rushed past. A light scent of damp soil and fresh water mixed with the aroma of spruce from the trees behind them.

She struggled to find an easy topic. "Salmon Festival will be in a week."

"Yeah. Coho's starting to run. I'm surprised we haven't gotten more than a few fish so far." He pointed toward the sealed cooler.

"The coho run hasn't peaked yet. It's downstream. Galena is seeing the peak right now."

"So, we're early." Hunter stared at her again. "The Salmon Festival will be fun. I haven't been in years." He paused, then said dramatically, "I want *all* the pickled salmon."

"I prefer smoked."

"You're too funny, Louise."

She pulled her head back. Her comment wasn't hilarious at all. It was only a comment. He was trying too hard and laughing too loudly. Why?

"Will your dad be at the Salmon Festival?" he asked.

"He and Mom wouldn't miss the fresh food and catching up with friends."

"I can catch up with him as well." He paused. "Sounds like you'll be there too."

"Wouldn't miss it!"

Regardless of her internal crisis, Lou could depend on comfort food and the warmth of community, even if she was shy. If there was one thing that Yukon Valley did well, it was throwing a food-laden gathering. Her mouth watered, eager to taste Auntie Ruth's salmon patties. Technically, she wasn't an aunt. Ruth Sampson was Tuli's grandma, but most younger people called the older women in the village *auntie*. No shade on Lou's parents, but Auntie Ruth cooked the best food in the village.

Hunter tapped her arm with a finger. "You're a million miles away. Am I boring you?" His confident, swaggering, star-quarterback expression wavered for a split second. He secured the fishing rod in the stand and reclined back on the picnic blanket.

"Er, no. Thinking about the fall events." Including Calvin and Deirdre's wedding.

A knot caught in her chest, and she rubbed her sternum while she clamped her mouth shut.

"Being here with me makes you think of festivals?" Well, that statement packed a lot of presumption into it.

Casting around for a safe way to skirt her thoughts, she said, "I think of all the festivals we attended as kids. How many free samples of food we got." How much fun those festivals were to attend with other people. Another person. A particular person.

Tuli.

Maybe she could attend the wedding with him.

No. She shook her head, as if to dislodge the thought. For so many reasons, that would be a terrible decision.

Why wasn't there a bite on the line? She sat up and jiggled the rod before giving up and securing it in the holder stuck in the ground.

"How about I give you something special?" Hunter said with a broad, boyish smile.

"Uh, what?"

He tapped on the cooler. "You know. Blackberry pie. Not as good as your mom—er, Aunt Melinda—might make, though. It's from the Yukon Valley Diner." He followed her line of sight. "Don't worry about the poles. We'll see the red flag go up if we get a hit."

Lou already saw a lot of red flags.

It was like he had complete amnesia for his support of Ryan last year. How he had helped spread the news of the breakup.

She pressed her lips together.

Get over it. Past history. Focus on the future. On family.

Except for the family she could no longer have.

Besides that family. A sigh caught in her throat, and she swallowed hard.

She scooted back from the rods, careful not to track silty dirt and pine needles onto the picnic blanket.

They ate slices of fresh blackberry pie in companionable silence, stowing all napkins and cutlery in plastic Ziploc bags, and then sealing everything in a cooler. No reason to tempt fate. Or bears with an excellent sense of smell.

He smiled. "This is a terrific day, isn't it?"

Fighting not to pull back, she made a positive, noncommittal sound. What was it about Hunter that put her defenses up?

Lou needed to keep the conversation superficial. "So, what brought you back to town last fall?" Besides hanging with his bestie, Ryan, who had broken her heart. "I thought you swore off Yukon Valley after high school. Heard you were heading out for big city riches instead of small-town living." Heard that from Ryan. The guy who never met a confidential fact he wouldn't turn around and share with others.

Anyway.

Hunter mumbled, "Why not have both?"

"Pardon?"

He stared at her, his brows drawn tight. "That came out weird. What I meant was, I'm back home with family, so that means I'm rich, right?"

"Uh. Sure." For some reason, Lou was certain that wasn't what he meant.

"To answer your question, our dads talk from time to time. Uncle Steve had mentioned an opening at the fire department last year." He flashed a megawatt smile that was handsomely blinding but didn't reach his eyes. "I enrolled in fire academy training. Realized that I missed the traditional life and our culture. So, it was good to return. Use my skills to give back. Hopefully, I'll continue helping in other areas."

Lou didn't recall Hunter being particularly involved in Athabascan culture growing up. Of course, most everyone attended memorial potlatches and celebrations. Enjoyed seasonal festivals. But really digging into the history and learning from elders? She didn't recall him doing that. However, their Koyukon tribe was one of the larger ones in the Alaskan interior. She didn't know every tribal member's activities. Or maybe something had changed, and Hunter truly wanted to get back in touch with his culture.

Who was she to judge? "It has to have been a change.

You were gone for several years. Big city and all."

"Big city. Yep."

Lou studied him. "You're really here to get back in touch with your roots and work as a firefighter?"

His eyes met hers briefly. "Well, my dad also mentioned that there was potentially gold or other minerals nearby. Thought that could make for a good investment in my future."

There it was. Truth.

Lou looked up at him sharply. "Not at this time, it's not a good investment."

"Yeah," he muttered. "Maybe soon. He said that the town and mine working group has got things tied up in red tape."

"The group includes the village and owners of land abutting the mining claim." It wasn't a secret that there were provable minerals in the ground in the Ray Mountain range outside of town.

It also wasn't a secret that a working group had been formed to decide how best to manage the resource. But something niggled in the back of her mind. She tried to focus on it, but it floated away like a yellow poplar leaf drifting off in the fall breeze.

"The group could use me." He sat up, shoulders pushed back. "I'd be great at managing the mine. I got my associate's degree in mine operations a few years back."

"But you're working as a firefighter."

"Opportunities show up in different ways. I enjoyed the safety parts of my degree. Firefighting was a good way for me to do more with that interest in public safety. It also allowed me to get back to Yukon Valley. Make some money."

Something still didn't fit. "You're a volunteer firefighter." Who apparently didn't have a regular job, not that it was her business.

However, for a guy about to move out of his dad's house, where did he get his income?

"We do get paid for callouts." He gave a serious nod. "Also, I have a plan to move up in the ranks."

There was only one rank higher than staff firefighter in town, and that was the fire chief position.

Lou peered at the confident set of his shoulders. "Hmm." So many questions. "What about the mine?"

"I can help while still working with the fire department. The mine, wow, it's an opportunity to create something special in Yukon Valley. Help the local economy and improve the area. Make Yukon Valley great. Develop a local mining business. Let everyone ride the gravy train."

Yukon Valley already was pretty great, in Lou's opinion. "That's not your call. It's not an operational mine yet."

"Seems unfair. That's an untapped resource just sitting there. It can make a lot of money if we get it up and running soon."

"That's for the working group to decide."

"Not everyone in the working group owns property in the target area. Doesn't that seem unfair?"

Alarmed, she leaned back. "No, but we all bear the responsibility for the resource and caring for our land."

"All I'm saying is, if you're not at the table, then you're

on the menu," he said. Hunter's smile froze for a beat, then he spluttered, "Of course. You're right. Sorry. I sometimes get excited about opportunities. I want to put my training to good use here. You know how that goes."

"I do," she conceded. "I'm starting the paramedic program next week."

"Really?"

"Got in under the wire for this semester's courses. It's a combination of online classes and hands-on courses in Fairbanks."

"You'd be great. Saving even more lives."

"Mm-hmm."

"I've missed this. The view. Being here."

"This is the perfect time of year. We're in the sweet spot between mosquitos and blizzards."

Hunter's laugh rang out, again too loud. Although volume was helpful for keeping bears away.

"So true." He turned toward her. "I'm glad we had time to catch up, Louise. This, us, together. It's nice." He paused. "After your breakup with Ryan, I didn't know if you would want to talk to me."

"You didn't break up with me." She made a face. "Ew, weird, right?"

He laughed for a few seconds, then sobered. "I know, but Ryan is—was—my best friend." Shoving a hand through his hair, he added, "At one point, he was a nice person."

"Well. Um, yes." On the one hand, she hated interpersonal conflict.

On the other hand, Hunter held out a proverbial olive

branch, even if accepting it meant she had to acknowledge that the guy who broke up with her wasn't a jerk to everyone. Just to her.

She didn't want to talk about Ryan or her shame.

His expression serious, he took a breath and opened his mouth. "Louise, I'm sor—"

Lou froze.

The brush shook—someone was walking up the path from the parking area. "*Gganaa*! Hi-de-ho-de there, neighbors!" a loud voice rang out.

Tuli's head popped into view above the thick green leaves of labrador tea shrubs.

Lou looked away.

Hunter scowled.

"Oh, I didn't realize this was a private party," Tuli said with a big smile and an *oops* shrug.

Chapter Eight

"WHAT ARE YOU doing here?" Hunter's tone was cold enough to make the Yukon River freeze up in September.

Tuli's grin held. Barely.

He didn't care if the guy was mad. Tuli could see the droop at the corners of her mouth. In a flash, all Tuli wanted was for Hunter to step away from Lou. He didn't care if it spoiled the family reunion.

She gave him a relieved smile, but her shoulders had a weary slump. Lou didn't talk a lot, but Tuli was fluent in Lou's expressions and body language. He had made the right call. He gripped his camera stand. Had Hunter's discussion been unwelcome? Did he hurt her? No way. He was her cousin. Family.

Family could hurt one another, though. Tuli's life was a testament to that fact.

For a few seconds, common sense fled, and buzzing irritation filled Tuli's brain. He took a few breaths to remain calm and maintained what he hoped was his typical friendly, aw-shucks smile.

"I'm doing clips for my socials." He held up his phone as he walked toward them. Ooh, picnic blanket overlooking the riverbank. Beautiful day. Lots of snacks. They were lucky a foraging bear hadn't joined in the party.

Hunter scrambled to his feet and glared at him. "Out of all the places in Alaska and you're here?"

"Ta-da!" Tule put his hands to the side and wiggled his fingers. "Actually, I'm *everywhere*. Ask anyone in town. Right, Lou?"

She smiled up at him, obvious relief written all over her face, and he felt ten feet tall.

"Besides, today is"—Tuli made a kissing motion with his fingers to his mouth—"perfect for creating content. This location is popular with *locals*." Yeah, he dropped some weight on that last word. Firefighting teammate or not, he wanted Hunter to understand that he no longer had the insider track on Yukon Valley. Or Lou's ear.

That was Tuli's job. At least, the Yukon Valley part.

Truth be told, his appearance wasn't simply a local enjoying a popular view on a nice day. Mav might have mentioned this morning about Lou meeting up with Hunter, including time and location. Then somehow Tuli had ended up here at the same time and location.

The world was filled with coincidences. "This is the best view around." He stuck a thumb over his shoulder toward the river. "Present company excluded, of course." He pointed at Hunter in what he hoped was a disarmingly joking manner.

Lou giggled.

Hunter did not. His head whipped around to stare at her, and she went silent.

Tuli clenched his jaw until it ached, but somehow, he held off physically inserting himself between the two of them.

Whatever was off about the guy sent Tuli's radar pinging all over the place.

However, Lou's family wasn't his business. Who she hung out with wasn't Tuli's business. He might not like it, but Lou made her own choices. But what if today she hadn't made her own choices? He glanced at the brow-raised relief written on her face.

What kind of friend would Tuli be if he didn't have her best interests at heart?

Hunter took a big step forward. His glare was all but palpable.

Tuli braced himself, ready for anything. He shifted his weight onto his bad leg, testing whether it would hold long enough for him to take necessary action. Adrenaline spiked fiery zaps through his veins.

"Don't you have someplace to be, Chief?" Hunter said. "Deli meat to cut? Fire engine to clean?"

"Don't get uppity with me, Hunter. You're still in your probationary period at the department. You're mine until I say you're safe to work on your own. I could assign you bathroom cleaning duties for the next month." Before Hunter could snap out a reply, Tuli continued, "But no worries, kids. I'll be out of your hair here in a few minutes." A cool breeze drifted past them with a clean, damp scent. He peered up at the quickly darkening sky. "Oh wow, would you look at that? Looks like it's going to rain soon. Mind if I set up here to do a quick shot? You're welcome to be in the clip. My subscribers would love to see other people from Yukon Valley and you, too, Hunter."

Lou scrambled to her feet and stood to the side of the blanket. "I don't want to be in it."

Hunter planted his fists on hips as he stood with his feet shoulder-width apart in front of Lou, making an absolutely ridiculous show of shielding her from Tuli's scary camera. Which was funny, considering that Tuli knew full well her aversion to public photos and posts. He had always respected that boundary. Always would.

Hunter lowered his voice. "You heard Louise. No videos."

The guy's protective stance was also laughable, considering he'd been Ryan West's wingman even as Lou's ex had advertised the details of their breakup for public entertainment.

"It's okay." Lou stepped around Hunter and pointed at the camera. "You have a job to do, Tuli. Shoot all the videos. I love following your page."

"Really?" Tuli pulled his chin back and stared at her.

He thought she never got on social media. He would need to take that info into consideration when shooting future clips. Make himself look even better.

She blushed. "Everyone in town probably follows it as well." Lou waved toward Tuli. "Get whatever you need."

"I said, don't shoot that stuff here." Hunter crossed his arms and tightened his biceps so they were on full display.

Nice gun show, but Tuli had originated that move. He

glanced at Lou. Little good it had done him. "Whoa there, caveman. There's a lot of undirected *aggro* happening." He lowered his phone. "First of all, Lou might be quiet, but when she speaks, I damn well listen." He glared at Hunter. "Hopefully, you're doing the same." Tuli tried to remain calm as he erected the camera stand. "Second of all, I can't put Lou in any of my posts. She would end up way more popular than I ever could be. I have to keep my audience focused on me."

Lou's snicker both satisfied him and soothed his amped-up nerves. "Since when do you listen to me, Tuli?" she said. "Or anyone?"

"Hey, I resemble that remark," he bantered back.

Hunter grunted and took a step toward Lou.

She took a step away from him.

Weird behavior for Lou and her cousin.

Hunter didn't seem to notice, but Tuli sure as hell did.

"Get your shot and leave," Hunter said, like he made the decisions. "We were here first."

Tuli turned to his stand and set the phone in it, framing the scene. "It's Alaska, bud. Lots of public land, which means all of us can be here. Together. Like one big jumble of friends out here enjoying the day."

Hunter muttered, "Sure. All the crappy land is public. The good stuff's owned by losers."

Lou frowned and studied Hunter, then crossed her arms and withdrew further into her frame. Something had happened between them. Hunter had upset her.

Tuli fought back another wave of need to wrap his arms

around her and become a physical barrier. As a friend, because that was what they were.

There was a weird flop in his chest as he watched how her hair fell forward to hide her face. Actually, she did have a claim to Tuli, but didn't know it.

And he had only started to realize it.

The darkening clouds overhead began to release fat drops. The popping *blaps* of rain hitting broadleaf shrubs blended with the rush of the Yukon River below as Hunter and Lou scrambled to pack up their supplies.

"Would you look at that?" Tuli said.

In a matter of seconds, they hurried off toward the parking area, Lou mouthing, *I owe you one* over her shoulder.

Tuli ignored the soaking rain as he strolled back down the path, humming a pleasant tune.

Chapter Nine

TWO DAYS LATER, on Tuesday, Lou and Mav off-loaded a stable patient with shortness of breath in room three of the Yukon Valley Hospital emergency department. Seasoned ER nurse Clyde had already begun his evaluation before she could exit with the gurney.

The department buzzed with activity this afternoon. The triage nurse-slash-receptionist was bringing back a man who clutched his arm. Judging by the angle of that forearm and the pain on the man's face, it looked like a cast was in his future.

Low whispers came from the health unit coordinator, an older woman, and another nurse on shift, Amberlyn, who had helped out during the recent fire. Johan, an environmental service worker, pushed his floor buffer over to them, shut it off, and joined in the quiet conversation. Lou smiled at the avid expressions and gestures as the three staff members chatted. Then Amberlyn looked up.

At Lou.

The words *picnic* and *river* and *Ryan's girlfriend* drifted over to her. Then she heard her name.

Lou froze.

After a few seconds, Amberlyn broke away and joined

her as Lou resecured the gurney straps for the third time.

"Good afternoon," Mav said, always amiable. "Hey, how are Wayne Sr. and Anna Beck doing?"

"Good. Stable, I mean." Amberlyn toyed with the badge on her lanyard clip. "Both were flown out to Fairbanks that night. Anna's recovering quickly. Wayne Sr. is still in ICU, but it looks like his airway swelling has gone down. Heard they might extubate him soon. Hopefully, he'll make a full recovery. Any word on what started the fire?"

Mav shook his head. "State troopers and the state fire marshal's office are still analyzing evidence."

Lou hadn't considered that the fire might not have been an accident. Who would have done this to the Becks? Why?

"Hopefully, they'll figure things out." Amberlyn looked at both of them. "How are things at the Yukon 911 department? Haven't seen you guys in a while. Not that I'm complaining."

"You know. Saving lives. Getting ready for Dee's wedding later this month." Mav secured the portable telemetry unit at the head of the bed.

"What about you?" she asked, turning toward Lou with a pleasantly feral smile. "Any interesting developments in your world?"

Lou suppressed the groan bubbling up from her chest and kept what she hoped was a neutral expression. She had known Amberlyn since middle school, but they weren't close friends. They were, however, work acquaintances. Unfortunately, the staff of Yukon Valley Hospital and its emergency department had quite the reputation for relentless matchmaking activities.

Lou fed the gossip beast a dry and tasteless morsel. "Mostly working with this guy." She lifted her chin toward Mav and then changed the subject. "How about you?"

Amberlyn toyed with the ends of her dark hair and utterly ignored the bait. "Any plans for the Salmon Festival this weekend? Or a date to the wedding?"

Mav snorted.

Lou's face burned.

For years, she had kept her own counsel for advice. Ever since she had opened up to a friend in high school, who then blasted her secrets all over the classroom, Lou had been intensely private. The disaster fallout from dating Ryan reinforced that decision. "No plans at this time."

Amberlyn frowned. "That's odd. I figured you'd be going with someone." She paused. "I could set you up with the new lab scientist, Reginald."

Lou gripped the handle on the end of the gurney with sweaty hands. Her world went off-kilter. She didn't want setups, especially public ones. She glanced over her shoulder, hoping that Reginald wasn't wandering into the ED.

Mav chuckled. "I've heard he's a nice guy. He's really into dogsledding in his free time. My babies and his had a playdate a few weeks ago."

"Huh?" Lou tilted her head.

Her partner shrugged. "You know, a play date. Running our dog teams on summer trails. Same thing." Mav's love for his dogs, his "babies," as he and Dee called the family's dogsled team, was local legend.

Then Amberlyn added, "Speaking of babies, you and Reginald would make amazing ones. Both of you are so good-looking. Good genes and all."

Lou froze. Her heart sped up double-time. Her vision dimmed at the edges. Was Amberlyn joking?

For a second, Lou considered sprinting out of the building and not stopping.

Babies. Exactly what she couldn't have. Shouldn't have.

Because her genes were anything but *good*.

"Um, I..." she murmured.

Was there a hole she could crawl into? It wasn't enough to want her personal life to stay personal. Now her future was a topic of uninformed speculation.

She opened and closed her mouth, but didn't move.

Mav studied her for a few seconds, concern creasing his features. "Oh hey, I think we need to get going," he said, too brightly. He met her stare with a brief, warm smile and a wink. "Let's roll. See you later, everyone." He waved to the staff as he pulled the gurney, dragging Lou along with him.

Amberlyn stood there, gaping like a salmon on dry land.

Lou had no idea how she made it out of the hospital.

Mav put the gurney in the rig and shut the door. "Get in."

"We're just going across the lot to the garage. I'll walk."

"Lou. In."

"Sure."

They both opened their doors, settled in, and out of habit, put on seat belts. In their line of work, they'd seen freak accidents. Always safety first.

"You looked like you'd seen a ghost a minute ago."

"I did?"

"Yeah. Are you okay?" That was her partner, checking on her, even when she didn't want to talk. Mav was a good guy.

"Yeah." He also deserved more than a single syllable answer, like *yeah*. "Thanks for running interference."

He started the ambulance to get some cool air blowing from the vents but didn't put it in drive. "Look, I've been subject to uncomfortable ribbing around here. Matchmaking is an Olympic sport in Yukon Valley." Clearing his throat, he rested the heels of his hands on the wheel. "While I'm always down for some teasing, I draw the line when someone's in distress."

"I wouldn't go that far." But close.

"Huh." His light-brown eyebrows rose. "Sure. Anything you want to chat about? I'm a good listener." He motioned. "In this ambulance, everything said is HIPAA compliant."

"Is that the protocol?"

"That's my protocol."

The EMS director had her back. Good to know.

However, there was no way she was prepared to go into the details of her inner turmoil and worries about her future. For five long seconds, a tight lump formed in her throat and she blinked against burning eyelids. "Thanks."

He studied her for a few more beats.

"It's not like that," she said. "Like what Amberlyn is thinking. Trying to set me up with someone."

"It can be whatever you want it to be."

"Sure. But I don't want a relationship."

"With anyone?"

She sighed. "Things are complicated right now. I'm still dealing with my feelings from my ex and all."

Mav halfway turned to face her, his mouth set in a serious line. "Whoa, do I need to step into an honorary big brother role and sort someone out? I'll track down that guy if need be."

In spite of herself, she laughed. "No, nothing like that."

"But?"

She didn't say anything.

He asked, "Is there anything else going on? Someone else?"

She froze. "N-no."

"You sure?"

Lou clamped her mouth shut. See, this was the problem with a small town. Everyone got into everyone else's business. Couldn't a gal get some privacy around here?

He put his hands up. "Never mind. Forget I said anything." He drummed his fingers on the wheel. "You should know that any guy would be lucky to hang out with you. You're high quality, Lou."

Would they still want to hang out after learning about her limited choices for a future? Would someone in particular want her? "That's not the issue," she murmured.

"Then what is it?"

"It's complicated."

He put the ambulance in gear. "It always is."

Chapter Ten

TUESDAY EVENING, TULI helped his grandma to her seat at the Yukon Valley Community Center. They were early, as usual. Grandma Ruth was anxious about the possibility of being late to anything.

As folks wandered into the meeting room, Tuli spied familiar faces of village elders, Yukon Valley town leadership, and people whose land abutted the Ray Mountains.

As involved property owners, the Becks were here, despite their homestead burning. Word was their daughter was coming home from the hospital soon and was doing well. He couldn't quite make eye contact with Natalie and Wayne Beck when they beelined it over to Tuli and thanked him for his part in the rescue. Little did they know how close Tuli—and his bum leg—had been from absolute failure. Wayne Sr. would be released from the hospital, likely late this week or next, and would be spending a week or so in a rehab facility before heading home. Even with all of that going on in their family, the fact that the Becks were attending this meeting underscored the importance of the subject.

Tonight was all about controlling access to the minerals and managing resources in a way that made sense for this community.

It was also about getting a warm jacket from the car for his grandma. He nodded at her request, patted her shoulder, then wove upstream past the incoming meeting participants.

After hurrying across the parking lot to his truck, he opened up the door with a squeal of rusty hinges, snagged the garment from the console, and headed back toward the building.

Near the edge of the parking lot, two men separated from what looked like an intense discussion that ended in a quick handshake. One man faded into the twilight shadows and the other walked toward the building.

"Hey, Chief. Looks like you got the night off your many jobs." Hunter's booming voice reached him.

To any bystander, Hunter would come across as friendly. Tuli caught the undertones. The emphasis on the wrong words. His smile that was a little too wide, daring Tuli to comment and look the fool.

To react was to be the bad guy. Tuli never was the bad guy, ever. He had a whole brand built around being the good guy. Given his parents' history, and especially his dad's abusiveness, Tuli strove to be the exact opposite in every way.

"What are you doing here?" Tuli asked.

"Whoa there." Hunter exaggerated his hands-up action. "Where's this aggression coming from?"

"Huh?" Truthfully, some days Tuli really wanted to be the bad guy. He rolled his hands into fists. Today was one of those days. "Was that a clandestine meeting over there?"

Hunter paused, like he was creating the story on the

spot. "I was talking with a friend."

"A friend on the edge of the parking lot?"

"It doesn't relate to my fire department work, so what business is it of yours?"

"Hey, as long as you're not doing anything illegal, you're right. Everything else is literally none of my business." Talk about overreaction. Tuli sized him up and thought of the worst-case scenario. "By friend, do you mean a friend like Ryan West?"

"No," he snapped. "You might think I'm a certain kind of person, but I wouldn't do that to Louise."

It's Lou. "You already *did that* when you supported him while he hurt her last year."

"You don't know anything, Chief." Hunter's expression narrowed as three more meeting participants filed into the building nearby. He flipped an attitude switch and said loudly, "It's always good running into you."

The friendly conversational whiplash caught Tuli off guard. Then he caught the glint in Hunter's eye. People were nearby.

Ah, acting. Two could play at that game.

"Same here. Great seeing you again." Tuli gave a social yuck-it-up laugh and smacked Hunter on his thick, hard upper arm, enough to make the guy take one step to the side. "Hey, look at you, all dried now."

"What?" he paused. "Oh, yeah. Dry." The blowhard's shoulders dropped. "Yeah. Because of the rain last weekend. Funny."

Except it wasn't. This interaction would make a good

video demonstrating how to subvert a bully. What he'd give to have this interaction filmed and posted. But Tuli wanted more than clickbait. He wanted to figure out this guy's agenda and keep him away from things that weren't his business. He might be Lou's cousin, but he could still hurt her.

"I don't control the weather." Tuli tapped his good foot on the gravel. "Hey, this gathering isn't public. Why are you here?"

"Dad said there was a village meeting and that I should go. I have background in mine management, so I thought I might help."

He had mine management training like Tuli had millions of dollars. "So, you weren't invited."

Hunter's smile tightened. "I'm a member of the Koyukon tribe."

"True. But you're not an elder."

He crossed his arms and lifted his cleft chin that begged for a knuckle kiss. "You're not an elder, either."

"Nope, but Grandma Ruth is. I'm her transportation." He stuck one hand in a pocket and grinned. "Sometimes I'm also her hearing aid." Tuli's neck tingled as a few more car doors closed in the parking lot.

Hunter grunted and glared at him, then in a split second, his face morphed into a big smile. "Hi, Uncle Steve. Louise."

Call her Lou, damn it.

Tuli turned. She preceded her father to the building entrance, with Maverick Steen trailing behind them. Seven p.m. Lou and Mav were in their navy-blue EMS uniforms.

Must have just finished a shift. Or they were still on call for a twenty-four-hour shift and needed to both remain together and close to the vehicle to respond to a call. That made more sense. The crew pulled longer shifts from time to time. Occupational requirement in a rural area.

"Ooh, it's a party," Tuli quipped.

Lou's small, warm smile did him a world of good. The neutral expression of her dad, a local elder? Not quite so much. Whew. Tough crowd.

"Tuli." Mav brought up the rear of the group and patted him on the upper arm. "Long time no see."

He laughed. "It's been, what, twelve hours since you two coffee addicts dropped by my deli?"

"Meeting's about to start." Mr. Wright held the front door open, shooting Lou an inscrutable expression.

"Right behind you, sir," Mav piped up, following him into the building.

As landowners with property adjacent to the Ray Mountains and the first citizens to be threatened by the speculators, Mav and his sister Deirdre had attended every meeting.

Lou paused before going in the door and half turned toward Tuli and Hunter.

Tuli took a deep breath before asking Lou to the Salmon Festival—

"Louise, I'll catch up with you and Uncle Steve after the meeting," Hunter interrupted.

She paused, her cheeks turning pink even in the twilight. "Okay." She didn't go in the building. As if she was creating space for Tuli and her to be alone. Good.

Tuli clutched his grandma's jacket in a sweaty fist. Damn it. This situation had become a mess. He needed to get over himself, stop waiting for the perfect moment, and dive right in. He'd waited several months after her breakup last fall, then was about to ask her out when he had his accident. Seemed like it was never the right time or place.

He opened his mouth. Closed it when he glanced at Hunter's eager and too-friendly expression. Tuli focused on the dude.

For real, what sort of kiss-ass showed up at the community resource management meeting just to *help*? Was this guy going for the Yukon Valley volunteer of the year?

Because pretty sure Tuli, with his social media promotion of the area boosting tourism, was in the running for that award. A shoo-in, really.

Hunter stood tall.

Tuli had been a shoo-in. Until this knob showed up.

"Hey, looks like we've got some loitering going on." Bruce Garrett's growly voice made the three of them look back as he slowly approached in his typical bow-legged, arthritic gait.

His son, Calvin, had been a victim of the speculators and was lucky to have escaped with his life. Seemed that if the speculators could not access the Ray Mountain-bordered property legally, they had no problem removing the barriers to access. Human barriers. Permanently. Yet another reason for the community to band together in their approach to resource management.

"Hi, Bruce," Tuli said.

Lou gave a quick wave and a small smile.

"*Hmmph.*" Bruce glowered under bushy salt-and-pepper eyebrows until his sweet but tough wife, Aggie, stopped and glared at him. Was that a whimper coming from the tough guy? "Um, I mean hi. Aggie says I have to be nicer to people."

"At least the ones who save your life," Lou said, brows arched.

Touché.

"She's lovely, and I love her," Aggie said, patting Bruce on the arm before heading into the building.

Bruce stuck around.

Lou's face turned a—yes, lovely—shade of crimson as she looked down at the gravel.

"What are you three stooges doing out here?" Bruce studied Hunter, Lou, and Tuli for several long seconds each.

"Just talking, sir," Hunter said.

"Mostly plotting world domination." Tuli shifted his weight off his aching right leg and hoped no one noticed.

Lou's gaze flicked down, then up to his face. Damn, she was observant. He locked his knees to maintain a stable stance.

Bruce pursed his mouth. "Oh, I know what this is." He pointed at each of them with a knowing grin.

He puffed his chest out, which would have been intimidating forty years ago, but now made him look like an old rooster wearing a flannel shirt, what with his thin bowed legs and his unruly gray hair.

"I know exactly what this is," he murmured, half to himself. "I have work to do."

Oh no. Tuli caught Lou's eye and gave a slight shake of his head. *Say nothing*, he tried to telepathically transmit to her.

"What?" Hunter said, obviously not getting the mental message.

"Well, this looks like a love triangle to me." Bruce crossed his arms and waited.

"Not at all," Hunter said, pointing at Lou. "We're cousins, remember?"

"Nothing's going on with any of us," she sputtered, shoving her hands in her work uniform pockets and avoiding everyone's gaze. She squirmed under the attention and Tuli's gut clenched in sympathy for her shyness.

Tuli thought fast. "You figured it out! What Hunter and I have is special, Bruce." He leaned his head onto Hunter's shoulder and batted his eyes. "No matchmaking needed. No judgment."

Hunter spluttered and tried to shove Tuli away. "No, not—"

"Huh. What?" Bruce pulled his head back.

Tuli could almost spy the virtual gerbil in Bruce's brain wheel running at top speed.

"Love is love. Right?" Lou said with the first relaxed smile Tuli had seen in some time.

Tuli slung his arm around Hunter's neck and hung on as the dude pulled back. Took all of Tuli's strength to hold him in place. The guy must be made of iron. "We're *friends*,

Bruce. Very good friends. Got it?"

Bruce froze. Stared at the group. Scratched his head. Then he turned on his heel and entered the building.

Hunter wrenched himself away. "Why'd you do that, man? We are—"

"Late for the meeting," Lou interjected.

Good job, Lou. Tuli gave her a thumbs-up.

"Um, so—" She pointed toward the door.

Hunter recovered quickly, making a big show of holding the door open for her.

Tuli trailed behind her. "Why, thank you."

Hunter let go, and Tuli walked right into the door with an *oof.*

Hunter stared at him from behind the glass and threw finger guns at him.

Oh yeah, buddy. Game. On.

Chapter Eleven

THE MEETING WITH the village elders and town leadership wrapped, and Lou pushed off from the back wall she was holding up. The room had been full as the group discussed mining rights, easement risks, and potential income from the vein of gold and rare earth elements in the nearby Ray Mountains.

As important as the evening's topic was, it had been challenging for Lou to concentrate. Bruce had way too much free time, seeing love blooming where it didn't exist. Seeing conflict where…

Yeah, there was conflict. Layers of it. In all directions. The tension between Tuli and Hunter made her skin itch. But the idea of confronting any conflict head-on, whether internal or external conflict, gave her hives.

Avoidance was the best medicine.

Case in point. She hadn't talked with her parents about the genetic report yet, a fact that weighed as heavily on her shoulders as the contents of the report itself. She wasn't keeping a secret. She just wasn't ready to discuss it.

Dad gave her a quick side hug. "How's your week going, Lou?"

She smiled and returned the hug with a lump in her

throat. She might be twenty-six, but Dad was still a dad. A twinge hit her heart before she could brace against the feeling. "Good. Work wasn't too busy. I missed a part of the meeting when I had to step out to take a call. What did I miss?" Truth be told, even when she stood in the room, her tumbling thoughts had made it hard to concentrate.

Dad took his job as a village elder very seriously. He patted a notebook that, for sure, held pages of his carefully detailed handwritten notes. He had notebooks like that about Gordy's health changes, medication regimen, appointments. The notes went back years. The guy might be old-school and a little over the top, but at least he was organized. "The USGS survey data was reconfirmed. Exactly what we had thought. There is basically an unbroken wall of private landowners and tribal property that abuts the Ray Mountains. Everything else is government-protected land. There's no access unless one of those parcels allows it. The initial bids for our community mining project look good. The companies we're vetting seem ethical and are good stewards of the environment. They think like we do."

We meaning the Athabascan population rather than the town of Yukon Valley. Dad worked well with town government, but at the end of the day, he prioritized the needs of the village and tribal culture.

With a grave nod, he said, "We have more digging to do. No pun intended." Then he laughed, clearly proud of himself for a quintessential dad joke.

"I'm glad you're making sure anything that's done is good for everyone," she said, looking up as Hunter approached.

Suddenly, she needed to go check the ambulance.

"Hi again, Louise," Hunter said, giving her a wave. He quickly pivoted and stuck his hand out. "Nice to see you again, Uncle Steve. It was good to hear the plans for mining. The sooner we get that ore out of the ground, the better it will be for everybody financially."

Dad shook his hand. "No one's in a hurry. We want to do this the right way and in a manner that cares for the land we're here to protect."

His gaze darted away. "Of course. Of course. But think about all you could do with that money."

Lou stared at his smile, which somehow didn't fit. She rubbed the bridge of her nose. This was her cousin. They'd grown up together.

"What are you doing here, Hunter?" Dad said in a neutral tone.

Hunter's Adam's apple bobbled. Yeah, her dad could be a little intimidating.

He said, "My dad asked me to come since he couldn't attend this evening."

"He isn't part of this working group."

"He should be." The words came out like spiky spruce needles.

"Pardon?" Dad said.

Lou studied her father. Then back to Hunter. A strange undercurrent ran between them. Like Hunter was a poker player bluffing with an iffy hand. Dad could pick up on BS a mile away.

So, what was Hunter doing?

"What I meant was, my dad thought I could help you all out," Hunter recovered. "I have experience in mine management."

"Do you?"

"Um, yes. Studied it when I was away."

"You were gone for several years, weren't you?"

"Yes, sir."

"Gained experience?"

Hunter nodded. "Experience I'm happy to use for the good of everyone here."

Lou watched his expression. His words were congenial, but his eyes were narrowed. Tiny beads of sweat popped out on his upper lip.

Hunter was as unflappable a person as she'd ever met.

Besides Tuli, who was the Houdini of any social situation and could make even the most argumentative person come around to his side of things. She flicked her gaze across the room, spying Tuli and his grandmother leaving the venue. Earlier, he had wanted to talk with her.

Part of her was eager to find out what Tuli wanted to say.

The other part—the realistic part—dreaded it.

"We should talk more," Dad was saying to Hunter.

"I'd like that." Hunter paused and glanced over. "If you don't mind, I'd like to have a word with Louise for a second."

Dad shot her a curious smile. "Of course. Let me step out of here while you two young people chat. I need to get out of here anyway. Mom's probably wondering if a bear ate me." He gave her a matter-of-fact nod before exiting.

Lou would have gone with him, but she would have had to step around Hunter. Make a scene.

She and Hunter stood alone next to the back wall of the mostly empty meeting room.

"I'm sorry we didn't get to finish our picnic," Hunter said.

"Around here, the weather changes a lot of plans."

"That wasn't what messed up our discussion."

"It wasn't a discussion. It was a nice outdoors lunch. As family. Friends."

"How do you figure that?" Hunter's eyes narrowed as his face turned red. He had shifted so that her back was pressed to the wall. No one else could see his clouded expression.

Her breath caught as he loomed over her.

After a few deep breaths, he seemed to calm down.

She couldn't get past the part where Hunter had stood by Ryan's side while Ryan had loudly shared secrets about her relationship to anyone in town. Slandered her. Controlled the public message of their breakup. Hunter had participated.

Hunter apparently hadn't felt like that was a big enough deal to step away from his friend. Not until after the damage had been done.

She gritted her teeth. *Avoid the conflict.* Get out. Get home.

"Um, yeah. I had a nice time," she managed to say. Anything to end the conversation and leave. "Well, I need to head on out." She took a step to the side.

He planted his hand on the wall next to her shoulder. "I'd love to try for lunch again. To catch up more as *family*."

The word twisted strangely in his mouth. Like he was saying *family*, but with strings attached. Like he was trying too hard for … what? Did his angle have to do with wanting to work with the mining project? Maybe he needed to get in Dad's good graces and thought he could do so by being her buddy. Or he wanted to use the family ties to get an insider track on the committee.

"If that's okay with you," he added.

A few lingering people glanced over. Lou unclenched her jaw. She hated the attention. She didn't want to hang out with Hunter. He was a decent person and a relative. But those memories of past privacy violations buffeted her.

What if the issue was Lou and her own trust issues?

Oh.

Rocking back on her feet, her head lightly bumped the wall behind her. She didn't feel safe with men.

Most men. Ryan.

Him.

Hunter.

But not all men. She felt safe around one particular guy.

Oh. A fleeing tightening in her chest came and went.

So that meant … what, exactly?

Nope. Lou mentally shook her head.

She wasn't prepared to evaluate her feelings. There was nothing to evaluate. Not before she had processed her genetic information and made some personal decisions about her future. Decisions she was putting off, because in her magical-thinking brain, if she didn't acknowledge the issue, maybe it wasn't real. Not yet, at least.

Lou swallowed.

"What do you say?"

"Um. Not sure about my schedule. What with starting the paramedic program, I'm studying more," she hedged. Really, Lou wanted to keep her plans and her life to herself.

His smile wavered. "We can catch up at the Salmon Festival this Friday."

"Might have work."

"I'll talk to Mav about changing your schedule."

Lou stared at him. "No! That's not right."

Hunter patted her arm. "Sorry I mentioned anything. I was just looking forward to hanging out with you again." His voice was too loud for her comfort. The few remaining meeting attendees looked up.

Edging away, she murmured, "Sure, sure. I'll see you at the fish fry."

Chapter Twelve

THAT FRIDAY AROUND five p.m., Tuli steered ladder truck 1-4 down Yukon Valley's main street, creeping toward the Salmon Festival. The parade ended at the school, and he could almost smell the seasoned salmon from here. He waved and smiled, turning on the siren, much to the squealing delight of the kids lining the route.

He checked the phone mounted on the dashboard. Yep, it was still filming out the front window.

When they stopped for a moment, he flipped the camera and gave a few lines of commentary that he'd edit into a post later tonight.

The brightly decorated fish-themed float in front of him started moving again, and he eased off the brake with more of a jolt than he had wanted. *Damn it.* The repeated press of his foot on the pedal had worsened the numbness and now the weakened muscles shook. He rubbed his leg.

"You okay?" Hunter asked from the passenger seat where he threw out huckleberry candies to waiting kids.

Like Tuli truly would give that guy any more ammo. "Absolutely fine." He rested his hand on the steering wheel.

Letting out a gusty, satisfied breath, Hunter said, "Don't know about you, but I'm looking forward to this evening.

Visiting with friends and family. All good."

The way he emphasized *family* again made Tuli flinch. Probably a subconscious response given his lack thereof.

Tuli would be nice to him. Personal feelings aside, Hunter was still on probation, training to be a full member of the Yukon Valley Fire Department. Tuli was his boss. He needed to remain civil and continue training the guy. That was literally Tuli's job. Frankly, he needed the help in the thinly staffed department. "Me too. Grandma Ruth has been cooking up a storm."

"Uh, yeah. The food should be good too."

"Anything you're looking forward to this evening?"

Obviously, the guy wanted to say more, but Tuli didn't like responding to conversation lobs.

It took exactly two more tossed handfuls of candy for Hunter to lean back into the vehicle and spill. He looked over at Tuli and sniffed. "The real reason? I'm this close to getting the mining supervisor job."

"Sounds good," he mumbled.

"You bet it's good, bro. I'll be raking in the money."

"What's your experience again?"

"Trained in the field while I was away from Yukon Valley. Time to cash in on a good education."

Every conversation with this guy was like a million little paper cuts.

"Say, you got a thing for Louise?"

Where'd that come from?

Tuli muttered, "You ever hear about privacy?"

In fact, he had hoped to see Lou at the festival and catch

up with her. Not just out of personal relationship interest. Tuli might not be as close of a friend with her as years ago, but he still could tell that something had been bothering her the past few weeks. He wanted to help. Maybe she was hiding something? Hard to tell.

Tuli, the most public face of Yukon Valley, wasn't the expert in privacy. He rested his hand on his traitorous, shaking leg.

Some things needed to be private. He, of all people, could appreciate that fact.

Hunter reached into the bucket with his meaty hand and gave a piercing whistle out the window before throwing more candy to the screaming kids.

The school came into view, with tents set up on the fields and a bonfire already going, even though it was another few hours before twilight. Days stayed long here into fall, and people took advantage of the extra light.

He pulled up to the parking area. Thank God he could stop pushing the truck's pedals with his quaking leg.

"She's family, and I protect family, you know."

Protect her from what? Lou was a grown woman who could take care of herself perfectly fine. Even if Tuli did want to participate in the protecting part. "Okay?"

"I want what's best for her."

He put the truck in park and whipped his head around. "You thought that public fallout with Ryan was what's best? Your chitchatting with anyone about the breakup details? She basically went into hiding for several months."

"What if he got the short end of the stick?"

Tuli gripped the wheel so hard his knuckles turned white. "How so?"

"Those two just had a misunderstanding. Things happen when people break up."

"'Things happen'?" What was Hunter's angle? Tuli couldn't figure the guy out. Talking with Hunter was like watching a movie but not following the plot. "So you believe that Ryan broadcasting the details of his and Lou's relationship across town and back was in some way okay? Justified?"

Hunter paused for a few seconds too long. "That part was kind of cold."

"Then what part in that situation did you agree with?"

"Look, Ryan was a good guy."

Not from where Tuli sat.

Hunter continued, "He got run out of town."

"Because of his terrible treatment of your cousin."

"Two sides to every story, man."

No way Tuli could accept a reality that Lou in any way deserved how that breakup had gone down. No way was she to blame for the drama. Lou avoided drama, even to her own detriment.

"Hmm." He let out a long breath, trying to calm down. "What's your point with all this?"

"My point …" Hunter leaned back in the seat, stretched out his legs, and crossed them. "Is that you think you know things, but you don't. You need to stay away from my family." He looked over and grinned. "And stay out of my way. Tonight is going to be a real good night for my future."

SEVERAL HOURS LATER, Tuli was not having a *real good night*.

Darkness had fallen and the festival was in full swing. People, people everywhere, but no sight of Lou.

He stumbled on a clod of dirt and gritted his teeth when Calvin and Deirdre, who were walking nearby, asked if he was okay.

Deep down, Tuli wasn't okay. Not by a long shot.

He eyed the smiling couple, gazes only on each other, standing arm in arm. Their excitement about the upcoming wedding was obvious.

No, Tuli wasn't okay.

However ... In addition to wanting to talk with Lou, he had bills to pay and an online reputation to maintain.

After checking for permission from the folks gathered around the bonfire, he held up his phone and went live.

"*Dzaanh nezoonh*! A warm welcome coming to you live from Yukon Valley's Salmon Festival. It's an evening full of bonfires, laughter, and wonder. This is the place to be! It's a night of a thousand fish, prepared in every way you can imagine. The Koyukon village and our Yukon Valley neighbors share in the salmon run up the Yukon River and give thanks for the bounty brought to us every fall as coho salmon return to their spawning grounds." He turned, getting the scene behind him in the frame. "Yet another reason to visit Yukon Valley and experience the local culture and good food! Don't forget to like and share my video to let others know about yet another amazing festival here in Yukon Valley."

The mayor stepped into the frame and Tuli asked her an easy question about the friendliness of folks in town. Then she waved along with Tuli. He turned off the camera and checked his account. Already engagement numbers were rising. The local festivals made for excellent posts on The Real Alaska handle.

"Did we go viral yet?" The mayor, Beverly Fowler, a local born and raised in Yukon Valley, pointed to the phone. She patted her short, gray hair self-consciously. "I'm working on my video presentation presence."

Chuckling, he said, "If we go viral, it's not generally in the first thirty seconds. Although, you never know." He checked his phone one more time before stowing it in his back pocket. "You're doing great. My audience loves you." Didn't pay to tell Mayor Fowler that she was stiff as wet laundry hung on the line in sub-freezing temperatures. Hey, at least she was sincere and genuine, which went a long way with followers.

Loud laughter boomed across the field. Hunter.

Not everyone was sincere and genuine. Tuli wiped his hand over his lower face. Before he could gather more information, Bruce Garrett waved him down and launched into a riveting story about his medical misadventures.

Tuli sighed to himself. The guy might not be from the village, but Tuli would be patient and respect him as his elder.

Tracing the broad laughter to the source, he spied

Hunter shaking Steve Wright's hand before Lou's father strolled away. Then Hunter motioned and Lou appeared, as if from the shadows. Tuli fought the urge to wave at her. Half listening to Bruce, he groaned as the man transitioned his narrative to the story of his heart attack. It was the fifth or sixth time Tuli had heard the tale. Got bigger and better each time.

"Then I gave that overstuffed Fairbanks doctor the what-for and said, 'No, I'm not taking that darn pill. I already have too many pills. Those pills make me worse, not better.' It's a conspiracy, you know." With an animated motion, Bruce ran a hand through his bushy hair, more salt than pepper these days.

Aggie walked up, handing him a steaming drink. "Then you took the pill. Didn't you?"

Bruce mumbled something.

"Sorry, I didn't hear you, dear." She stared at him until he stuffed a hand in his pocket.

"For now," he muttered. "But only because it was my decision. Probably isn't helping."

"You appear to be alive, as compared to when you were not alive," she said blandly. "No thanks to your love of caribou sausage and all thanks to those overstuffed doctors."

Above the beard, his skin turned pale, obvious even in the light of the bonfire. "*Hmph.*"

Tuli held back a laugh.

Bruce was like a bear—lots of grumpy bluster and throwing his weight around. But Aggie? She was a cunning wolverine, picking the best moments to strike with surgical precision.

Tuli glanced over Bruce's shoulder to check on Lou. At the edge of the open field, she crossed her arms while Hunter towered over her, leaning forward. Tuli inclined his upper body in their direction.

Then Hunter grasped her upper arm and led her back into the shadows of the Sitka pines that lined the field.

Tuli shifted from one foot to the other, chafing at society rules that required him to stay put and listen to his elders while they talked. Besides, Lou's life wasn't his business.

On the one hand, Lou was a fully formed adult who could make her own decisions. She didn't need Tuli's input or protection. She didn't need him butting into her family stuff.

On the other hand, Lou was Tuli's friend. And he wanted to hang out with his … friend.

Also, Tuli got weird vibes about Hunter, cousin or not. He'd love to solve the mystery of that guy's agenda.

Decision made.

Making his apologies to Bruce and Aggie, he took a few steps and then pulled out his phone, doing what he did best, narrating tidbits about the festival and responding on camera to his followers' comments and questions. All the while, he eased toward the place where Lou disappeared.

Hey, nothing like gaining a little internet clout while checking in on his friend. Two birds, one stone.

Friend. For some reason, that label sounded wrong.

He shook his head, unwilling to create another label. He turned off the feed but kept the phone up.

Low voices drifted over to him. Lou murmured something he couldn't quite catch, but he did hear her quiet but firm, "No. I can't do that for you."

Hunter's voice pierced the cool evening air. "No?"

Tuli glanced into the trees. Lou backed away, with Hunter stepping forward to maintain his proximity.

Still holding up the phone and pretending to film, Tuli tried to pull the innocent act of his life as he made a big show of talking into the phone, signing off, and hitting a button before stowing the phone once more.

He faced them. "What mayhem are you two plotting out here?"

"Could you be any more annoying?" Hunter said, turning halfway away from Lou.

A frown marred her shadowed face, but she didn't appear to be in distress.

"Having a good evening?" Tuli asked.

"It *was* fine," Hunter bit off, turning his back on Tuli.

"How are you?" Lou said, too brightly and with way more volume than usual.

"Good, good. Nice Salmon Festival this year, isn't it?" Tuli strolled closer, hands in his pockets.

Hunter glowered at him. "We were having a conversation. In private. We'd like to continue. In private."

One glance at Lou's pleading expression suggested that she did not want to continue the conversation in private.

Tuli might not be quick on his feet anymore, but his brain function was snappy. "Oh sure. Uh, you don't mind me grabbing some scenes for my social media account."

"I do mind." Hunter paused. "The festival is out there."

He lifted his cleft chin. "What are you doing here?"

"I told you. Social media," Tuli said smoothly. "The Real Alaska page is trending from an earlier post, and I want to keep up the momentum." He whipped his phone out once again and held it up before pointing at Hunter. "Oh, you mean me, here? Now? With you? Don't get too hopeful. It's a coincidence, buddy. Right guy, wrong time and all that."

"Huh?" Hunter said.

Lou snorted.

"Well. Go film somewhere else," he said. "Away from Lou, of course. She doesn't like being on camera."

She can speak for herself.

"It's okay. I was leaving," Lou said, turning on her heel.

"Forget it. I'm out of here." Hunter got close enough to bump against Tuli's shoulder. Under his breath, he said, "Keep your nose out of my business, man. I mean it." He kept right on stomping his way back to the bonfire and the gaggle of Hunter fans there.

Tuli caught up to Lou, stumbling on the third painful and numb-ish step, but regaining his footing. "Hey, Lou." He brushed her arm with his fingertips.

The urge to tug her into his chest and curl around her nailed him in the gut.

Instead, he dropped his hand and scanned her. "You okay? Can I help?"

Lou paused, her face half in shadow and half glowing from the light of the bonfire. Her dark gaze landed on him for a few seconds too long. "Just fine."

"That wasn't the answer to the question I asked."

"It's the answer I have to give."

Tuli ground his teeth. "What's going on with Hunter?" He waved his arm behind him, away from the laughing, chatting crowd of friends, family, and neighbors. "Is he bothering you?"

"He's my cousin."

Another nonanswer. So, it could be a yes. Damn it.

He knew Lou. She might be quiet, but her body language spoke volumes. He focused on the downturn of her mouth and the way she gripped her upper arms. "Seriously, what's going on with you? We used to share all kinds of insider secrets and laugh about stuff all the time. Lately, it seems like you're closed up like a frozen metal door."

Her flinch and the shimmer in her eyes told the tale. He had hit close to home. Too close. What gave?

Tuli cleared his throat. "Oh boy. Hey, Lou." He patted her shoulder. Suddenly, a wave of longing hit him harder than a falling pine tree. Every cell in his body needed to pull her into his arms and fight off whatever troubled her. "Look, I'm sorry if I said something wrong. Do you want to talk about anything?"

A pause, then she said, too brightly, "No need to worry."

"I do worry." His hands actually tingled, he wanted to touch her so badly. Connect with her. Provide support and comfort. He considered his state of mind and froze for a second. He wanted to provide way more than comfort. The realization made his head spin.

"Why?" she whispered before chopping with her hand to interrupt his answer. She pointed behind her shoulder.

"Gonna go grab some fish. See you back over by the fire."

Tuli stared as she walked away and wove between clusters of people talking. Even with her fleece jacket on, he could appreciate her cute butt wiggle as she strode across the field.

Since when did he think about his friend's backside?

He'd been thinking about Lou's backside and … other sides … for several years now. A lot during the past several months.

Tuli needed to think about other things, like figuring out the tension between him and Hunter. Clearing the air. They still had to work together. Tuli headed for the largest group of villagers. Perhaps the guy was there.

Lou's father nearby looked up from a conversation.

Gordy gave a jerky wave from his wheelchair and pressed a button on the small AI tablet he wore around his neck. "Hello," the voice said.

AI tried to make electronic speech as natural as possible, but Gordy's device still sounded a bit like a computer. Hey, at least the fellow could communicate his thoughts.

Mr. Wright cleared his throat. "Nice to see you, Tulim-ak."

Man, he'd known Steve Wright for twenty years, played at his house as a child, saw him at all the school functions growing up, but somehow, Lou's dad still scared the bejeebers out of him. More so right now. Tuli refused to venture a guess as to why.

Silence stretched between them as Mr. Wright watched him with a bemused expression.

Tuli scrambled for something to say. "Hey, Gordy. How

ya been?" Hopefully, that wasn't an off-limits topic. Everyone knew that Gordy had recent health struggles, but the Wrights, as a rule, were close-lipped about their family's business.

That said, folks in town loved Gordy and wanted him to be okay, Tuli included.

"I'm okay," the device intoned. Gordy grinned and met him for a fist bump.

Mr. Wright patted his son on the shoulder. "He's doing better, thank you for asking. Gordy's a tough guy."

"I'll say." Tuli cocked his head and pointed to the wheelchair. "You taking it easy after another day of walking all around town?"

Gordy gave a high-pitched laugh.

His dad smiled. "By the end of the day, he's worn out, so we bring out the ATW."

"ATW?"

"All-terrain wheelchair. Right, Gordy?" Mr. Wright glanced down and then met Tuli's eyes. "How about your health? Things going okay?"

Tuli bristled out of reflex but tried not to show it as he maintained careful balance on the balls of his feet—one half numb, but somehow also painful. "All better now. I'm back to full duties at the deli and with the fire department."

Mr. Wright took a drink from a steaming mug of what smelled like Labrador tea with birch syrup. "Good." Pausing, he finally said, "Are you still doing that internet stuff?"

He said *internet stuff* the way people insulted *day trading* or *online gambling*.

"If you mean social media influencing, then yes, I'm still working hard at it."

"Lots of people watch you?"

"Yes. I'm now getting options to monetize and promote some native Alaskan products on my page."

"So, you're a salesman?"

Tuli gritted his teeth for a beat, then relaxed his jaw. "Not exactly. More like a promoter of all things Alaska. In a way that features the best parts of Yukon Valley and encourages people to come visit or even move here."

Gordy gave a happy moan and patted his chest, then hit some buttons. "I will help."

Tuli gave him a thumbs up. "Yes, I told you before. You're a great ambassador for Yukon Valley! I mean, you walk all over town every day, waving at everyone. Yet you never get tired."

That screeching, happy laugh lifted Tuli's heart. Gordy might have gotten a rough draw in life, but every day the fellow managed to be positive.

Tuli could do well to learn from him.

Mr. Wright chuckled. "What are you hoping to do with this hobby?"

For some reason, Lou's dad's opinion mattered. "It's more than a hobby. It is an activity I hope will one day be a full-time job. Or open doors to other career options."

"Why do you do it?"

Wow, talk about the nth degree. Despite the cool evening air, sweat prickled the back of his neck. "On the most basic level, it's fun. I enjoy creating. I'm not shy. It's nice to meet new people and share with them how amazing Yukon Valley is." He motioned to the gathering. "Look around. There are new faces here tonight. There were more tourists during last summer than before. How much of that has to do with the Chamber of Commerce or general Alaska interest and how much that has to do with my social media efforts on The Real Alaska, I can't say. I'm just glad there are more customers in town, spending their money here."

Mr. Wright's eyes narrowed. "So, you think that the influx of tourists is your doing?"

"I'm not saying it's not."

"Interesting." He took another sip of tea. "Anyway, it's not a real career, but it sounds fun."

Tuli flinched like he'd been slapped, but kept his mouth shut.

Lou's dad continued, "Hopefully, now that you're recovered, you can get back to your other, more substantial work."

"Sir?"

"All of this"—he motioned with his hand—"is entertaining, but it's no way to support and raise a family the right way. Is it?"

"I—" He was so stunned by the question he couldn't come up with an answer.

Steve Wright had cut him off at the knees as surely as his injury.

"If I don't see her, please say hi to your grandmother. Good night."

He nodded at someone nearby, stowed his tea in the holder next to the wheelchair handle, and walked away, pushing Gordy.

Tuli knew only a small percentage of average-Joe influencers made a living out of their work. He knew it was a long shot. But that was why he tried so hard to make it successful. So that one day, he *could* support and raise a family with his efforts.

Unbidden, an image of himself and Lou, with a pair of cute, dark-haired children, flooded him until the air didn't move from his lungs.

Then his gut churned. *Raise a family the right way,* her dad had said.

Tuli's passion was social media. Connecting with people. Making lives better on a bigger scale than what he could do as a firefighter. Helping his community.

Tuli thought that people appreciated what he did to support the town.

He did it because, deep down, he always believed that if he worked hard enough, he could compensate for the parts of his life he wanted to hide from others. He could be successful on his own terms and gain respect.

But Steve Wright didn't have respect for Tuli's dreams and goals. For some reason, that man's opinion mattered.

Tuli halfheartedly waved at his grandmother, who was sitting and laughing with other tribe members at a table nearby. He glanced down at himself, dressed in his work gear, looking professional. He'd look great on a social media clip right now.

Not a real career.

Steve Wright's opinion mattered.

Because...

No. He couldn't mentally go to that place of future dreams.

Raise a family the right way.

Basically, the *right way* was the exact opposite of Tuli's entire childhood and adulthood.

Tuli had been the local kid abandoned by his drug-using mom and then by his abusive dad, who died of an overdose. Great lineage. In the Athabascan groups, family of origin and personal character meant everything. Tuli could read between Mr. Wright's spoken words. Hell, the Wrights were model parents, raising Lou and Gordy, involved in the Koyukon tribe and culture, and working to better their community.

The message from Mr. Wright reinforced what Tuli already knew—all of Tuli's best efforts would never be enough.

Chapter Thirteen

LOU SPOTTED TULI several hours later, after she strolled past the craft vendors. He was shooting a clip on his phone with an outstretched arm, expression animated and friendly. But there was a tension in his face. His neck seemed stiff, the happiness forced.

She wasn't in any position to judge someone else's exterior appearance versus interior strife, though.

Tuli had work to do.

He wasn't avoiding her. She had avoided him.

Why did the thought bother her? She had decided it was for the best.

Right?

Irritation popped like tiny bubbles over her chest, and she swatted at them, like she could swipe the frustration away. So many swirling thoughts filled her mind—the report from the genetic testing lab, starting paramedic school, Hunter's pressure for her to provide him an in with her dad and the mining venture, her fears of another relationship's public exposure.

Glancing at Tuli's broad smile, she suppressed a sigh. He paused and ruffled the hair of one of the young kids in town and answered questions. Then he knelt down with a leg she knew still bothered him and demonstrated how the camera and posting worked.

Lou didn't have much to offer a guy who had always wanted a family of his own.

Therefore, her childhood friend needed to remain only her friend. She needed to focus on that fact.

She didn't need to ignore him.

He didn't need to avoid her.

She sighed. Lou needed to figure herself out, stat.

Her mind continued to whirl.

By the time she strolled up to him, her stomach was churning. "Why do you keep doing that?" God, she hated confrontation of any kind, but she'd had enough of whatever weirdness was between them.

"And a good evening to you, Lou." He grinned. Then his brows pulled down and his mouth twisted. "I have no idea how to answer your very vague, yet somehow terrifying, question."

The words came out in a rush. "Sticking your nose in my personal life." Waving at the phone, she added, "In everyone's personal life. Not everyone likes it." Oh gosh, where had that come from?

"Whoa." He held up his hands and made an obvious show of turning off and stowing the phone in his back pocket. "It sounds like this might be more than just a Tuli issue. Can we talk about this?" He motioned for her to step behind the vendor tents so they had relative privacy.

Damn her, but she followed him, because this was Tuli. She always followed his lead. For some reason, that realization bugged the crap out of her tonight. Once they reached the unlit area behind the tents, she grabbed his wrist to turn him around, shocking herself with the action. With a gasp, she let go and popped her fist on her hip.

He stood in uncharacteristic silence, his dark gaze unreadable in the shadows. He absently rubbed a thumb over the wrist she had held. Then he stood there, waiting patiently.

Waiting for her.

Which also bothered her.

Why didn't he say something? Do something?

Why didn't she? Her thoughts had gone beyond a friendly discussion to encompass much more. No. For so many reasons, they were wrong to try to be anything greater than friends.

Lou tried to examine her own logic—or lack thereof—in this situation. Huffed. Tried again. Damn it. She blurted out, "You're everywhere."

He cocked his head, like she was a specimen in front of a scientist. "That's a problem how?"

"Sometimes you're really irritating, Tuli." Saying anything remotely aggressive made her stomach churn.

"Throw me a bone here, Lou. You caught me flat-footed with that opening statement." He shot her a half smile that soothed the sting of his words and caused a slow, warm swirl in her belly. "I need you to be more specific in your criticism. I'm cool with providing you with a blanket *I'm sorry* statement, but I'd like to know what I'm apologizing for."

That was just it. She didn't have any substantial criticism of him.

Which was the whole problem.

Aargh.

Even when she struggled to get the right words out, he patiently waited. He had consistently had her back over all those years. He worked hard at his jobs and tried to help people. He was friendly to everyone.

He posted videos of Yukon Valley and its citizens online.

He was considerate and never overstepped her boundaries.

She rocked back on her heels.

Maybe she wanted him to overstep a boundary or two.

But ... she'd experienced that before, and it resulted in a disaster.

No buts.

Damn it. He wasn't her ex.

He was her childhood friend.

She paused, really took a moment to view him in a rare moment of both stillness and silence. His broad shoulders slowly rose and fell. He'd bulked up. She thought back over the past six months since his accident.

The injury had been to his leg, not his upper body.

He rolled and released a fist, rubbing his right leg. Sinews and muscle shifted under the dark, button-down fire department uniform shirt.

The material strained over his chest.

She hadn't truly seen the transformation for what it was. Until now.

Yes, it was a change. Was it also overcompensation?

He shifted his weight to his left side with a low grunt and a forehead-furrowing wince.

He'd been hiding from her like she had been hiding from him.

Before she could work through this realization further, his voice reached her, low and soft like a stroke of his finger against her cheek. "You know I want the best of everything for you, Lou. Always have."

For some reason she said, "You have no idea what that is or whether you can provide it. The best, I mean."

He flinched. "I would if you'd ever talk to me. Like we used to."

"We talk. We see each other a lot. Just this morning at Three Bears, I told you about starting the paramedic program next week."

"Which is great. I'm proud of you. But for real, we haven't talked in weeks. Months. Longer. Not really talked in a way that matters. Not like we used to. Ever since you started dating Ryan. And then afterwards."

Now it was Lou's turn to flinch. The breakup with Ryan had exposed her in a way that still felt raw. Vulnerable. Nowadays, when someone paid her attention, it felt like alcohol getting rubbed over open wounds. Instead of saying that, she took a few steps farther away from the laughter and music of the gathering, stopping at several vendor trucks filled with boxes of supplies.

Next to a rusted chrome bumper, she turned around and rested her hand on the tailgate. "Mav and I drop by the deli all the time." Like that was adequate.

Tuli dipped his head. "You're not wrong. You guys do come over and we chat. As three good friends."

"We are friends!" She actually stomped a foot. "Ever since elementary school for us. And Mav's been our friend for several years."

Tuli took one step forward, somehow too far away but also too close. "What if we were more than just friends, Lou?"

For a few seconds, it was hard to breathe. "What?" She tried to ignore the hurt expression written stark on his face, even in the shadows and moonlight. "I mean, we *are* more than just friends, aren't we? We've been great friends for almost twenty years." That was all she had to give right now. It would have to be enough.

Yet it physically hurt her to see the pain cross his face.

Then, for the first time in forever, Tuli went utterly still and serious. His intense gaze pinned her in place. A muscle ticked in his jaw.

Her mouth went dry.

She'd never experienced him like this.

He stepped forward until they were a few inches apart. Heat rolled off him, bringing with it Tuli's light scent of soap and smoky aftershave. "We are the best of friends." He looked down at her. "What if there was more than friend-ship?"

Lou's thoughts swirled like puffs of smoke from a forest fire. One thought chased another to its inevitable, painful conclusion. The genetic report. His dreams. Her changed future. "There's a lot going on right now. Things are complicated."

"Complicated by what?"

She shifted, bumping the vehicle with her hip. "That's none of your business."

Tuli's Adam's apple bobbed. "Life is always complicated. That's life. But sometimes things are truly simple." He rolled his lips. "At some point, we will miss out on some awesome moments by keeping everyone out of our business."

"Sometimes keeping people out of our business reduces the chance of pain."

Nodding, he said, "Connection has risks. It requires trust. Respect." He patted his pocket containing the phone. "It opens us up to criticism and to not living up to others' expectations." His voice dropped to a decibel above a whisper. "It opens us up to being seen as a failure."

It was like he read her mind. "Why risk the pain?"

"Because letting people into our business can also be a joy. Trust. Simple connection." He extended his arms to the sides.

Lou pointed. "That phone attached to the internet makes things not simple."

"Huh?"

She reached for the only logical argument that didn't force her to share her deepest secret. "I had my personal business broadcast all over town once before. I can't do it again. I can't live that exposed of a life. Not like you do."

"No one's asking for you to be broadcast anywhere."

"Aren't you? That's part of the Tuli package. Social exposure." As if she had a shot at being part of that package. Lou knew the score. She did not have a chance.

"What are you getting at?"

"I'm a very private person."

"And I've respected that privacy. Always. Never mentioned your name online. Never put you on camera."

She kept going. "I can't deal with any relationship, friendship or otherwise, on display for others to see and examine. I don't know if I want to be around someone who thinks about life as a series of clips for thousands of people to see."

"Technically, over a hundred thousand people." He gave a self-deprecating snort. "That's literally my job."

"People aren't content."

He flinched like she had slapped him.

Lou blew out a harsh breath. "You're never off. This is why you're so ... you ... all the time."

A beat. Then two. Then he said, "You say that like it's a bad thing."

Horror dawned when she realized what she had said. Lou had undermined what he valued most in his life. She had attacked the person he was. Oh, God. Maybe she could take the words back. "Never mind. It's been a long day. Things are coming out wrong. I don't want to say anything else."

"Why not?"

She fought to form the words. "Because I don't want to hurt you."

"Lou." He was a breath away.

"Yeah?"

"I'm not talking about anything public. I'm not talking about filming things. I'm not talking social media. This conversation right here? It's about you and me. We've been through thick and thin together. Leaned on each other for help. Lifted each other up. All I'm asking is, what if there's more for us?"

Her heart hammered in her chest. The risk of pain versus the risk of ... something good ... tempted her. "I don't know." Even as she said the words, she leaned toward him like he was the anchor off the side of a fishing boat. The weight and the current pulled her toward the churning water.

The scent of woodsmoke and aftershave swirled around him.

What he was suggesting was akin to watching a fall wildfire blaze out of control. The act would be final, irreparable, and risky. Things would never be the same after the flame. Someone could get burned.

She tilted her head up. Somehow, she had ended up a hair's breadth away from him.

His rapid breath feathered over her, warm and familiar. "Lou," he said on an exhale.

She needed that heat like she needed oxygen. "I don't—" Unable to stop herself, she brushed her lips over his. Once. Twice.

Something deep down sparked to flame and crackled to life.

Blazed through her heart.

Then consumed everything in its path.

Tuli. Her friend. How was this possible?

He gave a shuddering breath, lifted her chin with his fingertip, and returned the kiss. Pressed to her lips, his trembled. His kisses drifting over her sent heated waves through her body.

Twenty-six years. She had waited her whole life for this moment.

A moment that had changed everything.

Tuli was familiar, but these fiery sensations were all new. She tilted her head up to better connect with him. He gave a low chuckle that was all Tuli and all satisfaction as he nipped at her lower lip until a small moan escaped her. She gripped his shirt fabric in her quaking fingers, bringing him closer.

No, these weren't completely new sensations.

What was new was the acknowledgment of her feelings. A willingness to experience them and take a risk of being burned.

With a sigh, she swayed into him, and he wrapped his arms around her, supporting her, surrounding her. Completing the circle that was Tuli and Lou.

He slid a hand up her spine, cupping her neck in a strong and callused but gentle grip. Another few strokes of his lips, and the warm moisture of his tongue swept over the seam of her mouth until her lips parted.

As surely as flame and dry tinder responded to a steady breeze, Lou couldn't stop herself from igniting for him.

The tentative but hungry sweep of his tongue against hers sparked electricity down her arms. Her knees softened.

But Tuli held her steady and supported her, even as he

kissed her over and over. His growls rumbled into her bones. Eddies of pleasure swept through her entire body.

"Well, well. Things make a lot more sense now." A deep, loud voice carried over to her.

Chapter Fourteen

Tuli's first thought with Lou in his arms was, *Why in the name of the Northern Lights had he waited this long?*

His second thought at the snide sound of the voice was, *Crap*.

Lou immediately stiffened, and he turned them so that her back was to Hunter. He kept his hands on her upper arms, providing support, while she took a few deep inhalations that he wanted to breathe into his own soul.

Hunter whistled. "So that's how it is."

Lou brushed shaking fingers over her lips, then stood straight and turned around. "No, it's not."

At the same time, Tuli blurted out, "Yes, it is."

Hunter laughed, the sound harsh and dry. "Sounds like you two aren't in the same zip code with this conversation."

Tuli caught a whiff of alcohol coming off Hunter. "We're fine."

With another snort, he crossed his arms. "Why would you pick this guy, Lou? He's a mess. He cuts meat for a living. He had deadbeat parents. Had to be raised by his grandma. Probably bad genes. I know the whole story. Everyone does."

Lou made a strangled noise, and her eyes popped open wide.

"Are you okay?" Tuli asked. He'd never seen her this rattled.

She visibly trembled. "You're way off base about Tuli and all of this, Hunter."

"Really? Because it gets worse," Hunter said. "He's disabled too."

Tuli's belly clenched. The last thing he wanted was for Lou to hear this. It was one thing for his past to be common knowledge around here. It was another thing to have someone air his dirty laundry right in front of him. In front of her.

Hunter sneered. "You know he still has problems with his leg. He can't even do his job."

Before Tuli could form words, Lou said in a flat, dead voice that he'd never heard before, "That's low, Hunter. I'm going to need to ask you to leave."

"What? I'm family who is sticking up for your well-being." His words slurred and he wavered on his feet but remained standing as he pointed. "Now you're actually defending this guy? You know I had to haul his ass out of the last fire because he has become crippled. Lame."

"Quit it." Lou's voice rose and quavered. "Don't use mean words like that."

Tuli caught the glint in her eyes. Of course. Gordy. That, and the fact that she possessed normal human kindness—something Hunter seemed to lack right now.

"He's a loser."

Tuli tried to diffuse the situation. "That's fire chief loser to you."

"Not if I have anything to say about it."

Lou and Tuli, at the same time, said, "What?"

Hunter smirked, a strange expression, with his face half in shadow. "Oh, did I not mention it to you? I've put in for the position, seeing as the current chief is unfit for duty. That'll make my dad and Uncle Steve proud too."

One part of Tuli really wanted this guy to leave so that his weaknesses would stay hidden. For as much as Tuli had tried to compensate for his leg, Hunter had a point. Tuli's leg was not fully healed. Not even close. The leg was a liability. But he could still lead and train others. He had skills and experience.

The side of his neck where he could feel Lou's eyes fixed on him burned.

What he would give for Hunter to be gone and for Tuli to continue kissing Lou.

This moment with Lou that started off amazing, then became a disaster had changed everything. Normal life would never be the same for Tuli.

"What, you have no answer for that?" Hunter said.

Tuli ground his back teeth. No way was he having this conversation right now. No way was his personal business getting aired at the festival by a tipsy Hunter. "Thank you for your concern. Have a great night."

Hunter watched them for a long minute. The noises of chattering people exiting the fish fry drifted over to them on a cool breeze. Tuli could sense Lou shivering next to him.

He wanted nothing more than to wrap an arm around her and keep her warm and safe, but at this point, any action would be fuel. Another minute passed. No one spoke.

Lou shifted from foot to foot. Finally, she shook her head. "I can't do this." She trudged away.

Her absence took a chunk of him with her.

Tuli turned to watch her leave, then rotated back.

Hunter smiled, his face dark and his teeth white. "Your move, *boss*."

Chapter Fifteen

LATE THE FOLLOWING Monday afternoon, Lou restocked the ambulance. She and Hilda had returned from an all-day transport to Fairbanks and back. Now it was time to check equipment and wait for the next call. Lou was hoping to get some studying done as well. The paramedic course-work started online today, and she was eager to dive into the material.

If she could focus.

Seemed like the hardest thing to do these days was calm the swirling thoughts and concentrate on one thing at a time.

"Hi, honey," a familiar voice rang out across the ambulance bay as the garage door opened.

Lou brushed her hands on her navy EMS cargo pants and waved at Mom. Gordy entered behind her, still wearing his high-visibility orange vest. They must have been out walking today, taking advantage of decent weather before the seasons changed.

Immediately, Gordy gave a barking laugh, his way of expressing love. Lou smiled.

Thanks to several months of physical therapy, he had gotten stronger after the severe seizures, which had been followed by a secondary pneumonia earlier this spring. Even now, though, he wasn't back to his full health, but he was better. That was all anyone could ask, given his underlying condition.

"He finished up his afternoon hike around town and wanted to stop by and say hi. I hope you don't mind," Mom said.

His thin fingers worked over the tablet suspended in a case from his neck. "Hug Lou-Lou," the machine intoned.

Lou let Gordy drape his arms on her shoulders and press his forehead to hers. "Anytime we're here, you guys are welcome to stop by." She leaned back and tugged at the vest. "You were busy today, huh? Getting free snacks at the diner, I bet."

Gordy grinned. Busted. He moved his hand on the machine. "Yes."

Hilda waved and said, "Hi, Mrs. Wright. Hi, Gordy!" as she headed into the EMT lounge.

Lou gave Gordy a proper hug. If his return embrace seemed weaker than usual, she didn't mention anything to Mom. Sweet love twisted into sour concern. Lou was looking at her future. This is what the genetic report meant.

Gordy was a walking, talking—well, not talking, but laughing—miracle of medical care and resilience, but he had already lived a difficult life and had more challenges ahead of him. The late twenties were when patients with Bledsoe Syndrome began to decline. Gordy was thirty. Her chest ached.

Lou couldn't willingly have a child who might be similarly affected. She shook her head, still trying to wrap her mind around the way her future had completely changed. Options were out of her control.

"What's wrong?" Mom said, touching Lou's forehead. "You're thinking really hard right there."

"It's nothing."

"Is it a boy?"

She resisted the urge to roll her eyes. "I'm twenty-six. There are no *boys* around."

"It's always about boys. They're a mess." She gave Gordy a kindhearted nudge with her elbow.

Gordy made his classic throat-slashing hand gesture to indicate he was not happy with the direction this conversation was going.

"Fine, fine. *Some* boys are trouble. Never you." Lou laughed along with him. Sobering, she said, "Mom, I got the results back from that genetic test."

"Oh?"

"The results weren't what I had hoped for."

Her face fell. "I am so sorry, honey. I don't know what to say."

Her throat hurt when she swallowed. "It'll be okay. I feel bad for you and Dad without grandchildren in your future."

"You can adopt."

"You know what I mean."

Her eyes shimmered, making Lou blink hard to avoid crying herself. Saying the results out loud hurt. The theoretical had become real.

Mom gave a practical nod and continued. "Grandchildren are the least of my concerns. Your dad and I want you healthy and happy and fulfilled, living the life that you want."

Which, for Lou, had meant having children eventually. Or so she'd always thought. She took a shaky breath and forced the enthusiasm. "I'm fine. I'm healthy. I have friends. I have a good job." She made a face—anything to break the tension. "I have goofball Gordy here." Thank God, he laughed. The guy was terrific for comic relief. "What's not to like about that?"

"You know as well as I do that there's more, but those options may not be available to you the way you had hoped they would be."

"It is what it is." Her words were light. Lou's chest was heavy.

"That seems like a cop-out."

"Yes, but it's my cop-out—"

At that moment, the garage door opened. Tuli appeared in the doorway, fall afternoon sunshine pouring in around him. In his hands was a bouquet of fall flowers.

On his face was a classic who-me? Tuli smile.

"What are you doing here?" Lou asked.

Would it be rude to ask Mom and Gordy to leave right now? Because things were liable to get embarrassing. Best guess was that her face had turned reddish purple, given the heat climbing her neck.

Gordy gave a jerky hand wave and made an irregular fist.

Tuli unwrapped one hand from the flowers to gently give a knuckle bump. "Hey, Gordy, you staying out of trouble this week?"

Gordy shook his head and stared at Tuli. "No way," came the computerized voice.

Mom patted Gordy on the upper arm and murmured, "We should go get groceries for dinner."

With a wink from Mom and a barking laugh from Gordy, they exited.

Lou's head spun as she stared at Tuli. "What are you doing here? What is this?"

"Taking the bull by the horns." His wry smile melted her heart. "I'm good at giving out advice, but it's time I take it."

"Huh?"

He thrust the flowers at her. Frankly, it was nice to have something to do with her hands besides nervously twist her fingers together.

Tuli continued. "I know we've been friends forever. You're one of my best friends in the whole world. I, uh ... things changed here recently with me, and I'm hoping it's changed for you, as well. I want more of what we did the other night. I want more of hanging out with you."

"Which means?"

He made a show of wiping his brow. "You don't make this easy, do you?"

Her cheeks radiated heat. Heart pounded. Thoughts swirled in a kaleidoscope of colors to rival the blooms in her hands.

Tuli stood there. After a minute, his broad smile wavered, but held.

Lou cleared her throat. "You don't give up, do you?"

"Not if it's for something—or someone—worthwhile."

Memories of playing house in the schoolyard and their friendship and their dreams and her test results raced through her brain one right after the other. She heaved in lungfuls of air but still felt like she was suffocating. Could she do this to him? Lou knew his desire to have a family. He'd made it clear from day one that all he ever wanted was to have kids and a family. Going down this path with her would only cause him pain.

She swallowed against a dry lump. This was going to hurt.

She couldn't do it. "Tuli, don't take this the wrong way," she began.

He whistled low. "If you're about to blow me off, then there isn't a right way to take this."

It took her a minute to come up with the words. "For a lot of reasons, I ... can't ... right now." Ever. Not with Tuli.

"Can you tell me why?" A reasonable question from her best friend in the whole world.

"I ... this isn't right. Us. Together. Now. We can't."

Tuli's expression shifted from brow-raised hope to something akin to a dog that had been kicked.

Lou felt like she had been kicked as well. "I can't go into the reasons. It's nothing you've done. I'm so sorry." The shaking in her limbs worsened. "I know you don't understand." How was she doing this to Tuli?

Because she had cared more for him than for herself.

For the first time in forever, his features drew into a mad scowl. "Yeah, I do understand. You've made it clear."

He turned on his heel.

The door closed.

Lou stared at the bright flowers that quivered in her hands.

SEVERAL HOURS LATER, when the shift ended, Lou was exhausted from fending off Hilda's well-meaning questions. The paramedic had caught the tail end of Tuli's visit and drawn all sorts of conclusions.

Lou walked home to her apartment, situated over the town furniture store. Normally, she loved her walks to and from work when the weather was good.

Today, she only wanted to be home. Not exposed. Locked behind a door, curled up on the couch. Away from people who knew her and smiled and waved when she walked past. Away from the people who wanted to chat about *how are you doing, how's your family, anything new in your love life, why are you carrying flowers?*

Trudging up the metal stairs, she entered her neat one-bedroom apartment, greeted by her white cat, Frost, who meowed in protest that she had left him at home once again. After the obligatory pat on his head, she unlaced and removed her work boots, laid the bouquet on the coffee table, then collapsed on the loveseat with a deep sigh. Frost jumped up and positioned his fuzzy frame on her lap so he could receive maximum pats. She smiled as his efforts to be standoffish were overridden by his need for scratches behind his white ears.

White fur appeared on her navy uniform top.

Her cat's low purring was the only sound in the apartment, and Lou took another breath in and slowly let it out.

The past several days—no, weeks—had been exhausting.

She glanced over at the flowers.

Rolling her lips, she sensed the ghost of Tuli's mouth on hers from the festival. Liquid heat spread through her veins.

What if?

No. She wouldn't dictate someone else's future. Bad enough that hers had been altered.

Why couldn't she let him know the truth and then he could make his own decision?

Lou sniffed. Because she knew Tuli. Knew that he would give up his dream. Sacrifice for a friend, because that was what Tuli did. Choosing her would hurt him.

She hugged Frost another time until he purred and made biscuits on her tummy.

Her phone dinged, too loud in the quiet living room. Lou jostled Frost, triggering an indignant meow, as she fished in her cargo pants pocket and opened the message.

Sorry.

The emptiness in her chest threatened to expand until there was nothing left of her. Her friend hadn't given up on their connection. He had apologized for something that wasn't remotely his fault. Finally, she typed back. *Me too. I was kind of harsh. There's a lot going on.*

It was just flowers and asking for a date.

He was right. She cast around for an excuse that wasn't a dodge but wasn't the whole truth. An excuse that wouldn't hurt him. *I know. I'm pretty allergic to public exposure with a relationship.*

From Ryan?

People are still talking about the breakup.

Makes sense you'd be leery of an influencer.

I'm really sorry.

Dots moved on the screen. Typing. Finally, the message popped up. *What if I promise to keep us a secret until you say otherwise? That way, if it doesn't work out, nobody has to know.*

Her heart cracked like a thick piece of wood finally breaking open in a burn pile. What he was offering felt like leftovers. A consolation prize for him. Suppressing his open, friendly nature to be with her.

He still didn't know her life-altering secret, either. Could she tell him?

Not like this.

He didn't deserve her waffling. He didn't deserve a relationship with conditions. Yet here he was, willing to accommodate her spoken and unspoken needs.

He didn't deserve to share in her limited future.

What. If.

Was this selfishness? Willfully ignoring her reality and leading him on?

What. If.

What if she told him and let him decide?

Still sounded unfair.

The image of his smiling, open expression floated before her. Years of friendship. Of history. She trusted him with her story. He deserved the truth.

Lou typed back. *Ok.*

More typing dots. *When is your next day off?*

Chapter Sixteen

FOUR DAYS LATER, on Friday, Tuli and Lou rode ATVs up to the top of Blackberry Hill. All the locals knew that the location was the best place to find late-season blackberries. At the top of the knoll, he inhaled the crisp fall air and took off his canvas jacket, leaving him in a black, long-sleeved thermal shirt. Temperatures had cooled, now that they were well into September. They'd have snow in the next month. He looked toward the higher mountains to the north. No termination dust yet.

But soon.

For now? Blackberries.

His mouth watered at the prospect. Hopefully, the bushes weren't picked over. He also crossed his fingers that there wouldn't be unwanted visitors. He patted his bear spray on one hip and his holstered pistol on the other.

He dismounted with a wobbly stumble, cursing to himself and glancing at the dust drifting away from his tracks up the hill. The second ATV was not in sight yet. Good. Lou hadn't seen him. He dropped a light fist onto his thigh. The ATV ride had fired up the nervy pain down his leg. The prickly half-asleep sensation never seemed to go away, no matter how much he rubbed on the skin.

He listened carefully. No rustling of large animals trudging through the shrubbery. Just the sound of Lou's ATV growing louder.

He pulled out his phone and snapped a few pictures of the scenery for a later post, then quickly stowed the device. He grimaced at the loss of a video opportunity.

Today wasn't about social media.

Lou appeared around a bend in the trail thirty seconds later, parked, and took off her helmet. Long, dark hair rippled down her back before she secured it in a low ponytail.

Tuli rubbed his thumb and index finger together, wanting to touch and see if her hair felt as silky as it looked. At her cautious expression, he rolled his hand into a fist and planted it at his side. *Go slowly*. First and foremost, they were friends, and he didn't want to ruin that friendship.

Whatever he had done wrong, it had spooked her. Today was a sort-of date. Tuli wouldn't push. Instead, he'd do what he did best—enthusiasm.

"Blackberry time!" he said, unhooking the nested buckets from the bungees on the back of his ATV and handing her one.

Lou's small, guarded smile changed into an open, relaxed one.

Point for Tuli.

If the day seemed to get brighter, she didn't appear to notice. Tuli sure as heck did.

"Let's go!" He motioned toward the thick bushes lining either side of the ATV trail. "Yes! Looks like there are still blackberries here. Grandma Ruth will be thrilled. She wants to make compote and preserves."

Lou dropped her thick leather jacket on the ATV. She had a blue-and-black-checked flannel shirt tucked into cargo pants. She looked up from where she studied the bush in front of her. "How long will the blackberries last?"

"With my appetite for her cooking? Not long. Actually, with my snacking ability, we'll be lucky if most of this makes it down the hill. But Grandma can dream about them lasting until spring."

Lou's laugh, rare and unrestrained, felt like liquid sunshine pouring over him, illuminating the world and making him smile. For several minutes, they worked in companionable silence, the only sounds the rustles of leaves and branches and the dull *thunks* of berries hitting the bottoms of the buckets.

"What about you? Are you keeping the berries or are these for your family?" he asked.

"I wanted them for myself, but when I told Gordy I was picking today, he really lit up." With a shrug, she said, "Guess these are his now."

Tuli looked over at her guarded expression. "How's he been doing? I know with his condition …"

Lou paused as several berries rolled out of her hand into the bucket. The soft impacts of fruit on plastic sounded wrong. Even the rustling of a ground squirrel in the underbrush was somehow too harsh.

He studied the stiff set of her shoulders and blinked. It wasn't about Gordy. Something else was going on. There was more to her quietness and downturned mouth. He'd bet on it. Tuli resisted his usual need to fill the silence and waited.

Finally, she said, "Mom and Dad think that Gordy is slowing down."

"What do you mean?"

"The syndrome he has ... it's progressive."

Tuli blew out a low whistle. Maybe her worry really was about her brother. "Oh man, that's rough. I didn't realize that. I had thought he needed an adjustment on his medications and some rest, and then he'd be fine."

"Nothing about Gordy's health is simple."

"I'll say."

Lou studied the blackberry bush in front of her.

A breeze teased strands of hair over her forehead, tempting Tuli to brush them to the side.

Her silence was his kryptonite.

He pressed his mouth shut, fighting against the discomfort.

They slowly worked their way up a game trail, the bushes growing closer together here. After another few seconds, she half turned toward him, her eyes bright. Was it the fall sunlight or were those tears? Tuli had never seen Lou cry, and the thought of it hit him like a punch to the gut.

She picked another berry, her fingertips now tinged purple. "Other patients who've had Bledsoe Syndrome generally don't live past age thirty."

Tuli did some terrible math. "Isn't he four years older than you? Thirty?"

"I never said Gordy followed the rules. We figure he's like a cat. Nine lives." She held the blackberry in her palm, jiggling it in a circle.

Her half smile, half frown triggered an overwhelming response to pull her into his arms and not let go.

Clearing his throat, he managed to quip, "I knew there was a reason I liked him."

"Well. Yes." She popped the blackberry in her mouth, chewing slowly. Then she said, "I think what that means for my family is, every moment with Gordy is special. We recognize that we're on borrowed time. The doctors will continue fine-tuning his treatment, but at some point, we know that it won't work."

He rocked back on his heels at the stark finality of the statement. A world without Gordy. The town wouldn't be the same. "That's a heavy weight for you and your parents to carry."

"Mom and Dad are solid. They have a good perspective on life and take each day as it comes. They cope with the situation in their own way. But yeah, it's hard." She looked like she wanted to say something else, but she turned away and plucked more berries. The cool breeze and her movements made the bush leaves *shush*. Nearby, a bird fluttered onto a high branch and called out *hey sweetie, hey sweetie.* Tuli smiled. Chickadee. Persistent in their calls for attention.

Speaking of persistent … He studied her frown in profile and gently pressed. "Is there more?"

She turned, but her gaze landed a few inches next to him. "What do you mean?"

"Gordy's been in your life, well, your entire life. You've known about his medical issues since before you could probably walk. You've rolled with all of the ups and downs. Been a great sister for him."

"But ..." That one quiet word hung in the bright, cool fall air, punctuated by the chickadee call.

He gulped. Time to dive in. This might hurt. "First of all, you have a life to live, and you deserve your own happiness. Second, it seems like you're dealing with more than Gordy's situation."

Another minute of silence. "It's tough talking about things."

He took the four steps to close the distance and curled his hand around her upper arm. "Hey, Lou, it's me. You know that you can tell me anything." He dropped his hand and made a key-turning motion in front of his mouth. "I will keep it in the vault. If you want to share, I'm here for it." *Here for you.* Then he stood there, being present.

The lack of conversation nearly killed him.

Her expression twisted.

Oh no. A cold wave rolled through him. There was something else, and it wasn't good. He studied her face for a hint. Did it have to do with her conversations with Hunter? Had the guy upset her? Because, supervisor or not, Tuli would give the guy a piece of his mind.

Was it something Tuli had done? He'd fix it. Make amends. Step back. Whatever.

Finally, Lou said, "You know how when we were kids, we would play house together?"

"Yeah, I liked that." Those were some of his best memories from an early childhood filled with pain and loss.

"We would talk about our dreams of growing up. Having families."

"I never stopped wanting that. Even after all these years," he said.

"Yeah."

Wait. Did that mean … they had a chance? For a guy who could always find the right words to say, the fear of saying the wrong thing rendered him silent.

A small sigh brushed past him like a soft caress. "Life doesn't always turn out the way we expected it to."

Something was so wrong here. Tuli knew it in his bones. Everything in the world was sitting one degree off plumb. Even the sunlight was wrong. His heart thudded against his ribs. "I don't follow."

"It's—" She shook her head. "Never mind."

No. He wanted to hear all of it. Whatever it was. "Come on, Lou, you've been my best friend growing up. What's going on? You're kind of scaring me."

She bent a small branch until it broke and dropped the piece on the ground, then wiped her fingers on her cargo pants. "You know how I was dating Ryan a while back?"

He gritted his teeth. That relationship had been hard to watch from the sidelines, but Tuli hadn't felt confident enough to ask her out back then. *You snooze; you lose*. This wasn't the time to share his opinions on her past love life. Might not even be the time to share opinions on her future love life, either. He had no idea the direction this conversation was headed.

"Yeah."

"Before we broke up and before he … anyway. Ryan and I had long conversations about family and future and what we wanted together."

Tuli did not want to hear any of this. Every muscle tensed. He gripped his bucket handle. He should have been there, not Ryan.

Tuli had doubted his own value and what he brought to the table as a poor guy from a broken family. He had hesitated. Hell, he still doubted his value, especially his value to a woman like Lou. Rubbing his leg, he clamped his jaw tightly and forced his hand to rest at his side. Thanks to his injury, now he had even less to bring to the table.

"I ordered some testing," she said.

"Testing?"

She glanced at him, her brown eyes and lightly tanned skin glowing in the sunshine. "We had agreed to get the testing but broke up long before the results came back."

The smooth line of her throat as she swallowed torment-ed him.

She continued, "I have a feeling the results would've ended our relationship anyway."

Tuli hated the direction this conversation was headed, but Lou was his friend, and by God, he'd hang in there for her.

Tests. Results. Her family. The pieces slotted together in a terrible logic. "Wait. Do you mean…"

Her voice was so quiet, he had to strain to hear the

words. "I got tested for Bledsoe Syndrome."

Tuli froze. He studied Lou's stiff frame, her knuckles turning white as she clutched her bucket in front of her. Her gaze focused on something a few feet to the side.

"I have it."

A rushing sound filled Tuli's head. His heartbeat thudded in his brain. He wanted to hold her and tell her something—anything—that would make this better. Her frame was so tight, he worried that one touch would shatter her.

Keep talking. Ask questions. Be supportive. "But you don't have any of the health problems that Gordy does."

A nod. Her gaze rose and met his briefly. "I have what's called a balanced translocation."

He racked his brain. Came up with nothing. "What's that?"

"Gordy has extra genetic material on chromosome 14. That's what causes Bledsoe Syndrome."

"Okay."

"I have that same extra genetic material on one copy of that chromosome, but there is a corresponding deletion of that same material on the other copy of the chromosome."

High school biology didn't prepare him to understand this information. "I'm not following. Doesn't that mean the extra material plus the reduced material equals a normal amount for you?" She looked normal. Not that appearance told the whole story of these sorts of problems, he guessed. Hell, he had no idea. He wasn't a doctor.

"Yes. The net result is a normal amount of genetic material for me."

"So that's good. Right?"

"It's good for me. It won't be good for any child. One hundred percent of offspring will have something"—she choked—"wrong with them. A genetic condition. Could be nothing major. Could be Bledsoe Syndrome. Could be something totally different and worse. No way to know." The corners of her mouth fell and her chin quivered, but she didn't make another sound.

Everything became clear in one big, giant rush. His friend, hurting. Her future, gone. Too late, he put down his bucket, eased her bucket from her clenched fingers, and set it on the ground. He pulled her into his arms, so gently, fighting the need to embrace her tightly until he completely surrounded her. He wanted to be the buffer between Lou and reality. He needed to protect her from this information.

But all he could do was to provide support and human touch. After a few seconds, Lou gave a shuddering sigh and slid her arms around his back. His shirt tightened around his chest as she fisted the fabric on his back, constricting him in an act of comfort for herself.

She could have all of it. Take up his space. Use him to squeeze the pain out if it brought her relief. He didn't care.

Her occasional sniffle gutted him more than a loud sob ever could. Raising one hand, he cupped the back of her head and pressed her face to his neck, dipping his chin to bracket her. He braced his legs shoulder width apart, wincing as her added weight made the muscles in his right leg shake.

He'd be damned if he would let her fall.

Her voice was so quiet against his neck that he had to strain to hear it. "Anyway, it was probably a good thing that Ryan and I broke up. That would've been a deal-breaker."

Deal-breaker. Tuli's thoughts spun out like an ATV stuck in silty mud.

Everything he wanted rested in his arms right now. His deepest dream, come to life.

Only … that dream had always involved children. His children. His chance at being better than his parents.

Their family.

That dream would never exist. Not in the way that he had hoped it would.

But this was Lou.

His Lou.

Lou from the schoolyard, the girl who always hugged her older brother, no matter how the other students snickered. The woman who had held Tuli's heart since … forever.

What did someone say to news like this?

Before he could come up with any consolation worthy of speaking aloud, Lou pulled back a few inches, briefly met his gaze, then stared near the top of his collarbone. "Now you know why I wasn't in a hurry to date anyone when I didn't have that information. Now I'm not in a hurry to date, *knowing* that information."

Her defeated, cracked laugh made him tighten his embrace. Press his palms against her flannel-covered back, spread out his fingers. Try anything to give more support and comfort.

"I know that at some point, you might have hoped for us

to go out," she continued. "But with your influencer stuff, I've never wanted, like, to be exposed socially. That was before. But now? I want exposure even less."

"But—"

She gave a sharp shake of her head. "We both have things we need in our lives. I couldn't take away your dream. You had made it clear from childhood that all you've ever wanted was a family with children."

Tuli held still, except for the thumb rubbing absently over the soft skin of her neck as they stood pressed to one another. She was right. He had always yearned for what he never had. Two parents who loved each other and their children. As he leaned back and stared down into Lou's dark eyes and sad but thoughtful expression, the truth hit him harder than a tree rolling off of a logging truck.

"You shut me out so that we wouldn't get to this point," he said. "So I wouldn't get hurt."

He felt her shrug.

Tuli took a big breath. "We don't always get what we want." No way did he want to admit his truth, but hell, it looked like all the Band-Aids were getting ripped off today. "I wanted my leg to work again after the accident, but here I am."

"It's still messed up?"

"Yep. Way worse than what anyone knows."

A silent *oh* preceded her murmured words. "I thought it gave you a little trouble. I had no idea."

"Docs say it will never be the same again. Permanent damage."

"I didn't realize that."

"I didn't want people to think even less of me." He let out a low chuckle and briefly pressed his forehead to hers. "Seems like we've both kept pieces of ourselves from each other for all the right and wrong reasons." Unable to resist, he brushed his lips over her hairline and inhaled her scent of fresh air and berries. As always, Lou's quiet, steady presence grounded him. Her presence also created other feelings that he wanted to explore. Not right now. Not in this situation. "So, the genetic condition means—"

Leaning back, she met his eyes. "If I have a child, they will either inherit the genetic duplication or the deletion. Both will cause a syndrome involving disabilities."

"There are other ways to have a family."

"I know that. My parents had really hoped that I would be able to have a natural child. It was important to them."

"That's their wish." He lifted a hand and brushed the windswept strands of hair back from her face. "What's your wish?"

"Similar to theirs. It's a fantasy now."

"What about something real that isn't fantasy? Something right in front of you?"

Lou didn't say a word, but as she watched him, her emotions flowed across her expression like fall leaves chasing each other down the trail, threatened to drive him to his knees. Her lower lip quivered, and a tear tracked from the inside of her nose down her cheek. In over twenty years, he had never seen her cry.

That one tear destroyed him. The ache deep in his chest

sucked the wind out of him.

"Ah, Lou. You're killing me."

He wrapped her again in his arms and dropped more kisses on her forehead. Then he trailed kisses down her cheek until he tasted salt. An imaginary fist wrapped around his heart. He drifted his kisses lower, until their lips finally met.

Locked together. Warm and soft pressure.

Everything clicked into place.

The sound that she made was a half sigh, half sob, and a one-hundred percent gut punch. He wanted to be the guy to erase that sadness. Replace grief with hope. He needed to be enough to fill her future.

Could he be enough?

Tuli had his doubts but pushed them to the side.

Right now, he just wanted to be Lou's shelter. Her lips parted on a soft sound, and he met her tongue with another scorching kiss. She tasted like blackberries and smelled like a cool fall afternoon. He snaked one arm more firmly around her lower back and buried his hand in her hair once again, tilting her face up to him. The kiss stoked a banked fire into a hungry flame.

This, right here. This was the moment that he had waited for his entire life.

He'd always known Lou was special, but he had no idea. The way they fit together, the way they kissed, the way they connected. He hadn't been prepared for any of it. Yet he'd known it would be like this. They had always been friends. He'd known the person she was.

At the end of the day, deep down, he'd known that it

would always be Lou.

Through the haze of kisses came a sniffling rumble and crackles nearby. He did a quick check-in on his stomach. Nope, not rumbling. There it was again. Low. Growling. Huffing.

Like a man buried in an avalanche and digging up to the surface, he pulled away, hauling in giant lungfuls of air.

Lou blinked, her warm brown eyes as glazed as he felt.

Another growling *whuff.*

Tuli gripped her arms. "Oh, shit."

Chapter Seventeen

L OU'S WORLD SPUN. She couldn't breathe.
From the raw sadness of revealing her deepest secret
to the heated honey kisses to the ice-water-shocking
realization that she wanted more of *this* with Tuli, she
struggled to regain her balance.

Then … enter a fat brown bear, apparently still hungry,
and possibly looking for one last big meal of delicious
blackberries before heading into hibernation.

She focused in a hurry. Like most people living in this
area, she knew how to handle herself around bears.

Step one. Don't encounter them in the first place. They
were way past that step.

She reached for the bear spray at her hip as the large bear
appeared about ten yards up the narrow blackberry-picking
trail. The ATVs were forty yards behind them.

Tuli reached an arm back for her and said in a low voice,
"Grab your bucket and back up. I think we'll make it to the
ATVs."

"Got it," she murmured, her movements slow.

He remained in front of her, his pistol in his hand.

With her hand resting on his shoulder, they took careful
steps backward until they emerged on the ATV trail. The

bear tracked their movements, now clacking his jaws, along with making pulsing huffs. Sweat iced her neck.

Crap.

"Go ahead and get your helmet on while I watch," Tuli said, resting the gun on his ATV seat while he poured one bucket into the other, nested the buckets, and stowed them on the back of the machine.

Keeping her movements deliberate, Lou eased the helmet on and buckled it, then mounted her ATV. Holding up her canister of bear spray, she said, "Okay. Your turn."

Tuli's actions mirrored hers. Once he was on his ATV, he nodded, and they both started the engines. The bear jogged toward them with a low, growling huff and stood on its back legs. Lou's heart leaped as she gunned the throttle.

Fifteen minutes and a lot of kicked-up dust later, they crossed a few fire roads, pulled off at an overlook, and dismounted. With shaking hands, she hooked her helmet on the seat back.

"We should be good for now," Tuli said. "You okay?"

From what? The bear or the kisses?

No. She wasn't okay. On either front.

The Yukon River, opaque with silty water, rushed below them in the distance. Late afternoon sun slanted through the nearby trees, and poplar leaves drifted to the ground in gold flickers.

She glanced over her shoulder and reflexively flinched. Tuli held up his camera and rotated 180 degrees.

Lou resisted the deep-seated urge to avert her face.

"I got you covered." He aimed the screen away from her.

"This is too beautiful of a picture to miss sharing."

Always the social media influencer. How many hundreds of thousands of people would see this exact moment that Lou was living?

He murmured as he rotated back to the middle of the view. A few swipes later and he stowed the phone. "Uploaded and sent. If this doesn't make people want to visit, I don't know what will."

"You could send it now?"

"Sure. Check your phone." He waited until she pulled hers out. "Enough bars from town to get the job done."

"Oh, you're right. Just like that?"

"Hashtags and all. This is a great place for a tourism post."

"Noticed you didn't get a clip of the bear."

"That's not good advertising!" He waved his hands in front of him. "Also, I'm not risking my life for a video."

"Do you think all the time about social media and how many views you'll get?" She almost tried to take back the words but held off.

"How I grow my brand and my reach? I don't think about it all the time, but having an eye for what people want to see comes with the territory, like interacting with followers through clips and commentary and responses."

"The way you interact with people is different than the way that I interact with people." She blurted out, "People aren't content."

He whipped his head up. "You mentioned that before. I'm in agreement, by the way." Then he tilted his head to the side, looking like the young Tuli of high school. "It's nice to be able to use my voice for others. Boost tourism. It's great to bring awareness and interest in the Athabascan culture."

"Why?"

"I like helping people, and I can do it with my platform."

"Like you helped the Steens with those land speculators?"

"The satisfying revenge at the Breakup Festival?" He grinned, all eye-twinkling devilry. "That was one of my most popular clips. That Randy dude brought the drama and caught some karma. All I had to do was record it."

It was on the tip of her tongue to question whether one truly experienced life if they were always recording it. But she kept her mouth shut.

After a few minutes of feeling the breeze and the sunshine on her face, she sighed. "So, no more berries, then?"

"We could go somewhere else. But I wouldn't return up the hill for another day or two."

The day was done then.

She had semi-dreaded this outing, but now she didn't want it to end.

She mounted her ATV. Tuli stood next to her, his thigh brushing against her knee. A zip of warmth at that small contact worked its way through her.

"We didn't get to finish our conversation," he said.

Her heart lodged in her throat. "Um."

"I'd love a chance with you."

After everything she had unloaded on him. "You sure about that?"

"You doubt me?"

"No. I doubt myself."

He tilted her chin up with a gentle finger. "What do you mean?"

"I don't know if I can handle being disappointed."

"By me?" That hand drifted down to her shoulder, sending a mixture of tingles and warm safety through her.

"No. Of course not. By me. By my situation. By the things that make me nervous."

"Then I will do my part to try to never hurt you."

"This is scary," she managed to say, reaching across and covering his hand with hers where it rested on her arm.

He laced their fingers together and brought their hands between them. "What part of it is scary?"

It took her a minute to organize the words. "All of it. My future. Our future. Feeling exposed socially. Knowing what you want out of life. New things."

His shrug came with a goofy smile. "What is life without trying new things?"

"Sure, but I don't want to hurt *us*." She let go of him and pressed her hand to her chest. "This. Our years of friendship."

"The friendship between us will always be there."

"But."

"What if we've been missing out on something even more special?"

"I don't want to be hurt." *I don't want* to *hurt*. There was a difference.

He cupped her jaw with his hands. "I would rather die than hurt you, Lou. I want to try."

Her mouth went dry.

How could she accept what he was offering, knowing that it wasn't what he had envisioned for his future?

Tuli was an adult. The cards were all on the table. He knew the facts just like she did and could make an informed decision.

Besides, what if they had a future together? Maybe not the future they had originally envisioned, but a new future. Together.

He cleared his throat. "So. How do you want to do this?"

"This?"

"This official us."

"Can we go slowly?"

"We go at whatever pace you want to go." He stroked her cheek with his thumb. "But if you could give me an idea of what you want the next step to be, that would be helpful."

Her laugh rang out in the crisp fall air. What felt right? "Dinner with my family?"

"Ooh, meet the parents?" He made an exaggerated collar-pulling movement. "Nothing like jumping right into the fire. Easy-peasy." He pressed a quick kiss to her lips and pulled back. "It's a deal."

Chapter Eighteen

TULI'S MOUTH TURNED to silt as he walked up to Melinda and Steve Wright's one-story house in the Koyukon village two days later on Sunday. The village was right outside of Yukon Valley town proper, and he knew the area well, given that Grandma Ruth lived four doors down.

He had parked at her place.

Now Grandma waved at him from the front yard.

He raised his hand in a quick greeting, then ducked his head and kept walking, aware that she was still waving. Despite the cool weather at dusk, sweat prickled his lower back.

Small towns sometimes were definitely too small. Point conceded to Lou on that one.

Why was he nervous? He had known Lou and her family for years. He'd eaten many meals here as a kid. Tuli had zero problems talking with anyone about anything. He was the most social person in Yukon Valley.

His stomach knotted.

If that first kiss at the festival was one foot perched over the cliff, then tonight was two feet off. The point of no return. Public acknowledgement of intent.

He glanced over at Grandma Ruth, her smile obvious

even in the twilight, and gave her another half-wave, half-*shoo* gesture.

As he reached the Wrights' front door, he paused, hand lifted to knock. Before he could make contact with the wood, the door opened, and a laughing Hunter appeared.

"Hey, great talking with you again, Uncle Steve. I look forward to working together. Let me know what I else can do to help," he called over his shoulder.

Tuli rocked back on his heels, his right leg buckling before he could shift his weight to the left side. He gripped the stair railing of the small porch. "What are you doing here?"

"Nothing that relates to the fire department. Therefore, none of your business." Hunter dropped his voice. "What are you doing here?"

"Same. None of your business."

Hunter planted his feet at the entrance.

Tuli glanced over Hunter's shoulder into the house.

One of them needed to enter. One of them needed to exit. Neither of them was moving.

Well, that made for a pickled herring if he'd ever seen one.

Thankfully, Mr. Wright appeared. "Tuli, right on time. Come on in."

Hunter muttered under his breath as he pushed past Tuli. His glare shifted into a superstar smile, then he called back to Lou's father, "Have a terrific night."

It was a mystery how Tuli managed to keep a lid on what he wanted to say. That guy was as fake as the white on his teeth.

With a smile of his own, Tuli entered the home and shook Mr. Wright's hand before the man headed to the kitchen. As Tuli removed his leather loafers he'd worn to only a few weddings and funerals in the past, he took in the familiar surroundings. Not much had changed. Woven throw blankets rested on the back of the well-loved couch. A decorated ceremonial paddle with salmon painted on it hung on the wall.

Pictures of Gordy and Lou from their high school graduations featured on one wall, their black caps and tassels framing smiling faces. Next to them hung a faded photo of a Melinda and Steve years ago at their wedding. He did a double take. Lou favored a young Melinda with her bright-eyed, smiling, open face, and dark brows and hair.

Lou walked up to him, her cheeks a dark crimson.

"Hi, Lou. How's it going?" He reached out to hug or kiss her, but at her raised eyebrows, he held off.

"Good." She bit her lip, and a jolt of heated interest shot right through him at the small gesture. Not the right time.

He made a big show of sniffing the aromas. "I'm hoping we get to have something that involves the efforts of our life-threatening berry picking." After they got back to town, he had given Lou all of their forage.

Because he couldn't face his Grandma empty-handed, Tuli had then bought out the Three Bears' supply of blackberries and put them in the empty bucket. That bill put a dent in his monthly budget. Groceries in Alaska were generally expensive, what with blackberries running ten dollars per pint and eight pints in a gallon. But no way would he come home with less than two gallons of blackberries.

So, it was probably good he was eating at the Wrights' tonight. Maybe they'd let him take home leftovers so he could save a little money on the next meal or two.

A high-barked laugh came from the recliner on the far side of the living room.

"*Gganaa'*, Gordy!" He waited for the guy to form a fist so Tuli could bump it. "You staying out of trouble?"

The sharp shake of Gordy's head made his response clear before he pressed the buttons. "No way." His smile stayed put.

Tuli leaned against the armrest on the end of the nearby couch and pointed at the TV. "Ooh, ESPN. Are we watching the Seahawks?"

"We are absolutely not watching the Seahawks." Mrs. Wright walked over, picked up the remote, and clicked off the TV.

Gordy pulled a face, but his unrepentant smile quickly returned.

Lou laughed as she helped Gordy to stand. He lurched up, bracing his hands on her shoulders. Tuli instinctively reached out but held back, unsure of how much he should assist. After a minute of steadying him, Lou took a step back and gripped Gordy's upper arm as he walked to the kitchen. One of his legs didn't lift properly.

Tuli knew all about that.

Gordy stumbled on the wood flooring, but Lou caught him.

"Everything okay?" her dad asked over his shoulder as he helped his wife.

"Gordy's just demonstrating the joke about 'have a nice trip, see you next fall.' Right?" Lou said.

Her brother laughed out loud and clapped once before he continued on to the table, where Lou settled him into a chair.

"Anything I can help with, Mrs. Wright?" Tuli asked. Normally, younger adults called elder women *auntie*, but it didn't seem like the correct name to call Lou's mother.

Thankfully, she didn't seem to notice. "No, I'm good. Go have a seat, and we'll have dinner out in a moment. And please call us Melinda and Steve."

"All right." Tuli wandered back into the living room, where Lou straightened up some magazines on the end table. He stopped a few inches away from her. "You okay?" he murmured.

"Yes."

"What was Hunter doing here?"

Her eyes darkened and her brows drew together. "Hunter was ... being Hunter."

"Which aspect of being Hunter are you referring to?"

She whispered, "The part where he's trying to butter up Dad for some reason. Wants to meet with the mining committee members." Tossing her hair over a shoulder, she said, "It also feels like dropping hints about you as well. It's all super strange."

Tuli wanted so badly to figure out Hunter's angle. Was it a con or simply a guy returning to his roots? He had to tread carefully. Hunter was also part of Lou's family.

His heart hammered in his chest and the prickles of sweat popped up again. "Hopefully, this evening will take care of any rumors circulating."

"I agree." She peered at him. "Don't worry. You're not surprising my parents. They do understand that you're here because we're starting to see each other."

He made a big, brow-sweeping gesture. "*Phew.*"

After everyone was seated around the pine table in hand-carved chairs, Tuli rubbed his hands together. "Dinner looks amazing and smells even better."

Steve gave a sound that was halfway between a chuckle and a grunt.

Sitting to Tuli's left, Lou smiled reassuringly.

Melinda waved her hands. "Dish up and enjoy. Guest first."

Somehow, Tuli managed not to drop or spill the first portions he took from the various dishes. Everything they were eating reminded him of many other times Tuli had spent here at the Wright house. The cinnamon wafting from the fall squash dish was particularly enticing. The salmon, likely fresh from the river, was broiled to perfection, with fresh thyme sprinkled on top of it. He inhaled deeply, his mouth watering.

The familiar tastes of well-cooked harvested foods triggered so many memories. There were times when he had to leave his father's house for his own safety and stay here. He'd hang out after school at the Wright household, sharing good food and company until Grandma came home from her work as a nurse at the hospital. She had retired only five years ago, when she turned seventy. If Tuli's father were still alive, he would have been in his early fifties.

Herbed potatoes and asparagus congealed in Tuli's mouth as pain and loneliness braided together with memories of safety and protection. He took a bite of something different, but the root vegetable salad was equally difficult to swallow.

"Thanks for getting the blackberries the other day," Melinda said. "It sounded like quite the adventure to pick them."

Tuli swallowed his bite and wiped his face with the paper napkin. "Apparently, you can outrun a brown bear as long as you're on an ATV."

"Lou, I don't like you being out with those animals foraging for winter." Steve pinned Tuli with a severe expression.

"Animals are a way of life out here. We all know that. Besides, she wasn't alone." He sat up straighter and forked a piece of squash. "She was with me." He popped in the bite and chewed.

"You know what I mean." Steve cut up a piece of salmon. "It's not safe for anyone to be out there in areas that are high risk for bear activity. Especially if you've got an injury."

Tuli stopped chewing.

Next to him, Lou stiffened and froze.

How would her dad know that Tuli's bum leg was still a problem? Based on her raised brows, it wasn't Lou who said anything.

Hunter. The biggest rat of them all.

Tuli took a sip of water and fought to stay calm. For whatever reason, this conversation felt like bait. It was tempting bait he'd normally bite on, but not tonight. "We both did fine. Took appropriate precautions. Didn't stick around but, instead, moved to safety as a team."

"Huh." Steve leaned back and crossed his arms.

"Dad, seriously." Lou's low voice cut through the tension. "You're telling me you never went to Blackberry Hill when you were younger?"

"Well …"

"You've had a bear approach you?" she continued.

Melinda smiled, eyes twinkling. "I remember a date years ago where not only did we have a mother bear and cubs crash our hike, but someone also slipped on bear droppings as he was trying to get away."

"No way," Lou said.

Gordy laughed, his adaptive-grip spoon clutched in his outstretched fist.

"Oh?" Tuli smiled. "Which of you would like to tell this story? Because it sounds fascinating."

"Neither of us." Steve sat back up and continued eating until Melinda caught his eye and gestured at him in a not-too-subtle manner. "It's nice of you to join us for dinner."

Tuli nodded. "Thanks for having me, if I didn't mention it before."

"Is there anything you'd like to talk about?" Melinda said.

Tuli glanced at Lou. She studied the food on her plate. A dark flush tinted the skin on her neck.

"Lou and I wanted to talk with you about us dating."

"Are you asking for my blessing?" Steve pointed with his fork at Tuli. Like he was taking aim.

"Um, not exactly. We're both adults. But we wanted you to know." There was a pause punctuated by the clinks of stainless steel against Corelle plates. He backpedaled. "Also, I couldn't turn down an excellent meal."

At least the chuckles cut the tension. Some.

"You guys have been friends since you were kids." Melinda reached over to help Gordy manage a piece of potato.

"Why mess that up by dating?" Steve muttered.

"Steve!" Melinda said. "Be nice."

Louise cleared her throat. "You and Mom were friends before you started dating."

"But you're such good friends for so long," Steve said.

Tuli put down his fork and rested his palms on the edge of the table. Calmly. Rationally. "I'm sorry. What is that supposed to mean?"

Melinda nodded toward the other end of the table. "I think what Dad is trying to say, but not very well, is that it's hard to go back to being friends if the dating part doesn't work out."

Louise blurted out, "Why would you think this won't work out?"

Steve raised his hands. "Whoa, it was just a discussion and a reminder to take things slowly."

"This is a super weird conversation." Leave it to Lou, stating the obvious in a gentle, but forthright, manner.

Tuli briefly patted the back of her hand, then turned to her parents. "You're right. Lou and I have been friends forever. We are dipping our toe into a different kind of relationship. No one's rushing anything." Not that he didn't want to. He consciously relaxed his clenched jaw. "This isn't permission. More like a heads-up on our status change."

"Is that what they call it on those social media sites?" Steve said.

Melinda nodded. "I think that's a Facebook thing."

Tuli laughed. "Oh no. We're not talking about social media."

"I'm surprised about that, Tuli," Steve said, like a hawk eying his prey. "Given how much you live on social media."

Tuli replied, "Tonight is not about social media or my internet presence. Tonight is hanging out with a friend and her family and having a nice meal together with nice people. And with one wild guy." He flashed a grin at Gordy across the table, who immediately smiled with a bit of food on his lower lip that Melinda swiped away.

"Lou, are you good with all the stuff that he does?" Steve asked.

"Steve, come on now," Melinda cut in.

"What? I'm only making sure that our daughter has the best prospects available to her."

"As opposed to what?" Melinda said.

"It's my job as her dad." He rested his button-sleeved arms on the table edge. "What are your plans for a job, Tuli?"

"Dad," Lou said, "seriously. We're adults."

Steve's curt nod was the only acknowledgement.

Tuli sat up straight. "I have a job. Two, actually. Three, if you count being an influencer."

"What was your college degree, again?"

Tuli bit back a frustrated laugh. "I completed summer fire academy in Fairbanks and trained with the Chena Fire Department before starting here six years ago."

"Huh. What are your plans?"

My plans are to kiss your daughter senseless, Steve.

"Steve," Melinda nearly growled.

Tuli lifted his hand. "I am doing well as a firefighter and as a productive member of society. I pay my bills, and I help people. How that work evolves in the future is to be determined."

"By taking videos?"

"You'd be surprised how lucrative that can be."

"So—" Steve began. "No way to provide, then."

"Hello, I'm sitting right here," Lou said. "I'm an adult who is involved in this conversation topic. I have a full-time job, and I'm working on my paramedic license now. I have a place of my own to stay and this isn't the eighteen hundreds. We're just letting you know that we're a low-key item."

"We had to make a dinner for all of this?" Steve asked.

Tuli's head swam. This was not how he had anticipated the evening going. But he could salvage a conversation. Change the subject. Do party tricks. Anything. "Yep, and now that the heads-up is done, can you tell me what your over-under is on the Seahawks game? Hopefully, we can catch the end of the fourth quarter after dinner."

Gordy laughed again and pointed toward the TV before touching the tablet around his neck. "Give me."

Steve muttered something about winning by one touchdown. The conversation settled into this year's playoff prospects and which rookies would make the biggest impact on the field. Everyone ate quietly.

After a few more minutes, Tuli asked, "Any new updates on the community resource management for the gold and minerals in the Ray Mountains?"

Steve frowned. "That's what Hunter was here about."

Lou, silent next to Tuli, gave a slight shake of her head.

Melinda steepled her fingers and rested her chin on them. "Your grandma is part of the elders as well. She can update you."

"Sure, but I haven't talked much with her since the last meeting. Last time I saw Grandma was literally a few minutes before I walked to your house." Tuli laughed. "She's probably calling up her friends to let them know that I'm over here. At some point, I will get an earful about why I didn't have dinner with her."

"She does make excellent blackberry pie," Melinda said.

"Speaking of which. Is it time?" Steve patted his slightly thickened midsection.

Gordy nodded vigorously and moved his hands on the communication device. "Give me," it intoned.

"Looks like someone thinks it's time," Tuli said.

Melinda dished up the fresh dessert and passed plates around.

Steve turned in Tuli's direction. "Hunter said that he has

some connections in mining that might be useful for our community goals."

"What kind of connections?" Tuli said.

"He worked with people who do ore extraction. He's happy to lead the community task force regarding how we access and use that resource. That guy's a real go-getter."

Tuli sat forward. Besides the inferiority complex setting up shop, something did not fit with what Steve was saying and what Tuli knew about Hunter. "Seems odd, Hunter coming back after all these years and then jumping right into the mining."

"We're lucky it's such good timing. I was telling my brother—his dad—the other day how lucky we are to have Hunter home now."

"Good timing. Very lucky." Tuli rested his fingertips on the table. "That guy has a lot of interesting timing," he muttered.

"Sorry, I didn't catch that," Steve said.

Lou glanced over out of the corner of her eye.

Tuli took a bite of steaming blackberry pie. "Nothing. Melinda, this is delicious."

Chapter Nineteen

"WELL, THAT WAS brutal," Tuli said as he and Lou walked across her yard.

Her tennis shoes scuffed on the dry gravel and grass in front of the house. Stars lit up the dark portion of the sky, fading to orange and pink light over the opposite mountainous horizon. She breathed in the cool air like doing so could clear her head of the tension from dinner. "Sorry about this evening. Dad can be like an underripe blackberry bush, all thorns and no sweetness."

"He's looking out for you. I get it."

She crossed her arms over her sweater. "That back there was excessive. I am a fully grown adult."

"He also takes his job as village elder seriously."

"What does that mean?"

Tuli shoved his hands into his lightweight jacket. "Means that your life choices reflect on his standing."

"Are you saying I am an embarrassment to him?"

"No, but I might be."

"No."

"That was a hell of a kick to the ego back there. I know that my family's history and my work are things he takes into consideration."

"That's not right. You're not your parents. You are successful at your work."

"Thankfully." Tuli's big breath raised his shoulders, making the canvas jacket fabric *shush* against itself. "So, after the inquisition tonight, are we still doing this? Us?"

She studied his proud profile in the low light, with his sturdy frame and the determined set of his jaw. "Are you giving me an out?"

His gaze briefly met hers. A muscle ticked in his jaw. "If you want one."

Rubbing her arms to ward off the chill, she said, "No. I don't want an out. Not like that, anyway."

He stared at her. "What do you mean?"

"A relationship should succeed or fail based on the two people involved. Not because of judgments of those outside the relationship."

"That's deep, Lou."

A giggle popped out. "Well, it's true." She brushed his forearm with her hand, and he grasped her fingers, his warmth seeping into her. Glancing around, she said, "So?"

Tuli grinned. "Here we are, standing here in broad nighttime, where anyone with a flashlight can see us. Are you okay with that?"

"Um, yes?"

"Not a resounding vote of confidence."

Lou resisted the urge to check over her shoulder at what would surely be an opening in the curtains with a face pressed to the glass. "I'm still licking my wounds from Ryan."

"Fair." He squeezed her hand. "Let me be clear. I'm not that guy. I'll never be that guy. I wouldn't spill the tea about a relationship to everyone in town. I'll stay low-key."

"How? With The Real Alaska site and all, you're recognizable."

"Recognizable for my handsomeness, you mean?" He lifted her hand and brushed a kiss over her knuckles. "If you don't want exposure, I will not expose you." His voice dropped low. "At least not on the channel."

Her face heated. "Oh. Well."

"Lou…"

"I think maybe … can we keep things casual between us for now?"

He dropped her hand. "I need you to define what you mean, so we're on the same page."

Her mouth was dry. "Dates, but not in public venues. Lots of texting. Conversations together. I have to make sure this is right before putting a relationship out there."

"Clandestine. Roger."

"It sounds bad when you say it that way."

His expression was obscured in shadow, but she felt the intensity of his focus. And his rakish grin. "Are you okay with a kiss or two?"

"When we're not visible to others." She rubbed her chin. "That sounds weird."

"It's not weird. It's the boundary that you have set, and I'll respect it."

"Yes."

"What about more than a kiss?"

Her lower abdomen tingled. "Um ..." She paused. "I can't right now." Too much closeness. Too much risk.

"Whoa, Lou." He raised a hand up. "I'm only getting a sense of parameters. I swear, even if you said *let's go for a no pants dance*, I would still make sure it was okay every step along the way."

She half-laughed, half-groaned, then gulped in a big lungful of air and let it out slowly. "Dad brought up a good point about future stability." Wow, she needed to change the topic.

After studying her for a second, he said, "How so?"

"I need to take some time to work on my own career. Complete my paramedic certificate before getting too far into a relationship."

"First of all, you're smart, and you're going to be a terrific paramedic. Second of all, I would never stand in your way of that goal."

"Fair enough." She stared at her feet for a moment. "So. Thanks for coming over. For what that was worth, getting the second degree from Dad."

"Hey, it is what it is," Tuli said. Looking up the gravel road, he nodded. "I should go check on Grandma. If I don't stop in while I'm right here, I'll never hear the end of it."

Lou couldn't envision Auntie Ruth giving Tuli a tongue-lashing, but the image made her smile. "Sounds good."

"Um, is it suitably dark enough for me to kiss you good-night?"

Lou froze, heart pounding. Outside. Here. Where people could see. She looked around. It was dark out. The houses were spaced pretty far apart in the village. Taking a deep breath, she pushed back on the uneasiness. At some point, she had to grow up and be a normal adult, having a normal relationship and trusting the person she was with. Who better to trust than Tuli? "Yes."

"I was hoping you'd say that." He gently gripped her upper arms and turned so her back was to the house. Then he cupped her face with warm, callused hands, the move hiding their mouths from prying eyes. He brushed his lips over hers as a zing of something new and exciting shot through her. "*Mmm*, blackberries. I love it," he said.

She fought the urge to press against him and wrap her arms around him. Lou could only do so much in public, and this was a big step.

"Well, that was a productive dinner, at least," she murmured before stepping back.

His arms dropped to his sides. "True. Can I call you?"

"Of course. *Neenihaal'yaa.*" *See you later,* she said.

"*S'idzaay.*"

He shoved his hands in his pockets and strolled up the street, whistling as he walked away.

As she reentered the house, she paused, reaching for the translation of his word.

My heart.

Oh.

Taking extra time to remove her shoes and collect herself, Lou finally sat down on the other end of the couch from her father. Gordy wasn't in the living room. He must be resting in bed.

"Why were you like that tonight, Dad?"

"Like what?" All innocence. Not going to fly. He knew what he had done.

"Giving Tuli the third degree."

Dad pressed his lips into a hard line and stared at the post-game Seahawks recap on the TV. "I only want what's best for you."

"Tuli and I were telling you what was best."

"Are you sure?"

"We are adults making choices, so it's right for us. Maybe it works out, maybe not. But I'm interested enough to want to see where this relationship goes."

Mom sat in the rocking chair, a crossword puzzle on her lap. "I like Tuli. Always have. Nice guy."

Dad turned toward Lou. "Are you sure you don't want to date other guys? Someone with a more solid future?"

"What are you saying?"

"Look, Tuli is a nice guy. Your mom is right. But he has that injury that's still affecting him." The words seemed to spill out, like a dam breached. "Both his parents had issues. He might be higher risk for addiction. And what kind of job is a social media influencer, anyway? All I'm saying is, don't settle. Look around first."

Lou reared back as her jaw dropped. "You do understand he almost died in that accident last spring, yet he is still back to work? Give the guy some credit. Lumping him in with his parents is kind of low, Dad." Dinner congealed in her gut. "It's even more testament to his character that he has made something of himself, given that start to life. Settling? You're kidding, right?" She paused. "Besides, I looked around before. That only got me hurt."

Mom said, "Honey—" Hard to know whether she was talking to Lou or Dad.

He lifted an outstretched hand. "You could go out with some other guys. See what else is out there. Hunter has some friends…"

"I'm sure he does."

"Why the attitude? He's your cousin. Besides, he's solid. We'll probably use him as our coordinator for the mining project."

Studying her father, she asked, "Why? He hasn't lived here in years. Did you check references? All of a sudden, he comes back to town and gets into the management of a future mine."

"He's from here. He's family. Hunter understands Yukon Valley and the Koyukon group's culture. That guy is going places."

"As opposed to a person like Tuli, is what you're saying."

"Louise!" Mom said.

"It's true." God, she hated conflict. "You've been sour on Tuli since I told you we were hanging out as more than friends."

"Well…" Dad shook his head.

Mom gently interjected, "Have you told him about the genetic issues?"

Lou's eyes stung. "Yes."

"And?"

That might be the bigger wedge. Not Dad and his vision

177

of a brighter future with Lou and Mr. Mining's superior friends.

"Tuli seemed to understand the test results and what it meant."

"Probably hasn't sunk in." Dad crossed his arms and leaned back on the couch.

Lou blew out a big breath. "You two have way too much time on your hands. Go stir the pot elsewhere. Hang out with Bruce and Aggie. They like meddling in people's lives."

"Lou!" Dad said.

She rolled her hands into fists, like doing so could keep back every inch of frustration from flying out. "I don't know what my future holds and who will be in it. But I want to find out for myself, and I think this is a nice start."

"If you say so." Dad turned up the volume on the football commentary.

Chapter Twenty

"DUDE, ARE YOU stalking me?" Tuli tried not to jump as Hunter appeared from the shadows next to the Wrights' house. That guy was the last person he wanted to see on his short walk to Grandma's.

Hunter flashed a smile that somehow didn't work. Sure, objectively speaking, the guy seemed casual and carefree in his Alaskan styling choices. Tech pants, nice hiking boots, button-down shirt. Also, he didn't have a bum leg. Point to Hunter.

Tuli had something extra. He could detect BS from a hundred miles away. This guy was ten pounds of crap in a five-pound sack. Nothing added up.

Hunter gave a guffaw that sounded more like an eighty-year-old's laugh. "You off tonight?"

"You know I am. Other folks are on call this weekend, so yeah, I'm footloose and fancy-free. Sky's the limit."

"Is it now?"

"Huh?" This guy was all swagger and no substance. Dude needed to get to whatever stupid point he was making so Tuli could find out if Grandma had freshly baked cookies.

"Just saying it looks like we've got some friendly competition." The way he said *friendly* was anything but.

A sinking sensation dropped in Tuli's midsection. "Not following."

Hunter's grin widened. "Your leg puts you at a disadvantage. A liability. Folks will figure it out, hopefully before it's too late and your disability gets someone killed. When people realize that you can't do the job and they see my application, I'll be ready to step in, with two functioning feet."

Tuli shined his nails on his jacket while his gut churned. "Good that you've gone to the trouble of setting up a succession plan for me, because I have recently been presented with some amazing opportunities. You may have freed me up to pursue greener pastures."

Hunter looked like he'd swallowed a tart salmonberry but crossed his arms. "Well, I've got an in with Louise and her dad."

Tuli dropped his hand into a fist and balanced on his feet. That square jaw was so tempting. "Do tell."

"Our dads are brothers. Go way back. They want quality partners for their kids and grandkids. I know guys with good educations, who Louise would be lucky to date. Also, I'm about to become the key to the community mining project. My words carry weight nowadays. More professional capital, less, uh, baggage."

A high-pitched, hot teakettle whistle sounded in Tuli's head, and his heart thudded. "Baggage?"

"You know, with the problems your parents both had. All of your struggles growing up. The bum leg. Not having a solid job. Baggage."

Tuli fought the urge to pummel the guy. "I grew up just fine."

"With your grandma."

"What's wrong with that?" He leaned forward. This guy, whose parents had divorced several years back, didn't have his own leg to stand on in the discussion.

Hunter raised his hands in an exaggerated maneuver. "Whoa, there. No need to get hostile."

"Who's hostile?" Tuli clapped him on the upper arm, like a buddy. But real hard.

"Ow." Hunter's eyes narrowed and he lowered his voice. "I can't wait to be invited to Louise's wedding."

"What, to one of your *quality* friends? The last one ruined her life, if you didn't notice."

"Water under the bridge." His teeth flashed white in the shadows. "Maybe they'll name their first child after me."

First of all, Tuli knew way more than Hunter about Lou's future baby situation, and boy, oh boy, did he want to tell him. But Tuli would die before he shared her secret.

He stepped into the guy's personal space. "You're an idiot. You know that?"

Hunter windmilled dramatically, like he'd been hit. "What are you doing attacking me? We're two friends having a conversation."

"Dude, you want an Oscar for that performance? Look, all I'm saying is, you don't know what you're talking about. You don't know Lou. You don't know anything about the situation."

"Don't I? Then you won't mind if I introduce her to a

friend or two at my next Wright family dinner. You think I've got the insider track now? Wait until I try my luck hooking Louise up with one of my buddies from Seattle."

A car drove by, and Tuli and Hunter waved out of habit, even though the driver likely couldn't see them well in the dim light.

"Try your luck?" Tuli spun back and growled.

Hunter might be an inch taller, but Tuli'd been working out. Hard. Overcompensating for his leg, sure, but he knew that his strong right hook packed a wallop. Just ask the punching bag.

He wanted to test drive his strength on Hunter's jaw. "She's not a fucking roulette wheel."

"You're a funny guy." Hunter turned on his heel and walked away. He turned halfway back and said, "Sit back and watch the master work. I'm about to become invaluable for the Koyukon tribe, make her family's dreams come true, and deconstruct your entire life."

Tuli's heart thundered in his chest, and every muscle in his body shook like live electricity ran through him. His fist tingled with the urge to realign Hunter's teeth.

No way would Tuli let that guy do the things he promised.

He ran a hand through his hair and looked around at the widely spaced village houses, some with warm yellow lights in the windows. Damn it. Hunter had already begun his work. Laid the foundation for destroying everything Tuli had built.

Stopping Hunter meant alienating the Wright family.

Damn it again.

Tuli would figure this out. He'd taken down bullies before. He could find a way to stop Hunter without ruining his future with Lou.

After taking a few more breaths, he got a grip on his anger and calmed the heck down as he trudged to Grandma's house.

Wow. He'd almost hit the guy. Truth be told, he could probably get one good jab in, but not two. Hunter was no shrinking violet. With a leg that wasn't cooperating, Tuli couldn't depend on footwork for stability or for a reliable generation of force.

Or to run away.

That, and there could be neighbors peeking out of windows. Tongues wagging. Didn't pay to make a scene.

His right foot caught on the step, and he grabbed the railing of Grandma's porch. Regaining his footing, he stepped on the landing, frowning at the creak of a loose board. He'd need to come back and repair it before she got hurt.

He knocked and heard her light footsteps. "Hi, *nok'eedonh!*" he called through the door.

"I was hoping you would stop by." She opened the door and hugged him, her head coming up to his chest. When she leaned back, her face creased into extra lines with her smile "Did you have a nice time with the Wrights?"

Dropping the stupid loafers off inside the front door, he followed her to the living room, where she perched on the edge of her easy chair.

"It's always good seeing Lou and the Wrights. Gordy's looking better."

She smoothed her blue cotton kuspuk hem over her thighs and tucked her hands into the slanted front pockets which were lined with white bric-a-brac. She peered at him with her dark, knowing stare. Then she sat back and got comfortable. Uh-oh. Grandma wasn't going anywhere until she was satisfied. "You didn't answer the question."

"Lou's dad was kind of rough."

Her smile fell. "Steve? What happened?"

"Talked about my upbringing, including that both my parents are out of the picture, and why. It was a tough discussion. Nothing like sitting at someone's house and taking slander about how I was reared."

"I brought you up, Tulimak!"

He grinned. "I'm all the luckier for it."

Sitting up straight, she scowled. "Do I need to go over there and set him straight? We might both be on the council of elders, but I have seniority. I was the nurse at his delivery. I can give him the what-for." She gripped the arms of the chair in her strong but work-worn hands.

"No need to scare the guy, Grandma. He's only looking out for Lou."

"By trampling on you?"

Seemed to be the thing to do these days.

Tuli unclenched his jaw and gave a nonchalant shrug that he tried to believe. "So, everything okay with you? Health-wise, things all right?"

"You always were good at subject changes."

"One of my many amazing skills."

"*Tsk*. Humility is another one."

Tuli laughed out loud. Grandma was cheeky when riled up.

She stretched her legs out, stretchy pants on, socks in sandals, in front of her. "Saw Dr. Moore earlier this week. My lungs are doing well. No sign of lingering problems from the infection this spring."

"Hey, I saw that woodpile you're making out back. You should let me do that."

"You're too busy with your firefighting and work at the deli and the cameras."

"I always have time to help you." Not really, but he'd make time.

"You're a good boy."

He clamped his teeth together. *Good boy.* He had heard that phrase from his dad once when Tuli was four. He was twenty-six and still craved the support of family. He would have given anything to have living parents who were healthy and sober. Grandma had filled the parenting gaps admirably and with love. Unfortunately, she seemed to think he was still in elementary school.

"So, what's your plan?" she asked.

"About what?"

Her graying brows shot up. "About the girl!"

"She's also not a girl. We are the same age. Both adults."

Grandma gave another noncommittal *tsk*. "Fine. Then, adult-to-adult, what are you doing? She seems like a nice … lady."

"She is." Tuli paused. "I believe we might be in a relationship."

"What does that even mean? *I believe I might fly* doesn't mean 'you're going to sprout wings and take off." She peered at him. "'In a relationship.' Is that like going steady?"

He laughed. Grandma's seventy-five-year-old memory was sharp. She must have been a firecracker back in the day. She'd given Grandpa a run for his money when he was alive. "Sure. Going steady works."

"Her family better be good to you."

"They will be fine."

"Well, you be good to her."

"I'm always good!"

"You always get away with too much." Grandma smiled and let out a sigh. "She's lucky to have such a nice boy— man—in her life."

Chapter Twenty-One

L ESS THAN TWENTY-FOUR hours after the tense family dinner, Lou shoved her whirling thoughts to the side as she parked the ambulance at the scene of the accident on Main Street. Oh, yikes.

Car versus timber hauler, and the hauler looked no worse for the wear.

The compact sedan, however, was completely crumpled. An accordion.

The driver was still in the vehicle.

Mav spared her a quick glance before unbuckling and launching himself out of the rig.

Lou followed, opening the back doors and pulling out bags of gear. Then she headed to the vehicle.

Bystanders milled around, their alarmed voices rising and falling. Even with the people nearby, Lou did her standard check for safety before moving closer. Oil and other fluids slicked the asphalt. No smoke. No visible flames. No engines running. No electrical wires. Safe to approach.

She and Mav peered through the spidered glass of the side window. The driver, a thirty-something male whom she didn't immediately recognize, lay unconscious, his head lolling to one side. The airbag had deployed, dusting the man's face in white powder. The steering wheel pressed into his chest. She couldn't see his legs with the dashboard compressed against him.

Maybe she could access him from the other side. She hurried around. Not going to work. There was even less space on that side, and the dash and door were both destroyed. Thank God there hadn't been a passenger.

The man's breathing rasped through his gaping mouth, a froth of blood dripping down one corner. He needed to get out of this car. Now. The golden hour to definitive care was counting down quickly. Outside of that hour, the chances of survival dropped significantly. Minutes mattered.

Yanking on the door, Maverick shook his head. "Won't open. Damn." Sirens blasted through the clear afternoon. They both looked up. Fire vehicle. "Hope they have their extraction tools," he said.

Louise ran back to the ambulance to pull out the gurney, so it was ready nearby. At least it gave her something to do in this hurry up and wait scene.

The late afternoon air cooled on her damp brow. Slanting sunlight through gray clouds illuminated the unnatural scene. Tuli and Hunter exited the fire engine as Mav called for the extractor. Lieutenant Kate Lucas and one of the other troopers directed bystanders to remain a safe distance away from the wreck.

Lou laid the equipment bag on the gurney and gripped the railing, waiting.

Like a well-oiled machine, Tuli and Hunter unloaded the generator onto the asphalt with a thud.

"Hook up the StrongArm," Tuli said, his voice carrying despite his helmet and the zipped up bunker coat.

Hunter attached the extraction device and turned on the generator. With a rapid, soft chugging sound, the hydraulic equipment drove a prying tip attachment as Tuli shoved it in between the destroyed driver's side door panel and frame.

Antsy, bouncing on the balls of her feet, Louise pulled on latex gloves, reset the stethoscope around her neck, and checked that bandage scissors were in her right pants pocket, ready to remove a seatbelt or clothing so she and Mav could examine the man.

With a screech of metal, the compressed door was freed from the crumpled frame. Tuli lifted the equipment higher, repeating the movement until the door opened about a foot away from the frame, still attached by the hinges. The back door was destroyed and compacted.

Still not enough room to remove the patient.

Hunter gripped the driver's side door and pulled, straining against thick, crushed hinges. "No good."

"Hold up. Swap out for the cutter tip," Tuli said.

The patient in the car moaned, and Lou glanced at Mav's tense expression. He, too, hovered, pacing, ready to act.

After another few seconds that felt like hours, Tuli had cut through the hinges to the point where Hunter, Mav, Kate, and the trooper pulled the door completely open.

"Let's clear the back door for access," Tuli said.

Hunter waved a yellow crowbar and pick tool. "I'll try the Glas-Master." He jammed it into the back window, shattering the surface. He cut through the remaining glass, removing it with a sweep of the tool. Yanking on the unlocked door, though, he couldn't budge it. "Bring the StrongArm back, boss."

After another few hydraulic pries and cuts with the machine, and more whines of unhappy metal, the back door was off.

Lou and Maverick surged forward. Hunter and Tuli dragged their equipment away.

"Lou, you're on C-spine," Maverick said.

Crawling into the back seat and being careful of the broken glass, Lou removed the headrest and reached behind the man, holding his neck in line. The odor of alcohol made her eyes water.

"Sats are 85%. I'm going to get the nasal cannula on him." He held up the tubing with a hiss of oxygen from the tank attached to the gurney.

Mav carefully slid the oxygen tubing under the man's nose and behind his ears and then maneuvered the cervical collar into place from the front.

"Get the KED," Mav said, sending Hunter to the ambulance. The KED, the Kendrick Extraction Device, was the semi-rigid upper body and neck brace that allowed for safe removal of a patient from a seated position to the backboard on the gurney.

Hunter ran back with the device.

The victim moaned as they worked the KED between his back and legs and the seat. Despite temps in the fifties, in the enclosed stuffy space, Lou had to duck her chin to wipe sweat on her shirt.

"Need help?" Tuli asked, taking off his helmet and peering into the vehicle.

"Sure."

She scooted forward as he wormed in behind her through the back door. Then he removed the passenger headrest, draped himself over the seat, and slithered a hand forward to reach a lever. He then lowered the passenger seat. "There. Much more room. Luxurious." He glanced at her with a rakish wink that triggered a warm flush of her skin.

Hunter added a helping pair of hands next to Mav. They moved the front seat back, making space between the steering wheel and the victim. With the access Tuli had gained on the passenger side, all three of them secured the patient into the KED. By the time they finished, Lou's back ached from the awkward angle where she maintained control of the patient's neck.

One quick check of the equipment before getting the guy out, and then Mav nodded. "Good enough." He looked at Lou, reached up, and said, "I've got C-spine."

"You've got C-spine," Lou answered as she slid her hands away and scooted herself out of the car. Pushing the gurney as close as possible, she then extended the backboard from the gurney to the car seat.

With a few careful, coordinated lifts and pushes, they had the unconscious patient seated sideways on the end of the backboard. In another maneuver, the four of them lowered the patient to the backboard and then eased him up the board and onto the gurney, all with a minimum of movement to his neck and back.

The man moaned softly but gave no more cooperation than that. Had they been here minutes? Hours? Time meant nothing and yet everything in these situations.

All of them quickly removed the KED so that the patient lay flat on top of the backboard. They secured him with straps to the backboard and gurney and then placed padded bolsters around the neck and taped everything securely in place.

Tuli and Hunter dropped off their helmets and jackets on the back of the truck and then returned to help further.

Lou reassessed the man.

Lungs clear, heart rate rapid. She quickly ran a new set of vitals. Blood pressure 80/40 and saturation was only 90% despite supplemental oxygen. Time to go. Now. The man's left leg was shorter than the right and internally rotated. "Looks like left hip fracture," she said.

"Likely chest wall trauma, based on where the steering wheel hit him," Mav said. "He's satting slightly better on ten liters of oxygen, but it's not great. I'm not going to do a full exam out here. He's protecting his airway and responded to my voice, so I don't need to intubate him. Doesn't look like I need to do a needle decompression right this minute. Leave any of that for the ER. This guy needs a hospital with a doctor, some nurses, and a scanner."

One day, Lou would have the training to perform those advanced paramedic skills like Mav. This situation made her want to study even harder. She pressed her hands to her tight lower back before grabbing the gurney.

"I've got it, Louise," Hunter said.

"Not arguing." She followed behind the gurney to the ambulance.

"You okay?" Tuli came up beside her, thick hair standing up in strange directions. Yet somehow it made him look even more handsome.

She couldn't help leaning toward him. "Great work getting that car opened up."

"Literally our job." He glanced at her. "That's not the answer to my question. Did you tweak your back?"

"I'm fine."

He grumped, "Again, not an answer." They moved to the driver's side of the ambulance.

Mav and Hunter secured the gurney. Hunter closed the back doors with Mav inside.

Tuli asked, "Hey, Lou. Are we still good? Us. Together. With your condition and all? I mean, I'm fine with everything."

Lou froze. There were onlookers.

Sure, the bystanders were a distance away, and no one had heard him.

Except for Hunter, who stuck his head out from around the back of the ambulance.

His face shifted into an avid grin. "What condition?" Hunter's eyes narrowed as he darted a glance between Lou and Tuli. "You have a condition? That doesn't sound good. Your parents know about this?"

She jerked, like she'd been kicked in the gut.

"Hunter, shut up. Get out of here," Tuli growled. He reached out, but she sidled away. "Lou, I'm—"

Her ears rang. Vision tunneled. Not again. "Not everything is meant to be broadcast."

"I didn't mean—"

"You never do." She swallowed what felt like shards of glass. "You can't help but be the person you are."

"Why does that sound bad?"

"I have to go."

As he stepped away from the vehicle, a girl ran up and tugged on Tuli's sleeve. He glanced up at Lou with a worried expression, then turned to the child. Based on the animated movements and his smile in return, he was telling her all about firefighting.

His face gentled as he knelt with a wince to talk with the child on her level.

As she put the ambulance in gear and pulled away, something inside of Lou's chest caught. Hard.

Chapter Twenty-Two

D AMN THE STUPID, giant gaping hole in his face and his inability to stop words from coming out of it.

He wrapped up the impromptu firefighting discussion with a local kid and stood up with a suppressed groan.

It wasn't Tuli's fault that all he'd thought about since last night was Lou. The minute he saw her he wanted to check in with her. Make sure that they were okay. See her smiling face again.

That wasn't his fault.

What was his fault? Time and place. Word choices. Volume.

And Hunter. Situational awareness would've helped.

"Well, well, Mr. Suave. Seems like you have some insider information on my cousin. Care to share?" Hunter cocked his head.

"Shut up."

"Hey!" He held his hands up. "No need for workplace violence. I'm just making friendly banter."

"Banter, my ass."

Hunter studied him, eyes narrowed. "It's you who stepped in moose poop. Not me, pal."

"Back off. I'm not your pal," he growled as he turned on

his heel and stalked off toward the fire truck, catching himself when his right foot scraped on loose gravel. Damn it. Last thing he needed to add to this disaster was falling flat on his face in front of pretty boy. He stopped and turned toward Hunter.

Exaggerating his defensive hands-up stance for all to see, Hunter said, "Does Louise know you have anger issues? Seems like that info would be helpful when making an informed decision about her life choices."

Tuli ground his molars until his jaw ached.

Hunter sneered at him. "Looks like even more doors are now open for me."

"How's that?" Tuli pretended to check the pump panels on the truck.

"Good thing I've been chatting up Uncle Steve. He likes me. Likes my new ideas to make money for the town and the corporation too."

"Through the mine?"

"I have insider connections."

"Huh."

"*Huh* is right, when you consider how rich this will make me."

"Thought you wanted to be a firefighter, not a miner. Besides, this discussion is unprofessional."

Hunter ignored the first question. "Like flirting with an EMT while they were on a trauma run wasn't unprofessional. I should write you up and tell my manager. Yet another reason you're unfit for duty." He rubbed his chin. "Only, my supervisor *is* the chief. So, who should I tell? The mayor, probably. She's the only one who can fire you, right?"

"First of all, I wasn't flirting while working. That was a brief pleasantry exchanged between friends." If he had a few more minutes and the patient wasn't unstable, it might have been flirting. Details.

"So, you're not dating?"

Tuli spun toward him once more. "This is insubordination."

"This is human interest. Besides, I'm family. What's wrong with her? I ought to know. We're family. She has a condition? Is she sick? Caught the cooties from you?"

He nearly bent the thick metal intake valve that he gripped.

Hunter said, "Never mind. You just blew your future with Louise and blew your job. With you out of the way and me taking lead on the mine and soon the fire chief job, the door's open for some Yukon Valley fun." He waggled his eyebrows. "I'm about to be the successful son the Wrights never had. And Uncle Steve wants me to set Louise up with one of my equally successful friends. Looks like the influencer can't shoot this video. Because he's out of the picture!"

That *har-har* laugh was all it took.

The movement of Tuli's hand, arm, and shoulder didn't register until his fist was an inch beyond Hunter's square jaw. The guy's head snapped back with an *oof.*

Would you look at that? All those upper body workouts had paid off.

After the three seconds of shock wore off, his knuckles stared to throb. Tuli looked up. *Uh-oh.*

Hunter had been working out as well.

"Now *this* is insubordination." The spark of light and flash of pain from Hunter's stone fist crunching Tuli's cheekbone left him seeing chirping chickadees.

Tuli staggered back, but his bad leg gave out on him, and he sprawled on his ass on the asphalt. When he tried to stand, the damned leg didn't cooperate. Sensation was all weird, like pain and numbness at the same time.

Tuli struggled to his feet, ignoring Hunter's outstretched hand.

"A little fisticuffs between friends. Firefighting hijinks. No hard feelings, right?" Hunter said as onlookers gasped.

A few held up their cell phones. Damn it. Hunter grabbed Tuli's aching hand and then smacked him on the upper arm, too hard to be a friendly strike, but not hard enough for others to tell the difference.

Tuli fantasized about using the fire hose to strangle the guy. Nothing drastic, just enough to shut him up. "Whatever."

Hunter pulled him in close and muttered, "By the time I'm done here, all you'll have remaining is a decent right hook and nothing else. No leadership job, no respect of the people in town." He paused and lowered his voice further. "No sweet Louise. And obviously, no leg to stand on."

Tuli rolled his fist, ready to take another swing, but the gape-mouthed spectators made him pause. "Damn you," he said through a smile with gritted teeth.

"I'm not the damned one, buddy. You brought this all on yourself. Lying about your injury so you could keep your job. Opening your stupid mouth one too many times. Don't get mad at me. All I did was shine a light on the cockroach in the corner."

"Get. Out. Of. My. Face."

"Gladly. However, we have to ride back to the station together. Want me to drive?"

Tuli opened his mouth to protest, but then he shifted his weight on that insensate right leg. Damn that guy.

Chapter Twenty-Three

TWO DAYS LATER, on Wednesday, Lou and Maverick were at Three Bears, holding their steaming coffee mugs. The morning was cool, with overcast conditions and drizzle. Coffee was a requirement.

They strolled toward the back of the store.

Well, Maverick strolled. Lou kind of lurked around the corners. Good thing she wasn't an avoidant personality at all. *Ha.*

She had texted Tuli the evening after the car accident to let him know she would go on her own to Deirdre and Calvin's wedding. Right now, Lou needed to take a break from her life and from all drama. Mostly, she needed a break from feeling exposed, and Tuli's offhand comment had triggered several prying texts from Hunter that she refused to deal with.

As she came around the corner to the deli counter, she took a sip of coffee and nearly spit it out.

"What happened to you?" she blurted.

Mav whistled low. "Nice."

Tuli's left eye was bruised and swollen.

"Surprised you didn't hear about it, rumor mill and all." He shrugged. "My face attacked a fist."

Mav smirked. "I think I know who won."

"You should see the other guy."

"You sure about that?"

Tuli's lopsided smile drooped. "Up for debate."

"So?" Mav said.

With a shrug, Tuli glanced at Lou. "Hey, I did what needed to be done in the moment."

She listened carefully.

Mav asked, "Which means what, exactly?"

Tuli blurted out, "I defended Lou's honor!"

"Wait." Rearing back, she clutched the coffee cup. "This had to do with me?"

Tuli leaned forward on the counter. "I couldn't have Hunter saying impolite things about you."

Her heart did a bizarre swoop up and then a stomach-churning nosedive. "You were the one who shared out my personal business in front of him."

Mav leaned against the end of a grocery shelf, crossed one ankle over the other, and blew on his coffee. A faint smile formed, and he pursed his lips, clearly entertained.

Lou hated a show.

"I didn't know he was standing there," Tuli said, ignoring their audience of one.

Lou replied, "We were in public."

"Who cares?"

She lowered her voice. "I told you that information in confidence."

"This isn't confidential now." He lifted his chin toward a very quiet Mav.

She shook her head. "Even if he knew what we were talking about—and he does not—Mav won't talk, even under torture."

"For sure under torture," Mav said with a wince.

Lou ran a hand over her ponytail and huffed. "Tuli, look, you're a good guy and all. Thanks for knocking around my idiot cousin, I guess. But I don't need my honor defended. I can take care of myself." As she would be doing in the future. Alone. "By the way, defending my honor doesn't count if you're the one blabbing my personal information and then getting mad if someone hears it."

If Mav's eyebrows went up any farther they'd meet his hairline.

"I can keep my mouth shut," Tuli muttered.

"Sure, and we might not get snow this winter."

"What are you saying, Lou?"

She waved at Mav. "We have work to do." Her face burned. Heart pounded. God, she hated conflict.

Turning on her heel, she exited not caring who followed or what anyone else thought of the scene.

Lou was over everything.

THAT CLOUDY AFTERNOON, Lou filled up the rig at the Three Bears gas station, enjoying the few minutes of time alone as Mav completed run paperwork back at the EMS garage. She leaned against the side of the ambulance, zipped up her navy EMS jacket against the nip in the air, and stared up at the low mountains above town. No snow yet. But soon.

Another vehicle pulled across the island from her, and a door opened and shut. Beat-up truck. Looked familiar.

"Hi, Louise." Bruce Garrett stepped down from his truck with an arthritic *ugh*, then raised a hand in greeting.

Aggie got out of the truck, waved, and headed into the gas station.

"Nice day," he said, his broad smile shifting his more salt than pepper bushy beard.

He leaned an arm on the side of the pump, his eyes narrowing as he looked at Lou. Uh-oh. This guy had nothing but time. Did no one in this town have things to do? Places to be?

She glanced at the old-school dial display slowly turning. Only ten gallons in the rig so far. Even the pumps worked against her today.

"Hi, Bruce," she said. "How have you been? Staying well?"

Bruce had almost died last spring. Here he was, not only miraculously alive, but apparently with an even more annoying level of energy, thanks to his newly cleaned heart vessels.

"Still have to visit with those fancy docs in Fairbanks every few months," he groused. "Don't know why I can't see the docs here."

"The docs here aren't cardiologists."

"They were fine when I needed them."

She remembered Bruce's gray complexion while the ER

team coded him for several long minutes. It really was a miracle to see him up and about nowadays. "That was a life-threatening emergency, and we could have used a cardiologist then."

"Hmph." He turned and fiddled with the gas cap, but seemed to be in no apparent rush to start pumping his own fuel. "Your brother okay?"

"Yes, sir. Thank you for asking. Gordy's doing all right. I think he's walking around town today. It's a nice afternoon."

"Anything else interesting in your life?"

After Bruce and his wife Aggie had conspired with pretty much the entire hospital staff to get Maverick and Dr. Tipton together, then successfully prodded Deirdre and Dr. Garrett into a lifetime commitment, Bruce had apparently decided it was time to focus his energy on Lou's love life.

Such as it was.

"Bruce, is this twenty questions?"

"Why, has someone else beat me to it?"

"You're down to nineteen remaining questions."

"Oh! Tough crowd." He winked. "My Calvin's getting married this weekend. I'm happy for him. Are you coming?"

"Wouldn't miss it." The wedding, yes. Certain guests, not so much.

"Got a date?"

Lou laughed, trying something—anything—to deflect the man. Unfortunately, Bruce was like a hound dog tracking a scent. "Are you offering?"

His rough laugh rang out. "I'm spoken for. Aggie would kill me." He pointed. "You. Any prospects?"

"Sixteen, Bruce."

"What?"

"Now fifteen questions left." She paused. "My life is uninteresting right now."

"You sure about that?"

"Absolutely."

He squinted as he peered at her from the side of the pump. "What about Tulimak? He seems nice."

"You're down to thirteen more questions. No, I'm not going with anyone. If that's okay with you." She planted her hands on her hip and glared at him.

"Oh, sure, sure. No issue." Then he pinned her with a stare that looked calculating. "Any particular reason why you're not going with anyone? Could it have to do with someone blurting out stuff?"

Was nothing sacred in this town? "We're at eleven questions left."

"The last one was more of a statement than a question."

She stared at him until he grunted to himself. The pump clicked off, and she took the nozzle out and secured it on the pump. Lou sighed and studied Bruce's too-eager expression. "Look, I'm not a fan of people sharing secrets that aren't theirs to tell."

"Fellow messed up, did he?"

"You could say that."

"I've done that a few hundred times with Aggie." He smiled. "Sounds like you are kicking the guy to the curb, as kids say these days."

"If you mean kids from the year 2005, then yes."

"See? I'm hip." He gave an awkward hip wiggle.

Lou suppressed a smirk, then sobered. "I'm focusing on me right now."

"Hmph. It's a date to a wedding. Not a joint bank account."

"Bruce, what are you getting at?"

"If I had a nickel for every time I shoved my giant foot in my giant mouth, I'd be a rich man. Yet, she said, I do, despite my bungling."

"Bungling?"

He rocked from one foot to the other, his arthritis-bowed legs making the movement look like a cowboy standing on a boat bobbing in ocean waves. "Back in the day, I told all my friends about kissing Aggie behind the school. The story spread through town like wildfire. You know how rumors are here. Aggie was mortified." He flapped a hand. "Things were different back then."

"I would feel mortified, too, even in present day."

"Anyway, that wasn't the last time I bragged or said something personal and it ended up hurting her feelings."

"Yet she's still with you." Lou pointed.

Aggie strolled up to the car and joined them. "Hi, Lou!"

"Hi, Aggie!"

"Is Bruce talking your ear off, dear?"

"He's reliving the good old days about when his mouth got him in trouble."

Bruce grumbled something about a *private conversation*.

Lou laughed, replaced the gas cap, and pulled the receipt from the machine. With a jingle to the ambulance keys, she opened the driver's door but paused and turned back toward him. "So. How'd you get past those things?"

When Aggie smiled, the lines crinkled over her face. "We had a few heart-to-heart discussions." She pointed. "Basically, I laid down the law."

"I don't recall it that way," Bruce said.

"Don't you?" Her steady glare worked its magic.

"Maybe a little bit." He turned his attention to studiously fueling his truck.

Lou bit back a laugh.

Aggie continued, "I saw the good guy he was beneath his foot-in-mouth problem."

"Hey!" Bruce complained.

She crossed her arms. "It's true and you know it."

"Fine."

Lou said to Aggie, "Look, I know that no one is perfect. All relationships take work and trust. But sometimes the effort is too much."

"Sometimes trust takes even more work. Trust takes time."

"I can't wait forever to trust Tuli."

Aggie stepped up and patted her arm. "I didn't mean him, dear. You have to first trust yourself."

Chapter Twenty-Four

WEDNESDAY EVENING, TULI sat down for dinner with Grandma Ruth.

He inhaled the buttery sage of the seasoned beans before spearing one with a fork. She made the best dishes.

"You want to tell me what that's all about?" She pointed at his face, her gray brows raised.

"Ran into a fire extinguisher," he said around the mouthful of food.

"Try again."

He took a sip of water. "Difference of opinion, now taken care of."

Then she stared at him for a solid minute. His fork quivered in his hand as he sat, frozen.

"Mm-hmm."

"What?" He pulled his head back.

"It's not the whole truth."

"Everything's okay, Grandma."

"That's not what I heard. You getting into it with Hunter Wright at a car accident scene."

Tuli rested the fork on his plate. "If you knew, then why did you ask me?"

She cut a piece of chicken and chewed thoughtfully, then

said, "To see what you'd say."

"You're spying on me?"

"Easy to do in a town with no secrets."

Actually, there might be a few secrets left, despite Tuli's screwup with Lou earlier this week. "Whatever happened to privacy?"

"This happened in public. Besides, Yukon Valley and the Koyukon village? We're all one community. Many lives, interconnected." Then she waited.

"You ever want to live in a different community? Less connected. More privacy."

"Why?" she asked. "What do you mean by different? Different from what?"

"Traditional life versus ... nontraditional."

"I'm not following."

"You're an elder, so you're involved in the Athabascan traditions and preserving local culture."

"Are you asking if I want something different than that? No. I love our home here. I am proud of our culture and heritage. I love this community. People look out for one another here." She paused and peered at him. "Mostly."

"What about the modern world? Would you want to be in a more modern home?"

"This one is plenty modern. I have a microwave and electricity. Running water!" She craned her neck around. "A TV and cell phone!"

"Um, it's a flip phone."

Grandma rested her chin on a fist. "I choose not to upgrade. It still dials your number."

"Huh. Good point."

"Besides, why can't you have both? Traditional and modern life."

Tuli absently rubbed his bruised cheekbone. "I don't understand."

"This place, this land, is a part of who I am. It's part of who you are too. Traditions are important because they connect us to the land and our ancestors. They guide how we move forward in the world."

He nodded.

"But you can make your own way by bringing the past to inform your future. Nothing is fixed in stone. Our culture has been around for thousands of years, like the Yukon River. During some years in the spring floods, even our solid, reliable Yukon River changes its course. It cuts new paths on its way to the ocean."

Still goes to the same place, though. "What if my future isn't turning out how I wanted it to be?"

"How so?"

He tapped the edge of the plate. Privacy was important, but he still wanted his Grandma's guidance. "What if I might not have a traditional family, like I always wanted?"

Ruth paused and gave him a thoughtful expression. "You know your father was a good boy growing up."

That was not the direction Tuli was going, but he leaned forward, respecting her words. Based on his memories, this description of Tuli's father wasn't accurate. Her statement didn't fit his painful experience. "Sure."

"He wasn't a good *man*, though. Or a good father."

"Yeah, I know." Tuli had fought against embodying the temper and impatience traits he recalled his father having.

"I think he wanted to be a good father." She sighed. "When he walked his own path in life, it meant that my dream of a perfect family didn't turn out how I had envisioned it, either," she said with a wistful smile.

For a second, he got a glimpse of the difficulties she had faced over the years. The problems that her son and daughter-in-law—Tuli's father and mother—also had.

"It must have been hard watching that happen. First my mom and then my dad. Watching addiction and anger consume them."

"Harder when I had to step in and become a parent. It was a blessing in disguise for me. I wouldn't have traded the years raising you for all the gold in those mountains."

He reached over and squeezed her hand. "That's sweet, *nok'eedonh.*"

"It was necessary. Who else would raise a restless Arctic fox like you?" She grinned and took a bite of salad.

"I could have been adopted out."

"Well, that wasn't going to happen as long as I drew breath. You are my blood. Anyway, you *were* technically adopted. By me."

"What a bargain that was!" Tuli pointed at the bounty of good food on the table.

"Yes. It was a bargain." She rested her chin on her hand and gazed at him until he squirmed. "My point being, life didn't go the way I had envisioned it. It was still a good life. A valuable life. One with meaning. One full of love … and a kid who got into lots of trouble."

"Do you mean my father or me?"

"Both!"

Tuli laughed, his shoulders relaxing. "You had lots of practice. Lucky for you."

"Anyone can have that kind of luck. I just did what was right for the people I loved."

A sour twist in his gut preceded distant memories of yelling and pain. "Doing the right thing was hard for a rageaholic like my dad. I don't want to be like that." Was it too late?

"That's him. That's not you, Tuli."

"Isn't it?"

"You're not like him. You never were."

He rubbed his cheek. "Some days it doesn't feel like that."

"So, you didn't really run into a fire extinguisher?"

"Technically, I did." Hunter extinguished fires, ergo, that was who Tuli's face had run into. He snorted at the joke.

"I was married to your grandfather. I know how love is. I understand having hot emotions. I know how love can make you do silly things."

"This is not about love."

"Oh?"

Something shifted and settled into place deep inside of him. No. He was defending his friend and protecting his own reputation. "Doesn't matter. I have a black eye now instead of a date to the wedding."

She got up and rustled around in the kitchen, coming back with frozen venison wrapped in cheesecloth, and handed it to him. "Was it worth it?"

He pressed the coolness to his bruised face. "Very satisfying."

"Things that matter in life are worth taking a risk. Things that matter are worth breaking from tradition and forging a different course."

"Is that Athabascan wisdom you're handing down to me?"

"If you want it to be." She patted the back of his hand. "But no, this is simply the lesson I've learned along the changing path of my own life."

Chapter Twenty-Five

"COME ON, YOU'VE gotten enough free snacks from the Yukon Valley Diner," Lou said as she nudged her brother out the door and down the street on Thursday afternoon.

Gordy grinned. The guy had zero remorse. Everyone gave him goodies, and he loved it.

"Give me please," he typed.

His uneven smile lit up the overcast day. That and his bright-orange safety vest he diligently wore on this thin frame when he went out walking.

Okay. Fine. He deserved the extra goodies.

As they strolled down the sidewalk, she breathed in the cool fall air this afternoon and zipped up her uninsulated jacket. A few leaves swirled over the street. People were out and about, getting supplies for the weekend. Yukon Valley's Main Street was basically a slowed-down part of an Alaska state highway that ran through town. Gordy was a town fixture, making his daily walking rounds.

Until last spring when his health had taken a bad turn.

At least he was back out here now.

He stumbled on a piece of concrete, and Lou resisted grabbing his elbow. *Let him do for himself,* Dad always said.

Easy for Dad to say. This was her brother. She looked out for him like it was her job.

Until she couldn't look out for him.

She could protect Gordy from tripping on pavement, but not the progression of his condition.

Genes. One of several links they shared.

Someone honked as they drove by, and Gordy gave a jerky lift of his arm. A couple walked out of Three Bears and headed in their direction, grocery bags in hand.

"Hi, Gordy," Calvin Garrett said. Next to him was Deirdre Steen.

Their smiles and loose-limbed walk spoke volumes about their comfort with each other. They waited a few seconds.

Gordy pressed buttons. "Hello."

"Hi, guys," Lou said.

Gordy made a hollow noise and, with a halting step forward, rested a hand on Calvin's shoulder in a half hug. He repeated the gesture with Deirdre.

"What am I? Chopped liver?" Lou said. "You're over here giving out hugs to strangers and I don't even get leftovers!"

He turned that big smile on her and leaned in, gently bonking foreheads and resting his thin arms over her shoulders as well. Lou dropped a quick kiss on his cheek. "Okay, you're off my blacklist." She shook a finger. "For now."

Gordy didn't even pretend to be scared.

When it came to him, she was a total pushover.

"You guys ready for the big day?" she asked.

Calvin exaggerated tugging at his collar. "T-minus one week until no more bachelor life for me."

"You should be so lucky!" Deirdre laughed.

"Oh, I'm lucky all right." His grin crinkled fine lines next to his eyes. His graying hair at the temples reminded Lou that these two weren't young kids in love.

Calvin and Deirdre and her first husband had grown up together. Been friends. Calvin had drifted away from them.

Then Deirdre's husband had died several years ago.

And now these two lifetime friends had reconnected.

Lou drew a few uncomfortable parallels.

Only, that future wasn't meant to be. Not for Lou.

She glanced over at Gordy, who slowly shuffled in place, clearly wanting to continue walking. Another passerby honked, and he laughed and waved.

"Everything set for the wedding?" she asked.

"As in, somehow we planned it in a matter of months? It's a whirlwind. Who knows if we got the details right?" Deirdre shifted her grocery bag in her arms.

Calvin took the bag from her. "Who cares about details? Let's get to the good stuff." The heat in his expression made Lou squirm.

"Um ..." Lou said.

"I meant the reception!" Calvin grinned.

Deirdre pointed. "Glad you're feeling causal about it, because the custom caribou finger foods aren't going to be here in time due to shipping issues."

He kissed her forehead. "I'll nibble on something else."

Lou put her hands over Gordy's ears. "And ... it's time

for us to mosey."

"Don't you want to comment on how quickly we're getting married?" Deirdre pinned her with an arch expression. "Everyone else has. It's a popular topic of conversation in town."

Lou knew all about being the subject of speculation. "That's your business."

Calvin cleared this throat. "Hey, I had to wait eighteen years. That was plenty long enough."

"Really?" Lou asked.

He made a sheepish expression. "Truthfully? I had been too chicken to share my feelings so many years ago. Missed out on a lot of living because of the fear of rejection and the fear of exposing how I felt. So much time lost."

"Then this isn't quick after all." Lou paused, then plowed ahead with her question. "You think things would have been different if you had said something sooner?"

"Depending on the timing, yes, I think our lives wouldn't be the same," Calvin said.

Deirdre frowned and tucked her shoulder-length brown hair behind an ear. "But here's the thing. My life experiences leading up to now? Like, going through all of that is what made me who I am today. It made me really appreciate what we have now. You know?"

Nope. "Mm-hmm."

"Not me. I was like, let's *goooo*! Am I right, Gordy?" Calvin moved both bags to one arm so he could bump knuckles with Gordy.

"Yes," his machine spoke.

"You know"—Deirdre studied Lou—"Mav talks too much sometimes."

Uh-oh.

She continued, "All I'm saying is that both Calvin and I are not perfect and we've both made mistakes. One day we both realized what we could have was worth taking a chance on. Warts and all. I'm thankful that we figured it out before life could throw another curveball."

"Hey, I don't have any warts!" Calvin said.

She laughed. "It's a metaphor."

Lou's chest ached, but she said, "I'm really happy for you two."

"You could have that, too, you know." Deirdre's gaze was confident but intense.

"Warts and all. Okay, let's get down the road." Calvin nudged Deirdre with his shoulder as they waved goodbye and strolled to their vehicle, heads tilted toward one another.

Lou gave a noncommittal noise and murmured something socially appropriate that they probably didn't hear.

Problem was, Lou's warts weren't small annoyances or personality quirks. They were genetic issues that impacted her entire life and her future and that of any partner. She rubbed her face with a full hand.

Today wasn't the day to deal with that reality.

"Come on, Gordy," she said. "Giddyap."

He gave a medium squeal, scuffing along with her slow pace. As they passed in front of Eddy's, a local bar, the door swung open and three men exited, one of them running into Gordy.

Gordy's poor balance didn't compensate in time.

He fell to the pavement in a flail of limbs and orange, high-visibility material. His communication device clattered against the ground. His high-pitched squeal turned cry scared her.

"Oh no!" Lou knelt next to Gordy.

He grabbed his elbow. Then he looked at his tablet. A crack ran through the screen. Tears formed in his eyes.

Lou's heart dropped to her feet.

"Hey, watch where you're going, buddy," one of the men said from above her.

He was in his early thirties, thin beneath a light flannel shirt, his brown hair longer than the current style.

Lou glared up at him. "Why don't you watch where you're going? Can't you see he's disabled?"

"I'll show you disabled," the guy said.

"What?" she spluttered.

"Bud, shut up," a familiar voice reached her.

Lou froze. "Hunter?"

"Oh hey, sorry about this bonehead here. He's had one too many today." He cut off the man's retort, bent, and hooked his fingers under Gordy's armpits. "Come on, let's get you up."

Lou batted him away. "No, please don't do that until I check him out." She scanned her brother with a medic's eye.

He lay on the concrete sidewalk, moved all extremities, breathed fine. Below the fleece jacket sleeve, the heel of his right hand was scraped raw with a small amount of bleeding.

"Come on, Hunter," the second man, older by twenty

years and with a thicker build, said. "We're late for our meeting."

"In a minute," Hunter muttered.

"Kid really should watch where he's going," the first guy said. "Why are you letting someone like that walk on the streets?"

Hunter remained near Gordy, but he didn't say anything. He just stood there, looking vaguely sympathetic.

Lou couldn't think. A buzz of imaginary hornets filled her head until the humming sound drowned out the cars going down Main Street. Her vision tunneled in, and a pulsing sensation began at her temple.

Someone like that.

A war began inside of her as she crouched next to Gordy. One side wanted to help her brother. The other side wanted to implant a better attitude in the jerk standing there.

Implant won out. She assured herself that Gordy was stable and then stood. "What do you mean *someone like that*?" She glared up at the guy, who looked to be a few inches taller and about forty pounds heavier than she was. Every inch of her body shook as her hands rolled into fists. Never had she confronted anyone before. Not like this.

"You know." The thin man motioned. "A person who needs like a nurse or something."

She glanced at Gordy, who was now sitting up, cross-legged. "Nurse?" she said.

"For babysitting."

Hunter stepped partially in front of the man. "Dude, shut up. You don't know what you're talking about." For all this bravado, he hadn't done much else to help. "Let me check him out."

"Seriously, who the heck are you?" Lou asked the brown-haired guy. No one answered, and she looked at Hunter. "Well?"

"Um, this is Zach. He's a friend from Seattle." He punched his friend in the arm. "Zach, this is Louise, my cousin I thought you should meet."

"Meet?" she said.

Hunter ducked his head. "You know, go out. I told your dad I had some friends who would be great for you."

She glared at Hunter, then Zach, then the other guy. Everyone took a step back. "You're serious."

"Well, I was, until"—he lifted his chin toward Gordy—"this accident. Zach's a good guy. The beer just made him mouthy."

Even more reason not to go out with him. If alcohol took away his mask and this was who he truly was? No thanks.

"Nice to meet you, Louise," Zach said, hand outstretched.

She didn't return the gesture. "Why don't you all head on? I'm going to get Gordy sorted out."

"Sure you want to touch him?" Zach snorted. At the nasty expressions from everyone else standing there, he added, "What? Because he's bleeding, that's all. I'm sure he's a nice fellow."

The drone of imaginary hornets quickly turned into a high-pitched teakettle scream in her head. Lou cocked a fist, shocking herself with the willingness to take this action. That was it. "He's not contagious," Lou said, voice coming out high and quivering.

"Yeah, but that bad attitude is contagious," came another voice from behind her.

Chapter Twenty-Six

TULI WAS POSTING deli prices in the front window of Three Bears when he saw the guy barrel into Gordy but was too far away to do anything but lift an arm in helpless warning. He dropped the Windex and dashed down the street, grunting against the awkward gait and weird pinprick sensations shooting down his leg. Thankfully, everything held together until he reached the accident.

Tuli did a five-second assessment.

Gordy sat on the crumbled sidewalk, wincing—but he still gave Tuli a watery smile.

Lou stood in front of her brother, an icy death stare aimed at the man who had knocked Gordy down. By the looks of it, she was about five seconds away from removing the guy's spleen. Well deserved, in Tuli's opinion.

Hunter stood between Lou and the other two men. To Hunter's minimal credit, he appeared concerned.

And bruised on his jaw.

Tuli mentally patted himself on the back.

The dude who had run into Gordy looked to be older than Hunter by several years. In addition to a blue flannel shirt, he wore stiff, new-looking, leather lug-sole boots that somehow appeared out of place, like he was trying too hard to blend in.

Another shorter, stockier guy around fifty stood off to the side, hands in the pockets of his puffy jacket. Temps were in the fifties today. Too early for puffy jacket season, at least for hardy Alaskans.

Tuli suppressed the urge to rip someone's head off and instead focused on how he could help. "Hiya, Gordy. You tackling people again?" He didn't understand all of what Gordy had going on medically, but getting dumped on his butt sure wouldn't help. Tuli sure as hell wasn't going to stand by why this tool picked on Lou's brother. "What did I tell you? You're supposed to greet visitors, not attack them." He paused and stared at Hunter's companion, then back down. "Gordy, you gotta quit making dumb people look stupid."

Gordy tapped the cracked screen of his device, but nothing happened. His expression crumbled.

Lou made a gasping sound.

Tuli's heart twisted. Then he squared up to flannel and fancy boot boy.

"Wait a minute. It was an accident," the guy spluttered.

Lou made to step forward, but Tuli held out a hand to hold her back. Gordy looked stable, so Tuli figured he could focus on the men standing there, catching air with their gaping mouths. At least Tuli kept his shit together. Barely.

He could only imagine what Lou was going through. Her worry for her brother. The need to protect him.

A rush of adrenaline drove Tuli to protect both of them.

The man recovered. "Hey, the fellow got in our way.

Shouldn't be out here if he can't walk."

Tuli glanced over his shoulder. Yep, Lou's face had turned a lovely shade of pissed-off purple.

"I don't know you," Tuli said. "But it seems you like to pick on folks with disabilities. Real big of you." He laughed loudly and turned ninety degrees. "Is this the kind of company you keep, Hunter?"

Hunter muttered, "I was here helping."

"Clearly," Tuli said in a droll tone. "Lou?"

Eyebrows raised, she shrugged. "Hunter's also trying to set me up with Zach."

"This guy?" Tuli leaned forward and pointed to blue flannel who, to his credit, took a step back. "Quality friends you've got here, Hunter."

"At least I have friends," Hunter snapped. "You've got—"

"Top notch crew, like Gordy. And Lou. I'll hang with a select few good people rather than multiple bullies any day of the week." Tuli braced his stronger leg behind him and faced Hunter. "We'll talk about this later at work."

"This isn't work-related. There's nothing to talk about."

Tuli clamped his mouth shut for a solid ten seconds, holding back what he wanted to say. Instead, he settled for a more civil alternative. "If you're not going to be helpful, then why don't you three musketeers move on? Unless you want me to broadcast you." He patted the phone in his back pocket.

Hunter sneered. "Everything's a video moment for you, isn't it? You're not here helping anything but your online clout."

"Maybe it's two birds, one stone. I can do more than one thing at once, like how you are able to talk *and* be an idiot. What's to say I haven't already filmed you and posted it online? Hashtag, Bullying. Now I'm looking after my friends. You're lucky I don't report you to the troopers."

Blue flannel—Zach—said, "Tattling to the police. That's rich."

"If it keeps the good people of my town safe, I'm down for it."

"This town isn't yours for long, idiot," pudgy vest guy said before Hunter whipped his head around and hissed at him.

"What's that mean?" Tuli peered at the trio of tools.

"Anyway. Looks like Gordy's in good hands," Hunter said. "No harm no foul, right, Gordy?"

Gordy looked at his device, but the screen was cracked and blank. His big, friendly smile was gone.

So was Lou's. She hovered near her brother like a mother bear, tense and ready to charge.

"Skip along with your friends, Hunter." Tuli waggled his fingers. "Play some patty cake. Plan world domination. Pretend to pan for gold. Whatever you losers like to do."

In a blur of movement, Hunter whipped around and kicked out, his booted foot glancing Tuli's bad leg.

It buckled painfully, and down Tuli went, landing next to Gordy.

"Oh wow. Now you can't walk either," Zach said.

Hunter had the good sense to look offended.

Tuli rubbed his leg, pushed to a standing position, and

reset his shoulder-width stance on one good leg and one burning, unreliable leg. He'd protect Lou and Gordy or die trying. "This is getting to be a habit, Hunter."

"What? With the inability to fight because of your bum leg?" Hunter sneered. "You're useless."

"Don't need my foot to fight." Tuli feinted a jab toward his face, then swung and connected with the guy's gut. Hunter doubled over, his wheezing *oof* music to Tuli's ears. "Anyway, I'd hate to make your ass-kicking public." He forced his throbbing leg to keep him upright and stepped into an upward punch, catching his nose.

Blood spurted and ran from one nostril.

Thank God for extra core and upper body workouts over the past six months.

Tuli's leg burned like a hot poker had been shoved into it.

Shutting up Hunter took away some of the pain.

Deep down, Tuli didn't condone violence. But he'd use it for the right reason on a special occasion.

Several cars slowed down. One pulled over and doors opened.

"See you at the station for next shift, Hunter." Along with a discussion about professionalism in the community.

A lesson Tuli would need to reevaluate for himself. Fine, he was down for soul-searching as long as Lou was safe.

Hunter spat blood on the sidewalk. "Looking forward to it."

I just bet.

The guys headed off in a mumbling gaggle.

Tuli grunted as he tried to kneel next to Gordy. His shaky bad leg gave out, so he sat down hard on his butt. "You okay, buddy?" He eyed Gordy from head to toe and nodded in satisfaction. "How about your sister?" He rested his hand on her arm when she knelt next to them.

Lou pinned him with a curious expression. "He looks okay. Some scrapes."

"You didn't answer my question. What about you?" Tuli said gently. He scanned her, as if he would find some injury from Hunter and his friends.

"I'm fine. Just super mad. At Hunter and those jerks. Also, Gordy's communication tablet is broken."

The bar owner poked his head out, and Lou asked for some paper towels. In a minute, she pressed the squares against Gordy's scraped hand.

"You never get mad, Lou. This is a new side of you," Tuli said as he brushed his hands from head to toe over Gordy in a secondary medical assessment. He didn't find any obvious neurological deficits, worsening pain, or broken bones. Thank God. He waved off the onlookers and bar owner. "All good now. Thanks for the concern."

Lou hugged Gordy and tapped the tablet hanging from the strap. "We'll get this fixed. I promise."

"Stupid bullies," Tuli muttered.

After a minute, Lou pinned him with that fathomless brown gaze. "You've always hated bullies."

"Allergic to them." He rubbed his leg and winced. "The feeling might be mutual."

"Never took Hunter to be that much of a jerk, what with

him being family and all." She paused. "Hey, is your leg okay?"

"Worth it." He rested his hand on her forearm, needing to touch her, reassure himself that she was right here. Safe. He needed to ground himself in her steady gaze. After a second, he continued, "Who were those guys with Hunter?"

She shook her head. "Zach, the big talker? He was a guy Hunter had wanted to set me up with. I don't know the other man. They're both new to town."

"Damned strange. Guess they could be Hunter's friends, hanging out for a long weekend. Not sure what that one dude meant about the town not being mine for long. It's not mine now."

"One guy mentioned a meeting. I wonder if they are working with Hunter on the ore stuff?" She paused and tapped her lip. Tuli was jealous of her finger. "Seems like you and I would have heard if the community working group had hired people already." She stood up and looked down at him.

"If they're hired, then I want to know how to fire them." He slowly got up, not ashamed to use Lou's outstretched hand for extra stability until he locked his leg in place under him. He took a few test steps. It held, but man, it ached. "I know we like new people in town with tourism and economic opportunities, but those guys are not welcome."

Together, they carefully helped Gordy to get to his feet. He had a tear in the knee of his pants. His hand had stopped bleeding. He took a few halting steps. To Tuli's eye, Gordy seemed back to his usual mobility and balance. Which was to say, not great, but functional.

Lou kept a hand on her brother's upper arm. "Want to head home, bud?" she asked.

Gordy's smile crumbled. He shook his head and made a low noise. Then he looked pointedly down the street.

Tuli studied the direction of his stare. So that was his angle. What a scammer. "Need something to help you feel better?" Tuli asked.

The smile popped back on Gordy's face as he pointed at the seasonal sweet shop a few doors down. Then he patted his broken communication device.

Lou rolled her eyes. "Ice cream? You're turning this accident into a play for ice cream? You want sympathy because your machine is busted."

The returning grin was completely unrepentant. *Way to work the situation, Gordy.*

She let go of him and crossed her arms. "No way. It's getting close to dinnertime. Mom and Dad will kill us if we get ice cream now."

Gordy huffed and took a few steps, thin limbs stiff and jerky. Tuli reached out to steady him.

"Let's go home," she said.

The pitiful baby moose noise Gordy made would have ripped out most people's hearts.

"Not going to work on me, bud." But her expression softened.

Tuli smiled, but kept his mouth shut.

Gordy took a halting step toward her and pressed his cheek to her neck, resting his arms on her shoulders.

Tuli almost clapped, the acting job was that good.

After a second, Lou slid her arms around and gave her brother a hug. "Fine." Her voice dropped to a whisper as she threatened him. "But we're not telling Mom and Dad. And you'd better act like you're hungry and eat your dinner." She stepped back and pointed at him. "If you're up all night on a sugar high, you're just going to have to count sheep. I don't want to hear any complaints."

Tuli smiled as Lou stalked off toward to the sweet shoppe.

Lifting a fist for a bump, Tuli murmured, "Nicely played, Gordy. You're a master."

Chapter Twenty-Seven

AFTER THE SIDEWALK incident, Lou found herself agreeing not only to contraband ice cream for Gordy but also to a date with Tuli after work the next day.

That next day was today. Friday.

An actual date.

As the sound of a truck grew louder outside her apartment above the back of the furniture store in town, she checked her outfit. She had dashed home from work twenty minutes early, hedging her bets that no calls would come in. Mav had agreed to pick her up if they needed to do a run. She loved having a flexible and supportive boss.

Lou had quickly showered and changed into a long-sleeved, black knit dress with an open neckline. The hem came to above her knees. Leather booties added a little heel and looked dressy, but not fancy. A beaded pendant hung from a silver chain on her neck and rested on her sternum.

She peeked out the window. Tuli's old but reliable truck. Footsteps on the metal steps grew louder until there was a knock at the door.

Lou smoothed her unbound hair and opened the door.

Tuli, with faded bruises on his face, stood there with a bundle of late season wildflowers and pine boughs in his hand and a broad smile. He wore dark denim, thick-soled work boots, a brick-red cotton button down, and a black leather vest with embellished fringe. His broad shoulders filled out the shirt until there was no space left. Material strained over his arms.

"We're really doing this?" she asked, heart pounding.

His brows drew together. "The flower part or the going out part?"

"Both."

"First things first." He held out the flowers. "You look beautiful tonight."

Needing something to do with her hands, she clutched the bouquet. "Thank you," she said.

He paused, his smile twisting into a silly expression. "Or as a third option, we can stand here for a while."

"Oh. Come in. I don't want Frost to escape."

He quickly stepped inside and closed the door behind him. The space between them became charged. Hot. An invisible strand between them stretched tight. The weight of his dark gaze pinned her in place.

Finally, he blew out a breath. "Hey, Lou, if you're not into this, we can stay in. I'll grab a frozen pizza from Three Bears. Or we can punt. Your call."

She thought hard and then gulped. "No, we're going out."

Leaning a hip against the doorjamb, he said, "You make it sound like a prison sentence, not an enjoyable activity."

"I just ... need to get over some things."

"Like privacy stuff?"

"It's silly, I know." Unable to stand there beneath his scrutiny, she gently laid the bouquet down on the entry table. A wide orange ribbon wrapped around the stems, protecting hands from sap and keeping the bundle together. The lopsided bow suggested the entire display was home-made.

"No, your privacy concerns are valid." His warm hand on her upper arm sent shivers through her. "Hey, my phone is here only for emergency fire calls. Nothing else, I promise."

"What if there's a really good opportunity to get a clip for your site?"

"Not happening."

She peered up at him. "Are you working tonight?"

He shook his head. "I swapped shifts." Then he lifted his hands in a shrug. "But as the fire chief, I'm never not available."

"Got it." A door shut below them, the sound muffled and faint. Store closing. A few minutes after seven p.m. She was truly all alone with Tuli in her apartment. A wave of warmth rushed through her.

He laced her fingers in his, and she couldn't stop staring at their joined hands.

"Lou." The intensity of his serious expression hit her hard. "Let me cut to the chase."

Her heart thumped against her ribs. "I was thinking that I might try that."

"What?"

"Cutting to the chase. Being plain in what I say."

He rubbed his thumb over the back of her hand. "Ladies first."

Her mouth went dry. Finally, she stammered, "I want to try. Us. Together."

"That's what we're doing. Going out. Together."

"I know. But ..." She hesitated, unable to find the words.

"You're thinking about dating for real and not dancing around in casual-friend world?"

"Exactly." Her breath left her in a relieved exhale.

Tuli didn't speak for her, but sometimes he seemed to have an easier time voicing the hard things out loud.

"I, too, want to not dance around with you, Lou!" He tugged her forward and snagged her around the waist until they were pressed together. The warmth from his lean torso flowed into her. Lifting their joined hands, he dropped a tender kiss on her wrist. A whiff of his spicy aftershave triggered goose bumps on her arms.

"Since we're no longer dancing around, I'd like to kiss you." His breath, minty and warm, moved tendrils of hair off her forehead.

His smiling expression changed into something serious. More intense. It took her breath away.

Wow. She had never really seen serious Tuli. Not like this.

"Me too."

He tightened his arm around her back and pressed her palm to his chest. Then he let go of her hand, sliding his fingers up her arm to rest under her jaw, tilting her face up.

"Man, Lou."

"What?"

"I—" He shook his head and pressed his lips to hers, igniting sparks along every point of contact.

Changing angles, he swept his mouth over hers. When she let out a murmured gasp, the tip of his tongue teased along the seam of her lips. Her knees went weak, but he held her steady, the muscled cords shifting as he adjusted his grip.

The low rumble in his chest sent shockwaves through hers. Pulling back, he looked down at her, a half smile on his damp lips. The next featherlight kiss he brushed over her mouth wasn't enough. She stood on her tiptoes to gain precious inches. Unable to stand the teasing, she dragged her hand up his chest and then rested it on the back of his neck, drawing him down to her.

The kiss went on and on, all sighs and moist heat. She answered the questioning probe with his tongue by opening to him, tangling her tongue with his. She inhaled, and mint and aftershave scent filled her nose. A loosening sensation in her hips made her gently rock against him until she was shocked back to reality.

More needed to be said first. More cutting to the chase.

She pulled back a few inches. "Tuli?"

After another brush of his lips against hers, he pulled his head up with a low groan. "Yeah, Lou?" He was breathing like a guy who had run a mile.

"Before we go … out … I want to be clear. You have dreams." Her voice cracked. He reached both of his hands around her back, supporting and circling. "The future you wanted since we were kids. Back when we played house together." A hard lump lodged in her throat. She rested her palms on his chest. "Those dreams involved a family. Kids. Grandchildren."

He kissed the top of her forehead. "Yes, those were my dreams."

"So, if we're going out … I can't provide that future for you. Be honest with yourself and what you want. In the end, it'll just be disappointing."

His eyes darkened. "Nothing about you will ever disappoint me, Lou."

"You don't know that."

"I do." He bent down to kiss her again.

Turning her head to the side, she let his lips glance off her cheek. Lou hauled in a shaky breath. "I don't want to hold you back from your future."

"Maybe I want to see if we can make a new future together."

Deep inside, she knew this was wrong. She couldn't do this to him. But in the circle of his warm embrace, she couldn't help herself. "Are you sure?"

"You're what's important in this equation, Lou."

She sighed, melting into his tall, strong frame, and looped both of her hands behind his neck.

With a growl, he went in for another kiss that went on and on until she couldn't tell where he started and she began. The world tilted. Still, he kept her upright and steady.

Her toes tingled.

You're what's important.

For now.

She should stop this. For both of their sakes.

He slanted his mouth in another interesting angle, and she hummed.

Tomorrow. She would worry about that tomorrow.

Chapter Twenty-Eight

TULI SHIFTED IN his seat at the restaurant table. He had never gone to a dinner he had looked forward to, while simultaneously wanting it to be over as quickly as possible. On the other hand, he also wanted this evening to last forever.

What he wanted was to hold Lou's hand. To maintain a physical connection with her and show everyone how proud he was to be here with her. But he knew that she didn't want public displays of affection. Or attention from others.

It was enough that they were on a date in public. That was a huge step for her.

He nodded at a few diners who walked by their table. He and Lou were Yukon Valley official by now.

At least there were no fire calls. He patted the phone secured in his vest pocket. Felt weird not to have it out so he could respond to comments and other content.

"Hey, how's Gordy after yesterday's fall?" he asked.

"A little sore, I think, but none the worse for wear. That guy is tough."

"I'll say. He gets it from his sister."

"Hmm." A crimson blush climbed her neck.

Tuli fought a wave of desire. He needed to drop kisses on

that redness to see if the skin was as heated and smooth as it appeared.

He needed more than that.

Oh boy, he was in trouble.

Planting his hands on the table, palms down, he focused on the conversation. "What about his tablet?"

Her eyes narrowed. "It's off to get fixed. Hopefully, we'll have a new one in a week or so."

"Good. Anything about those guys who were with Hunter?" he asked.

"No information. Dad didn't know."

"That's strange. It's small enough of a town that gossip about anyone new gets broadcast within a minute of arrival." He tapped a fingertip on the laminated wood surface. "The fact that we have no information on them is weird in and of itself. I poked around online but came up with nothing."

"Think it has to do with Hunter taking on the mine development duties?"

They paused as their food arrived, the steamy, delicious aromas wafting over them.

He cut into the baked salmon. "Maybe."

"Dad said Hunter has experience managing a mine, so the local working group has asked Hunter to help out."

He chewed thoughtfully. "They asked him, or he volunteered himself?"

"Second one. I'm questioning what mine management experience he really has. He's a year younger than we are." She shrugged and took a bite of meatloaf.

He followed the movement of her lips around the fork

and the line of her throat as she swallowed. How had he not noticed how pretty her lips were until today?

Oh, he'd noticed all right. He had just not been brave enough to risk acknowledging it.

"He said he has training, right?"

"He says. Folks in town know Hunter from when he lived here before," she said.

"Knowing someone isn't for the same as a line on the ol' resumé."

"You really don't like him, do you?"

"I know he's your cousin, Lou. But I don't know him that well. What I do know hasn't impressed me. At least not his character. How about you?" That was a question Tuli didn't want to ask. He took a risk being perceived as attacking Lou's family, legitimate reason or not. He reminded himself to tread carefully.

"He's a known quantity in our family. Likes hanging out with Dad." She paused and took a sip of water. A drop rested on her lower lip, torturing Tuli. "He seemed to want to help Gordy yesterday."

"Kind of."

"Yeah. He comes on strong at times. He's still family."

What Tuli didn't have. The veggies turned to silt in his stomach. "I noticed."

"Hey." She pointed with her fork. "We're all family in Yukon Valley."

"Community isn't the same as blood." He chewed thoughtfully before swallowing a bite. "Your dad seems to be all in on Team Hunter."

"Dad doesn't get the final say. It's a committee." She sighed. "Dad's looking out for my future and our family's future. He also is focused on Gordy's welfare. And he's a village elder with responsibilities."

"So, your dad looks at the mine decisions as part of how he takes care of his family?"

"We're more like the to-do list."

His head whipped up. "You're not a project to be checked off a list."

"I know."

"Do you?"

"I also think that … my folks are coming to grips with the change in their own hopes and dreams. With Gordy and"—her voice dropped to right above a whisper—"with the DNA results."

He didn't know what to say to that, so he nodded.

"They want the best for their kids. It's understandable." She toyed with the stem of her water glass. "But years ago, their dreams were changed when Gordy came along. Happened again when I got the test back."

"What about your dreams? Did the test change those?"

"Of course." So matter-of-fact. Like it was a mundane event for her.

How did she not show any emotion? Years of practice. Lou was always so stoic.

Wait. There. The corners of her mouth turned down. Gaze slid away from him. Eyes shimmered.

Reaching out, he ran his fingertips lightly over the back

of her hand. "You know I like you for being you, right?"

"Sure. But—" The pause almost killed him.

He gazed at the rapid pulse at the base of her neck. He needed to know that she was as affected by him as he was by her.

She darted a glance around the restaurant, pulled her hand back a few inches, and pressed her fingertips against his. "First of all, I need to get over my privacy issues. Second of all, I am not pushing you away. I'm processing."

"Good, because I would like the opposite of being pushed away. Whatever that is, I want it."

"Me too."

Her quick, shy smile satisfied more than the good meal in front of him.

"As for privacy," he said, "I'm an open book. You can have access to everything I do online. I won't ever create a post involving you unless you give me permission. I want to promise that."

"I know."

"I want you to feel safe."

"Thank you."

"I want you."

He brushed his fingers over hers. Virtual sparks arced at the contact, arrowing to other areas of his anatomy. He put down his fork. She did the same.

Their eyes locked.

Held.

Tuli cleared his throat. "Can I pay the bill so we can get

out of here?" Whatever this new, delicate thing was between them, he wanted to explore it. Nurture it. Protect it.

Her eyes turned into dark, sensual orbs that caged him in place. "Please."

Chapter Twenty-Nine

WHETHER IT WAS the company, the night, or the realization that her genetic makeup hadn't ruined her chances with Tuli, Lou couldn't keep her hands off him as they climbed the stairs to her apartment together.

Every few steps, those little touches, deep kisses, and breathy sighs all took up space in her heart and mind until every sense focused on Tuli.

She fumbled with the lock on the door but finally managed to turn the bolt and step inside. Two steps away from the door, she flipped on a light and toed off her booties, shooing Frost away.

Tuli stood right there, staring hungrily as if he hadn't just had dinner, taking up all the space in front of her. His serious facade cracked when he quirked a dark brow and shot her a half smile. Then, without taking his eyes off her, he reached out and threw the bolt from the inside. The *thunk* of metal into the door jamb was loud in the quiet apartment.

Lou didn't breathe.

Tuli stared at her, his broad chest rising and falling.

Neither of them moved.

Until they both moved.

They closed the two feet between them in a sensual collision of lips and arms and chests pressed against each other.

She set and reset her hands, restless, desperate to touch all of him all at once.

His arm banded around her back, tightening up, then easing off the pressure, over and over, as if he consciously forced his muscles to loosen up. Yet kept failing.

Her head spun as she locked her arms around his neck. He was her north star in a swirl of bright lights and emotions. He walked them until she bumped against the back of her loveseat. Still, he moved forward. Trapped in the sweetest of prisons, she throbbed as pressure and heat built between them. He crowded her. His eyes darkened. This was a side to him she'd never truly seen before. She couldn't move. Didn't want to move. She needed more.

He pulled away from a soul-stealing kiss. "Lou, I want you so much."

Blasts of images and thoughts raced through her mind—the two of them playing together as children, growing up together, working to help patients, hanging out at festivals, chatting over morning coffee in the deli. Two orbits intersecting as they circled in proximity.

Her childhood memories and her adult memories were all filled with one smiling face—Tuli's.

This moment would change everything. Hell, it had already changed.

What he was asking. What she desperately needed. She'd never be the same again.

She never wanted to be the same again.

She needed her best friend, her rock, her colleague. The

guy who always understood her, even when she didn't speak. A full body shudder rippled through her.

She wanted him.

"Please," she said.

"I can't … I—" He didn't finish his sentence before dipping his head and taking her lips in another sensual kiss that went on and on.

The world tilted and shifted. He held her steady. He was her anchor, like he'd always been.

He slid his hands over her waist and breasts, teasing nipples into tight, hard peaks even through the knit dress. His kisses along her neckline set off tremors. When his hands drifted down to fist the skirt material, he dropped his forehead to hers. His chest heaved.

"You good?" he asked, voice harsh and raw, like he'd been running.

She lowered her hand and rested it over his fist, lifting the dress hem together. "Absolutely." She kissed him again, their tongues tangling against each other in the most sensuous of battles.

He slid his fingertips over the panty material covering her hip, and she arched into him.

"No," he murmured against her mouth.

"No?" For some reason, she couldn't stop kissing him and rubbing up against him.

"No."

She forced herself to hold still. Of course, *no*. She would respect his boundary. With a gasp, she said, "You want to stop?"

"Not at all. I want to go, go, go." Beneath her dress, his hand tightened, fingertips pressed into her flesh. "I want to rip this off of you."

She shuddered. "But?"

"No buts. Other than I'd like to temporarily pause so we can move to the bedroom. Not that I'm opposed to using this loveseat in all sorts of fun ways."

"Oh. *Oh.*"

His rakish grin pulled a giggle from her. He continued, "I mean, we can work with the loveseat later if you want. Hell, if you're committed to living room furniture right now, I'm game." He brushed a hot kiss over her lips and drew back once more. "But I want to make this perfect for us. For you. Always for you, Lou."

Oh God. How could a heart ache and swell at the same time? She wanted all of him, period.

"So?" he said with a sideways grin.

Her friend, her confidante, her rock, her ... Tuli.

"Yes."

"Hot damn!" He nearly danced as he tugged her to the bedroom, kicked the door closed on Frost's indignant meow, and pulled her into another deep embrace full of kisses.

At some point, her dress and necklace went missing, and the cool air made her shiver as she stood there in her bra and panties. Amazingly, she didn't feel shy.

This was Tuli.

Her Tuli.

He rested his hands at her waist and leaned back, a rapt expression on his face. "My God, Lou. For the first time in my entire life, I have no words." He bent down and swept his lips over the exposed upper swell of one breast, then the other. His mouth created warm fire that raced along her nerve endings like dry tinder ready to flare at the least spark.

"Mmm." She dug her fingers into his hair and arched back as he tongued the cleft between her breasts.

He lowered his voice, his eyes heavy-lidded. "I want more, Lou."

"You can have more."

Shucking off the black leather vest and unbuttoning the top two shirt buttons, he said, "You're beautiful and amazing. I can't believe we waited this long." He slowly rolled up his sleeves.

"Less talking, more kissing." She gasped.

He let out a broad laugh, then concentrated as he pulled one bra cup to the side and lifted her breast in his palm. His thumb drifted over the taut nipple until her knees shook. "You have no idea how many times I've fantasized about this. Never thought this dream would come true."

Lou tried to answer. Honestly, she did. But then he reached around and unclasped her bra, sliding it off and away. When he latched his lips over one tip, the sound coming out of her was half groan, half squeal and all pleasure. Her brain short-circuited for a split second.

He kneaded the other breast while he sucked the nipple and flicked his rough tongue over the sensitive flesh. Then, when her voice cracked on a hoarse moan, he switched sides. She plunged her fingers in his thick, dark hair and held on tight.

After minutes, he eased her back onto the bed, hand cupping her head like she was made of fine China. "Still good?" His lips were wet, mouth open.

She needed more of his kisses.

Her breasts throbbed, her belly ached, her hips shifted toward where he crouched over her, needing connection. Pressure. "I'm very good." She reached up and smoothed her hands over the material stretched tight across his upper arms and chest as he knelt over her and made the bed dip with their combined weight. Her lower legs still dangled off the edge of the mattress.

"Fabulous. Because I'm just getting started." He palmed her breasts again and dropped kisses beneath them, licking and kissing his way lower. He dipped his tongue into her belly button, and it sent off a sensual jolt straight into her core.

"Oh God, Tuli." Her hips bucked beneath his hands where he gripped her waist.

"I'll say."

He slowly licked his way lower until he reached her underwear. Caressing the skin over her waist, he paused and studied her.

"You have no idea how much I want you," he said.

"I have a good idea." She reached for him. "Less talk, more Tuli."

"You got it." Hooking his fingers under the garment, he drew the panties down and off her legs.

Suddenly, Lou felt exposed. Vulnerable. She didn't know where to put her hands. She wanted to cover back up and also wanted him to see all of her. Touch all of her.

"Tuli?"

He sat back, his face creased with raw emotion. "You're beautiful, Lou."

In a flash, he had his shirt off, and the breadth and ridges of his bare chest stunned her.

Then he swept his palms down her thighs, so close but so far from the place she needed him to touch. He lifted and slowly caressed each leg and ankle, moving back up to settle his hands at the junction of her pelvis. His fingers dug into her thighs with a firm, warm grip. With a steady press of his palms, he eased her open.

Lou panted.

It was too much.

No. Not enough.

She closed her eyes. Then opened them. She wanted to see everything. Experience everything.

"Talk to me, Lou." His voice had dropped an octave.

He knelt at the edge of the bed, positioned between her legs, face close enough that her sensitive skin tingled with his heated breath. Her legs dangled over his arms.

"More, Tuli."

"Show me. Guide me. You're in the driver's seat."

Sitting halfway up and propped on one elbow, she used her other hand to cup his face, then laced her fingers into his thick hair. She held eye contact while she brought his face closer to her throbbing flesh. So close.

"Yes. Show me what you want, Lou." When he exhaled, her skin quivered, hips loosened. Everything ached for him to touch her.

In a rush of hot desire, hesitation fled, and raw need took over. She let go of him, lay back, and flexed her hips so her legs rested near her chest.

"You're beautiful." His reverent words made her eyes sting. "I want you to see everything. Feel everything. All of it. For you. You're amazing. So strong and sexy. Show me more."

Blinking hard, she watched his face as she slid her hands down her abdomen, between her legs. She checked for any hesitation or doubt on his face. There was absolutely nothing there but an expression of gape-mouthed wonder.

She lowered her hands to her folds.

"Yes, ma'am," he growled.

Then she opened for him.

"Damn. Please, I need to touch you. Please. I have to taste. Lou, I need you."

"Tuli, I—" She reached up for his hand and pressed it against her center.

With a satisfied rumble, he stroked her damp skin with a finger, teasing her entrance. Not enough. It wasn't nearly enough. She closed her eyes and gripped the bedspread.

"Watch me, Lou. This is all yours. All for you."

Her eyes flew open as he met her gaze. Then he slid the pad of his finger over that bundle of nerves, over and over, until eddies of sensation threatened to pull her under. The intensity of his concentration and—she watched him through her lust-hazed vision—his sheer enjoyment of touching her sent another shudder through her.

"You're a miracle. This is a miracle," he whispered, the words dragging like roughly woven cloth over raw nerves. "Beautiful." His words made her fly.

Lou let her knees drop even further to the sides. She was completely open to him. Trusted him.

Loved this connection. Craved more pleasure.

So did he. He chuckled as he dipped his head. The first lick of his tongue over her hot flesh nearly made her levitate off the bed.

"Oh, God."

"Should I slow down?" he asked, lifting his head up and peering at her.

She panted, hips shifting restlessly. "Don't you dare."

"I'm on it." Holding her steady with his strong grip on her inner thighs, he licked and sucked, throwing in random gentle nips that showered her vision with sparks. Tuli teased and tasted until she vibrated, so close to the top of the mountain. He dipped his finger into her and curled it in time with the strokes of his tongue up the seam of her folds. She choked out a guttural cry.

"Yes," he said with a quick grin at her before diving back down. He settled into a relentlessly sensual rhythm of pressing one finger deep into her and licking at the same time.

Closing her eyes, she allowed her hearing to center on the wet sounds and his hums of appreciation as he changed angles and the pressure of his mouth on her flesh.

"Lou, look at me."

Her eyelids flew open.

Sweat beaded his forehead. The expression of sheer lust and wonder when he lifted his head and met her gaze stunned her. Then he flashed a rakish, goofy Tuli smile, full of mischief and promise.

A second finger joined the first one, and the stretch drew out a bone-deep groan from both of them.

"Look at what I'm doing to you. Look at what you're doing to me. Watch how I can't get enough of you." He pressed his two fingers deeper. "This is for you, Lou." His words were as sexy as his actions, and she met his gaze until he dipped his head back down to suck and lick some more. Sensations coiled up, up, up. Tighter the spring wound.

He didn't stop the movements of his mouth or his fingers.

All of this was for her pleasure. Tuli. Here. He was hers.

As sparks danced along the edge of her vision, she squeezed one breast. A swirling reaction deep inside tightened up her inner muscles. Higher.

Higher.

Until she released in a burst of desire.

"Tuli! Oh my God." She gasped, muscles clenching and tightening. He held onto her thigh while continuing to thrust and lick, pulling more response from the depths of her body. On and on it went, waves of pleasure that seemed to last forever.

Finally, the aftershocks subsided, but he kept one finger inside and continued to gently lick her folds, letting her enjoyment skim along at a low level that persisted.

She rested her arms limp at her sides, every joint in her

body relaxed and loose, heat coursing through her.

With one last kiss, he finally pulled away and then prowled up her body, scooting her up the bed. He kissed her belly, her breasts, then her mouth. She tasted his scent and her essence mixed together on his tongue. Perfect.

Sitting up on his knees, he kept his weight off her chest while she stroked his lean torso. When she reached for the belt at his waist, he shot her a half smile, swung his good leg off the bed, stood, and shucked off his pants and briefs. The scar from his femoral artery surgery was an angry slash marring his upper thigh.

"It's not pretty. I know." He didn't meet her gaze.

Beneath the dark curls at his center, he jutted out hard and proud.

She sat up and stroked him, then skimmed her hands down both of his thighs and back up to his center. Pulling him toward her, she bent and dragged her lips over his legs. Over the scar. Over his stiff erection.

He shuddered and gripped fistfuls of hair at the base of her neck.

"Everything looks pretty to me." She leaned back after a few minutes of tasting and licking.

"Damn—" The word was cut off as she circled his length with both hands. "You know exactly what to say." He panted. "Don't you?" His erection pulsed hot and hard in her light grip.

"Hope so."

He reached down and fished around in his clothing on the floor and straightened, holding out a packet. "Condom?"

"If you want. But I'm on the pill. Recent checkup was normal."

He nodded and pointed a thumb at his chest. "No partners in quite some time, but I stay up-to-date on testing." He paused, foil packet in hand. "So?"

"So … I'm okay without one if you are. I trust you."

Chapter Thirty

F OR REAL, TULI was the richest man in the entire world. No one could ever have felt better than him. No one would ever be luckier. Not with a beautiful woman like Lou in front of him.

Lou.

His forever friend.

His family.

His center.

His love.

Oh shit. His love.

He pushed that realization to the side as he knelt on the mattress and lined himself up at her hot, wet entrance. When he nudged her opening with his dick, he shook with the urge to drive into her hard and chase his completion.

No. This was Lou. They would do this together. He wanted this moment to be special for both of them. This wasn't the end of a need that he'd had for years.

It was the beginning of something amazing.

How long had he wanted this? So long.

Inch by satisfying inch, he sank into her, and their twin groans filled the bedroom.

He focused on his breathing, needing to make sure she

was right there with him. He needed her to understand so much more about how he felt. "Lou, you're—I want you to know, I—"

No. It was too much. He bent forward and pressed his lips against hers to keep the words back.

She pushed his head up and stared at him for several long seconds before she slid her hands down, gripped his butt, and guided him deeper inside.

So perfect, the fit of them together, like they'd been made for each other. This connection was the best present he'd ever been offered.

He seated inside of her with a slow, deep thrust, every inch of their skin pressed together. She filled his vision. His senses.

His soul.

"More, Tuli."

He grinned. This shy person was able to tell him what she needed. Who was he to refuse that gift?

"You got it." He worked his hips, adjusting his position to relieve the tingle of pain shooting into his right thigh.

No way would a stupid injury stop him from enjoying this evening and ensuring her pleasure. Each thrust brought them closer together, and he cupped her head and pressed his damp forehead to hers. Their panting became one.

When she locked her ankles around his backside? He became a man happily drowning in the rushing river of sexiness that was Lou. She could do that move any day of the week, and he'd be the luckiest guy in the world.

A blast of pleasure took him by surprise as he chased his

release. "Oh God. I'm coming, Lou!"

She clung to him. He kissed her with everything he had but somehow held off long enough for her to join him as they crested together in a tangle of limbs and cries. The grip of her inner muscles rippled around him. He never wanted her to let go. He didn't want to leave. Ever. Sensations rolled on and on until Tuli couldn't tell where he ended and Lou began. Words utterly failed him.

He shuddered under the light drift of her fingertips over his back. The press of her cheek against his was life. Bliss. Perfection.

It was Lou.

Home. This was home. No. This was more than home. It was family. Like cracked ice melting and refreezing, something shattered and then re-formed in his chest.

Lou was his family.

Lou was his everything.

A hard lump in his throat choked him.

Unable to move or say a word, he simply rested there in her arms. She was part of him. She was the missing piece of his world.

Only, she hadn't been missing, had she? Lou had always been right there.

At her low hum, he lifted his head. A shimmer in her eyes brought him back to Earth in a hurry.

He pushed up on one arm. "Lou, are you okay?"

She sighed. "Very okay."

"These are good tears?"

"Yes. What about yours?"

He lifted his head and swiped. Yep. Wet. No shame in that. He earned it. "Very good tears, Lou."

Leaning down, he wrapped his arms around her once again and they lay entwined for several minutes longer until he softened and eased out of her. Standing, he looked back at her sprawled body and sated smile. Stepping away, even for a minute, challenged his self-control. He quickly cleaned up and then brought back a warm washcloth to take care of her.

After setting the cloth on the nightstand, he pulled back the covers and helped her under them. Then he turned off the bedside lamp and pulled her against him, back to chest. A perfect fit, of course.

Twining his fingers in hers, he murmured, "Where has that been my whole life?"

"It's always been right here."

"Lou, I want this to work. Us." That was more of a commitment statement than anything he'd ever spoken in his life.

"I know. Me too." She swallowed. "I just … don't want you disappointed by your life later down the road."

"If I'm with you, I won't be disappointed. Period." He nuzzled her neck, the words muffled. "Besides, we can always have kids other ways if we want. Adoption." He kissed her on the shoulder. "I don't quite understand how the genetics work, but can we roll the dice? Use a fertility doctor to help us get a good egg and sperm?"

"It won't work that way for us."

"That's okay."

"Is it?" She looked over her shoulder at him. "I mean, I

love Gordy, but I want to be sure I don't have a child with Gordy's health challenges. It would break my heart to know that every day might be a struggle for a child to survive. They would have to exist in a world that isn't designed for them. In a world that, on some level, doesn't see them as a complete person. To realize that my child could be gone"— she snapped her fingers—"in the blink of an eye, due to the severe health problems associated with Bledsoe Syndrome." Her voice cracked. "Those are the thoughts that go through my head when I consider a future like his."

"That's a lot of weight to carry, Lou." He kissed her temple. "I would like to take some of that burden off of you."

"That's amazing for you to say."

"I would love any family we had. Or didn't have. We don't have to have kids. At the end of the day, Lou, it is entirely your choice. At the end of the day, I am ride-or-die with you."

"Tuli …" The word came out choked.

He swallowed against a hard lump. "I've got you," he murmured.

"Thank you …" She paused. "For being the person you are. I'm lucky that you're in my life."

He chuckled. "Just another day of being awesome, really."

She laughed in return and sighed. Then she yawned and pillowed her head on his arm in a movement so natural, it was like they'd been here, in bed, together, thousands of times.

Wrapping his arms around her, he murmured, "So does

that mean you'll be my date to Calvin and Deirdre's wedding?"

"Mm-hmm." Her breaths evened out as she drifted off to sleep.

TULI GOT UP early the next morning to grab a quick shower. He needed to start his shift soon, but first he wanted to check his social media accounts. After five minutes of standing in last night's clothes in the chilly kitchen, posting and responding to online comments, he walked in bare feet back to the bedroom.

Paused.

The morning light slanted over Lou's sleeping face. A pang of longing twisted in his chest at her tiny smile and peaceful expression. Her neck and the top of her exposed shoulders begged him to stroke her soft skin.

He would be a happy man if he had the privilege of seeing this face every day of his life. This one perfect image.

The thought drove the air from his lungs.

Holding up his phone, he snapped a picture of her beautiful face.

As if he could ever forget this moment.

"Lou," he whispered, hating to wake her, but determined not to walk out without saying goodbye.

"Mm-hmm?" She cracked one eyelid. As she homed in on him, a crimson blush bloomed from her neck up to her cheeks.

He had done that.

They had done that.

Leaning over to kiss her forehead, he said, "Shift's starting for me, and I think for you too."

"Got it." Her voice, roughened by her moans during sex and by sleep, sent jolts of heat deep into his core.

"I'll text you today."

"Sounds good."

"Hey, Lou." He perched on the edge of the bed and gave into temptation, trailing a finger along her shoulder. When she slid her hand out from under the covers, he lifted it and kissed her wrist. "This is something special. Something good."

She nodded and cupped his cheek, the sensation of her fingertips against his rough whiskers sending shivers down his back.

"I'll be thinking about you at work," he murmured, dropping one last kiss on her forehead.

She chuckled. "Same."

He exited and slowly eased the apartment door closed behind him.

Chapter Thirty-One

"YOU TYPING OUT a book on your phone, boss?" Hunter's sarcastic voice cut through Tuli's thoughts several hours later on Saturday morning.

Tuli hit SEND on the latest smiley heart emoji-filled text to Lou and put his phone down on the arm of the recliner in the fire station. "Nope." He crossed his foot over his knee, the black uniform cargo pants loud with the movement.

"You must have something good to text about. You've had a goofy smile on your face all morning. Website stuff?"

After their brief discussion on professionalism as they started today's shift and an agreement to try and work together, Hunter seemed to be overcompensating in the other direction. Extra friendly. Extra buddy-buddy.

At least they weren't busy punching each other. Tuli would call that a win.

He gripped the phone. "Something like that."

"Lady stuff?"

Tuli's dick tightened right up. Hunter had no idea how much *lady stuff* Tuli had enjoyed last night. And hopefully, would enjoy more later this week if things continued to go well with Lou. "Hmm," he said noncommittally.

Hunter's smile drooped. "So that's a yes. Spill the beans.

Sharing is caring."

"Not always, man." He pushed to his feet. "Enough sitting around. We've got equipment checks and bay cleaning today." He pushed a piece of paper over the station table to him. "I'm going to the restroom, then we'll tackle the list together."

"Roger that, boss." He raised an eyebrow and sneered. "Ah, you taking your phone into the bathroom?"

Yes. The phone went literally everywhere with him. "No." He deliberately put it face-down on the table and headed down the hall.

AFTER AN HOUR of checking equipment was cut short by a call about a gas leak at a business, Tuli hung up his turnout gear on pegs with a weary sigh. He trudged into the station lounge. He needed to prep some sandwiches for lunch, then help Hunter finish cleaning the garage and trucks.

His hand was on a package of sliced meat when a text message from Mav popped up on his phone. Before he tapped on it, he spotted a red dot with thousands of notifications on the Instagram app. Huh. One of his posts must have gone viral. Which one?

He tapped on the text first.

"GET YOUR ASS DOWN HERE NOW."

He sat up straight, heart slamming against his chest. *"What happened?"* he wrote back. Had someone gotten hurt?

"You screwed up. Big time. Get over here."

"Be there in 5." His thoughts raced. What had he messed up? Damn it.

Tuli bolted past a brow-raised Hunter, who held a sudsy sponge over the side panel of an engine.

"Where are you going, boss?"

"Mav needs help. Keep working on the equipment, and I'll be back in a flash. Call if anything comes up."

"Everything okay?"

"No idea."

Chapter Thirty-Two

Earlier that morning, Lou relaxed in bed, stretching until all the sore spots from the night with Tuli eased away. What a night.

Tuli. She smiled and traced her lips with her fingertips, remembering his hot kisses and so much more. She pressed her legs together.

It was like everything in the universe had come together perfectly.

She had gone from the devastation of her future dreams to the man of her dreams in mere weeks. *Her man*. It terrified her to let the thought see light, but Lou could picture Tuli as *the one*. Forever and always.

That was something she'd never truly considered calling anyone before.

Because no one had ever measured up to her childhood friend. Checking the clock again, she'd leaped out of bed. She needed to get to work. She set out food for Frost and cleaned the litter box. Then she rinsed off in the shower and threw on her navy EMS pants and button-down shirt, snagging a scone from the basket on the way out the door. She gave Frost a quick pet before hopping on one foot, then the other, to tie her work boots.

Coffee could wait. She had a hundred percent chance of getting Mav to take her to Three Bears. He was a sucker for a freshly brewed cup of coffee.

Her heart skipped a beat as she hurried down the metal stairs to her car. No, Tuli wouldn't be at the grocery store. True, he sometimes took a fire department call while working at the deli, but he'd mentioned they had some inventory or equipment duties, where he had to be at the station all day.

He got to hang out with his bestie, Hunter. Hopefully, those two were done hitting each other.

She finished her scone on the short drive to the hospital, pulled up to the building that was stationed across the parking lot from the hospital, got out of the car, and dashed in the door.

She checked her phone—7:01. Not bad.

"Hey, great. You're here." Mav walked toward her. "We just got a call."

"All right." She stowed her phone, grabbed the keys to the ambulance, and hopped into the driver's seat.

A TRIP TO the ER later, after transporting a man with chest pain, Lou and Mav had their nice fresh cups of coffee in Three Bears to-go cups. She pulled into the ambulance garage, parked, and lifted her cup out from the holder.

Her phone beeped.

Another text from Tuli.

Her cheeks heated up as she smiled.

"Huh." Mav threw her a wink before exiting the vehicle.

But he didn't say anything further. At least her partner knew how much she craved privacy. He wouldn't press unless she offered up information to share.

Another text popped up, then another.

She got out of the ambulance and shut the door but stood in the garage and checked the texts. What the heck?

One from Tuli. *"Hoping we can have another date like that soon. Minus the going out part."*

She laughed out loud and hit a heart response.

From Mom: *"Call me. Gordy's fine."* Okay, *phew*. She'd contact Mom in a minute.

From her friend who worked in food services at the hospital. *"GIRL, WHAT IS GOING ON?"*

"What?" Lou typed back.

"You're internet famous."

Her heart thudded. Her head spun. Sweat broke out on her forehead. What? How? Only people in Yukon Valley knew who she was. Heck, she had only created a social media account a year ago, just to follow along with Tuli's The Real Alaska page.

"??" she typed.

"Here." Her friend sent a link and Lou clicked on it.

Her face, sideways, eyes closed in sleep, filled the frame. The post read: "Relationship status: it's complicated. Can't wait for more mornings like this with my Louise. We'll work through life together, genetics and all." That picture must have been from this morning. Dimly, she acknowledged that she looked extra-kissed and well-loved in the photo. On one inappropriate level, a tingle from last night's passion shot through her. Yeah, it had been a good night.

But her picture? Online? She rocked back on her heels and checked the post statistics, hand pressed to her chest.

Oh God, there were thousands of likes and comments, with more popping up every few seconds. Her hands shook.

She couldn't breathe.

Mav's voice reached her, from a distance. He said something, but she couldn't understand him with the pulsing in her head.

When had she sat down on the cement? She patted the cold, dusty ground. Solid. Real. Her ears rang.

"Lou? Are you okay?" His big brotherly voice undid her. "Are you hurt?"

To her absolute horror, she burst into tears.

"Oh, wow. Uh, what can I do?"

"I d-don't know." She gestured weakly at the phone clutched in one hand.

"Did something happen? Did you get bad news? Is it Gordy?"

All she could do was shake her head and drop her forehead to her knees.

For a few minutes, he knelt and patted her awkwardly on the shoulder until she wrestled control over her emotions with sheer force of will. She never cried in front of anyone. Ever. Until right now.

She forced air in and out through her lips, gripping her work pants in her free hand. Over and over. Her thoughts raced one another for attention.

Her face was online.

Her face was *like that* online.

The mention of genetics.

Everyone in town followed Tuli's account.

Mom's text. Her parents. *Oh no.* They had seen it.

What had Tuli done?

What else had he posted?

If they got an EMS call right now, Lou didn't know if she could show her face outside of this garage. She couldn't do her job.

"You're kind of scaring me, buddy," Mav said, his boot making a dusty scuff on the concrete floor as he shifted position. "Want to talk about it?"

"Gordy's fine."

"Okay, that's a good start. Your parents?"

"Fine."

"So…"

Her heart was breaking. She had been so exposed last night with Tuli, so vulnerable. Beyond vulnerable. But she had trusted him.

Now, here she was, exposed in ways that brought up her past issues and rammed them down the throat of her present issues.

Rather than explaining it, she pulled up the post and handed the phone to Mav. Why not? Everyone else had seen it.

"What the hell?" He scrolled up and down. "This has to be a mistake."

"It's right there."

"Yeah. Damn it. Tuli, you idiot," he muttered to himself, pulling out his own phone and texting. "Hey, let's go into the work area. Take a break. Get something cool to drink."

"Sure. Sure." She let him pull her to stand, and she weakly brushed the dust off her butt before following him to the office/kitchenette/lounge/sleep area that the medics used when on shift.

Mav said nothing while he poured a glass of water and brought it over to her where she sat at the small table. He glanced at her, then exited, returning with a box of hospital-grade tissue.

She laughed, a high-pitched, inappropriate sound. She couldn't even score a name-brand tissue for this meltdown.

He sat across from her and waved for her to take a sip of water.

It tasted cool and wet and did nothing to relieve her humiliation and horror.

Mav had the most worried expression she'd ever seen on him.

For several minutes, they just sat there, with Lou picking at the scratches on the linoleum tabletop.

He occasionally checked his phone, then turned it back over with a huff.

More minutes went by.

A door slammed and footsteps grew louder. She looked up. Someone was running through the ambulance garage.

Bursting in the lounge door, Tuli yelled, "Lou!" making her jump.

Fresh tears burned.

Through blurry eyes, she spied him hovering in the entrance of the lounge. He gripped the doorjamb, balancing on his black work boots. His dark hair was wild, like he'd run his hands through it.

Like she had done last night.

Damn it.

She sniffled and glanced at Mav.

He rolled his lips and looked from Tuli to Lou. "It seems like maybe I should go check the truck. Um, unless you want me here for support? Or to perform some ass-kicking?"

"I'm fine." She waved her hand.

"Clearly." He stood and dropped his hand on her shoulder with a gentle squeeze. "Holler if you want me back, okay?" He glared at Tuli on the way to the garage.

"It's about the post, right?" Tuli slowly approached the table.

He'd better not touch her, or she would lose what little control she had over herself.

"Why?" she whispered.

"I didn't do it. I swear." He sat next to her at the table, one hand planted flat on the surface, the other one rolled into a fist on his knee. His forehead creased with pain and his eyes were filled with sadness.

She wanted to believe him.

He continued, "Never in a million years would I do something like that. I know how private you are." He reached out but stopped short of touching her. "The post is already deleted."

"How many screenshots are there of the post? Never mind. Just ... why?" she asked again.

"I promise you on my parents' graves that this wasn't me." He ran his hand through his hair. "Seriously, Lou, I must have been hacked."

"That's the weakest excuse I've heard in a long time." She took a sip of water and regretted it when her stomach churned. "You have security on your accounts and your phone. Or you should."

"I do—"

Like a dam burst, the words tumbled out. "I mean, the one thing I asked. No pictures. No social media. None of it." She gulped. "I hate it. People I don't even know are commenting. Critiquing me. The post even mentions genetics and all." She covered her face. "Oh my God."

"You have to believe me. Lou. I did not do this."

She smacked her hand on the table, startling herself. "Who else could have?"

"I don't know. Someone could have logged in or—" His brows rose, then slammed down in a thunderclap. "Hold on." He pulled his phone out and tapped on the screen, then swiped his finger up, scrolling.

"What?" she asked.

"I screenshot it."

"That's not any better—"

He briefly touched her hand with his fingertips. "In case I needed to evaluate the post later. The timestamp of the post was right after I texted you this morning." He paused. "No way."

"What is it?"

"Had to be him." He dropped one fist into the other hand. "Hunter did this." He half stood, then sat back down. "I'm going to kill him."

For a split second, she believed him. Or at least wanted to believe him.

But her own cousin wouldn't do this to her, would he? He was family. Her mouth went dry.

"I asked for you to do one thing," she said. "I know you love social media. But that was the condition."

"Lou—"

"You took a picture?"

"Damn it, Lou. This morning, waking up with you was the most amazing thing I've ever experienced in my entire life."

Every word kicked her in the chest.

He rushed ahead. "I saw you laying there. You were so damn beautiful. I wanted to remember that moment forever, and so I snapped a picture. For myself. Nothing racy at all. Only to remember. You. Us. How perfect it was. I'm so sorry. You have no idea how sorry I am that this happened." He swallowed. "I will do anything—anything—to fix this."

This was Tuli. Her friend for life. The guy who always had her back. The man she had—Lou gulped against a rock-hard lump in her throat. She scanned his devastated expression. His mouth hung open and his forehead was furrowed, like he was the one about to cry.

Right then, she knew.

He hadn't posted the picture. He wouldn't have. Not

even unintentionally.

But that didn't fix the other issues rising up right now. The questions rising from deep inside of her psyche and boiling to the surface. The things that had little to do with Tuli and all to do with Lou.

Nodding, she blew out a shaky lungful of air. "I believe you. I do."

"Thank God. Look, I'm going to figure out how to make this right, so we can move past this." He made to stand.

She reached out for his hand, stilling him, and shook her head. "It's not about the post, Tuli. This shook me down to my boots. I feel so exposed."

When she paused, he settled back in the chair and said, "I get it. You're a very private person."

"I didn't realize how private."

"Huh?"

"You have a good thing going with your page and all you're doing to help this community. You're … you. Open, friendly. I mean, you don't know a stranger. You're making a career out of this work. It's important."

His voice went still and low. "I don't like where you're going with this, Lou."

Hot, wet tears burned behind her eyelids, and she blinked hard, clenching her jaw until it ached. Once her eyes were dry again, she said, "I need to take a step back and make sure this is what I want."

"You mean *who* you want?"

Every second it took for her to answer him took a chunk out of her soul. Finally, she said, "I already worried that you'd be giving up too much to be with me. This might be a sign for us to reassess."

"You're breaking my heart, Lou." His eyes glistened.

She almost crumbled. Almost. She curled her hands into fists, letting the nail tips dig into her palms. Anything to center her pain anywhere else but her heart. "I don't want to hold you back. With your work or with your future."

"Oh no, Lou." His voice was a raw, torn sound. "Please don't do this."

She had to. She wouldn't hold him back or limit his future. His dreams. She couldn't do that to someone she loved.

Her heart cracked in two as she stared at the gape-mouthed, horrified expression on his handsome face.

She loved Tuli.

Always had.

And now she was going to set him free.

Chapter Thirty-Three

TULI WAVED OFF Mav as he staggered out of the ambulance garage, emerging from the darkness and blinking in the bright midday light.

Breathing hard, he bent over like he'd been punched.

He leaned against the corrugated exterior wall of the building.

Breakfast came right up on the asphalt.

He wheezed until his head and stomach calmed down.

He'd had the one thing he always had wanted in his life. Right there, in his hands.

All his.

Now?

Gone.

Fucking Hunter.

He stumbled to his truck, leg buckling under him on the last step, and he gripped the handle to remain upright.

Hunter. Why?

He and Lou were cousins. Family. Blood relatives.

Was the guy somehow jealous that her attention had been focused on Tuli, not Hunter? Still didn't make sense.

Besides, Tuli had won Lou fair and square.

Actually, she wasn't a prize to win. She made her own

choices, a fact that she had just demonstrated.

Turned out, Tuli hadn't won a damned thing, after all.

BACK AT THE fire station, Tuli burst through the door, stomping toward the lounge.

Empty.

He checked the bunk room.

Empty.

Walked around the trucks.

No sign of Hunter.

He looked out back. Hunter's car was gone.

Well. AWOL Hunter meant that Tuli had no crew for today. Hopefully, nothing would happen, because Tuli could barely function right now.

He could dismiss Hunter for abandoning his duties today.

Or he could be a decent boss and figure out first why Hunter had left. Make sure he didn't have an emergency.

At least until Tuli *gave* him an emergency.

A puff of air made a piece of paper wave on the kitchen counter. Tuli's name was on it. Reading, he gritted his teeth. Hunter had resigned due to *opportunities elsewhere* and *no confidence in his supervisor's fitness for duty*. He noted his lack of confidence in Tuli's ability to provide Hunter with a safe work environment, citing abandonment of his post as a reason.

Damn it.

This would end up in an uncomfortable discussion with the mayor.

Fitness for duty.

Abandonment of his post.

Which, fair enough, Tuli had abandoned his post temporarily. But he was the town fire chief who carried a pager and a damned cell phone. He hadn't gone far.

He was also a fire chief who wasn't functioning at one hundred percent, physically or emotionally.

Now he had no extra staff today, and he might be out of a job soon. Damn it.

Tuli reentered the lounge and dropped into the recliner, his body weighted like an entire burning house had crumbled down on top of him.

He pulled up The Real Alaska page again. Even though he'd taken the post down, several direct messages remained, congratulating him on the *hot babe* and *cute girl*. One poster, Angelfire, pointed out how Tuli could *do better* and provided examples as she offered herself up as an alternative.

THE NEXT WEEK was as hollow as Tuli's chest.

Meetings with the mayor.

No morning coffee at the deli.

No joint fire and medical calls.

No posts.

No Lou.

Even the skies remained gray and heavy.

Chapter Thirty-Four

THE LAST THING Tuli wanted to do the next Saturday was escort Grandma Ruth to Deirdre and Calvin's wedding. The city park pavilion, with the mountains behind it, made for a beautiful setting. Fall flowers and leaves highlighted the decorations in rust and gold colors. The late afternoon breeze was cool, but not chilly. Late September. No bugs. No rain. No snow. A perfect day.

Perfect for someone else.

He helped Grandma to her folding chair seat and glanced around, nodding and waving grimly at familiar faces.

Most of the men affiliated with the Koyukon village wore moose, deer, or caribou hide vests with intricate bead designs on the chest and back. Many vests had beaver fur trim. Tuli wore his best pale-tan leather vest with decorative fringe and a black button-down shirt beneath.

A few village women wore vests as well, but most had on the traditional kuspuk, with beautiful necklaces and earrings made out of colorful beads and elongated, smoothed bone. Several women also had feathers attached to their hair.

He recognized multiple staff from the hospital, some of whom were in traditional garb and others in business suits and pretty dresses.

The mix of colors and styles, all here together for a celebration, should have warmed Tuli's heart. This was everything Yukon Valley was about.

His gut clenched.

Several rows up, he caught sight of a woman with beautiful dark hair, pulled back on one side in a beaded clip. Lou. When she turned her face to the side, her cheek and profile made him want to reach out and stroke a finger over her soft skin.

To one side of her was her dad and then her mom. And Gordy. The guy was looking stylish today in his brown vest with beaded salmon designs on the upper back.

On the other side of Lou?

Goddamned Hunter.

The asshole glanced back, caught Tuli's eye, flashed a quick smile and a wink, then draped an arm over the back of Lou's chair. Tuli almost climbed several rows.

"Something wrong, honey?" Grandma tugged at Tuli's sleeve. She smoothed the hem of her special-event blue kuspuk with a butterfly pattern in the cloth. The trim had gold thread in it that picked up the light. The top of the slanted center pockets were finished with an embellishment that was unique to the local Koyukon village.

"I'm good," he replied, patting her hand as he settled in the chair.

He snapped a few pictures that he would de-identify and save for later to promote the town, then he turned off the volume on his phone.

The music started.

Dr. Garrett—Calvin—wore a smart black suit. He walked from the side of the gathering to stand at the front of the pavilion, joining the officiant. A DJ played light, classical music that Tuli associated with weddings. A minute later, Aggie and Bruce marched down the aisle, arm in arm, looking every bit the proud parents. She wore a pretty orange-and-gold dress. Bruce wore a suit that he tugged at as he walked with his wife.

There was a moment where no music played. Per the program, this was a time to remember Deirdre and Mav's parents. There were a few sniffles in the crowd. The Steens had made a long-lasting impact on the town, with their love for Deirdre and Mav.

Then the music started again, soft and rising. Murmurs and the shifting of seats built in anticipation.

Mav, in a black suit, appeared, arm in arm with Deirdre. Her flowy white dress moved in the light breeze, and her hair was pinned up with a few sprigs of delicate white flowers tucked into it. She carried a bouquet of colorful beaded flowers wrapped in decorated, tanned leather, courtesy of one of the village artisans.

Everyone stood. The whispered excitement created a swirl of happiness that flowed through the crowd, but only partially affected Tuli.

He wanted to ask Lou what she thought. Instead, he had to settle for agreeing with Grandma's comment that Deirdre was beautiful and Calvin was handsome.

Only, it wasn't their suit and dress that made them glow. It was the fact that they locked their gazes on one another and their smiles lit up the gathering. To them, the crowd didn't exist. Only the other mattered. This was the end of a lifelong journey for them.

This was also the beginning of a whole new journey together.

Tuli gripped his knee. He wanted that.

He'd almost had that.

Up at the front, Mav kissed his sister on the cheek, then joined Lee in the front row.

The rest of the ceremony was full of warmth and love and friendship. Everyone present had a smile on their face. This day would have been perfect for Tuli. Except …

A wave of need to have Lou in his own arms hit him like a boulder breaking loose from a mountaintop. He wanted to take her away from the crowd and beg for a second chance. He needed her like Calvin needed Deirdre.

Like salmon needed the river.

Like fire needed oxygen.

After the couple were pronounced husband and wife and everyone cheered, the members of the crowd, chattering, drifted to the nearby tent for food and more celebration. After a while, locals from the village brought out instruments, and soon the beats and jingles of traditional Koyukon music and singing blended with the conversations and laughter of everyone at the event.

This experience should have been rich. Enjoyable. Heck, Tuli wanted to be thrilled that two people in town found love and each other and would live the rest of their lives together.

Tuli only felt empty.

He was empty without Lou.

Every time he tried to get near her, it seemed like Hunter was hovering right at her elbow, or they were in a discussion with her dad.

It wasn't only jealousy that made Tuli grind his molars. Sure, that was a part of it. He wanted to be right next to her. But something else was going on with Hunter that had nothing to do with Tuli.

Hunter's return to town last fall, joining the community meetings to offer up his services for mineral resource management, and then quitting his job at the fire department so abruptly—none of it added up. Tuli's BS detector had been pinging off the wall.

If only he could figure out the guy's deal.

At the moment, Hunter was in an intense discussion with Lou's dad, who nodded several times and then waved over other elders.

Finally, after dinner, Tuli worked his way through the crowd to Lou. How had it only been a week earlier that she'd been in his arms, as they shared that perfect connection?

Right before everything had shattered.

"Hi, Lou," he said, stumbling as he approached her. Had nothing to do with his bum leg. It was the sight of a beautiful woman in a dark-maroon, floor-length dress. The color made her brown eyes glow. The top hugged her curves like he wanted to, and the neckline tempted him to stroke her smooth skin. His mouth went dry.

"Hi," she said softly. A flush pinkened her neck and

cheeks. Classic Lou.

"Would you like—"

"Care to dance, coz?" Hunter reached in and grasped her hand before waiting for an answer.

Her gaze darted from one man to the other. "Not right now."

Hunter tugged. "Of course now. What better time? We're family." His voice got louder.

Lou's neck worked as she swallowed and looked at the ground. She hated attention, and Tuli hated that Hunter was using that issue against her. "Sure," she said.

As much as Tuli wanted to intervene, that action would only create more drama. He stepped to the side.

With a backward smile and a wry lift of his shoulders, Hunter led her onto the small dance floor, joining Deirdre and Calvin as well as other couples. He made a show of carefully wrapping his arms around her and guiding her through some turns.

Tuli wanted to maim the guy.

"Tuli," Lou's father said politely. So politely.

"Sir."

"Hear you've been busy on social media."

"Someone has been."

He crossed his arms. "I don't follow."

"Lou must have told you. I didn't post that picture of her. Someone got into my page." He stared at Hunter, who slowly twirled with Lou. "Someone with access to my phone."

"You sure about that?"

"Bet on my Grandma's life."

"Huh." He frowned at Tuli. "You going to fix it?"

"The access? It's fixed." He stared at the man. "Thought you would be happy that I'm out of the picture."

The weight of Steve's stare felt like blocks of ice pushing Tuli down, down, down into the cold river. "I want my daughter happy and healthy. I want my family happy and healthy. I want my community happy and healthy."

The implication being Tuli had ruined all three.

Tuli looked over at a stiff Lou in Hunter's arms. Her mouth was pressed into a tense line. Hunter lifted his chin at someone on the periphery of the dance floor.

Then Hunter glanced over at Tuli.

And winked.

Community happy and healthy.

Tuli mulled those words over and over, rocks tumbling in a rushing flood.

Community healthy.

Community.

Tuli excused himself and stepped out of the tent into a dark, quiet area of the park, pulled out his phone, and started typing.

Chapter Thirty-Five

TOO EXPOSED.

Lou's skin twitched. She couldn't help but hear the whispers and sense the subtle pointing of friends, colleagues, and various aunties as Hunter glided with her around the dance floor. Sure, he was handsome in his brown leather vest and black shirt underneath, with bone and bead regalia in a thick choker around his neck. He loved the attention and made a big show of being her super nice cousin in public.

But she saw something different beneath his too-solicitous smile.

She hadn't been able to ask him about posting that picture. Couldn't speak the words. Why would he have done that?

He was Hunter. She'd grown up with him. She didn't choose her relatives.

For a very brief period, she had chosen Tuli.

Lou wasn't right for Tuli. Her chest ached. What she needed and what he needed and who he was, these were all very different things. Too different. Bridging them would be like walking across the flowing Yukon and expecting to reach the other side dry.

She lightly stepped on Hunter's toes and jumped. "Sorry."

He tightened up his hand, gripping her fingers. "Never a problem. Walk all over me anytime, coz." He laughed, too loudly.

Others around him looked up and joined in the chuckles.

She ducked her head, then let her brain whirl, trying to talk about something safe. "Glad no one got called out for an emergency today."

"Anyone going to have a medical emergency is here. No one's at their homes to set fire to stuff. We're good." He paused and gave her an almost-boyish smile. "Besides, I don't work for the fire department anymore."

"Why?"

"Problems with management." The words dropped like lead sinkers.

She pressed her lips together. He'd left. It didn't make sense. He had been on track to becoming a full-time firefighter. Nearly done with his probationary period.

There was no room in her heart for extra empathy or inquisitiveness today, so she went with another benign topic. "It was a beautiful day."

"Sure was. Maybe one day you'll have a wedding day like this." Why did his statement sound like a taunt, not a wish?

When she tugged her hand, he didn't let go. His other hand had locked around her waist. She was trapped in a smiling prison.

The wedding photographer appeared and snapped a picture.

She ducked her head, but it was too late.

"Why are you so shy? You're beautiful in pictures," he said.

These were the words she wanted to hear, but not from her cousin.

"Um, thank you." They danced for another minute until the music changed to an upbeat tune. "I'm going to sit with Gordy for a for a while."

The corners of his mouth dropped for a split second. "Sure. I'll join you soon."

It wasn't what she wanted, but Lou shrugged. Then she worked her way to their table and sat next to Gordy. "Doing okay, bud?"

Gordy grinned and looked at the half-eaten plate of food and the punch poured into his adaptive cup. "Love Lou Lou." The communication tablet company had rushed the repair and returned it yesterday. He had been typing away ever since then.

"You always know the right things to say." She shot him a smile.

Lou snagged the cloth napkin off the table and wiped a bit of food that had fallen onto his vest. Several guests came up and said hi to him. Gordy smiled each time and waved or fist-bumped. Folks knew to wait for him to type a reply, which warmed her heart. Gordy loved people. He loved the attention.

He also loved the extra snacks people brought over.

She had made an effort to avoid Tuli all evening. At some point, they would have to work together, and she would need to be professional. Tonight wasn't about being professional. She spied Deirdre and Calvin laughing with friends, even as they kept their arms around each other.

Tonight was the view of a future she would never have.

She patted her purse, with her cell phone in it. That picture Tuli had taken.

Her sigh caught in her chest. No more anger remained, only sadness. It wasn't that she didn't believe his excuse for why her picture got out into the world. She believed him. For real. He had always been careful to exclude her from posts and seek permission from others before uploading pictures.

But the more she thought about his social media livelihood and dreams, the more her chest ached. Yet another chasm between them.

Sure, Lou could ask him to change who he was. Ask him to stop doing the social media. Ask him to discard his dream of a family.

A sob lodged in her throat, and she patted Gordy's hand. Knowing Tuli, he'd do all of it and more.

She couldn't be that person who asked for him to change. He was her friend.

At the end of the day, she wanted him to have the life he had always hoped for, and on his terms. She wanted him to have choices.

With a sigh, she turned to her brother. Having a mostly one-sided conversation with Gordy, she chatted about the wedding and the people present. At one point, she whispered about one of the aunties' bobbing double chin, and Gordy barked out a laugh that turned multiple heads.

"Shh, you're going to get me in trouble. Again."

He laughed, utterly unrepentant. Then he accepted a plate of cookies when Lou's paramedic colleague Hilda stopped by.

Lou pointed at the plate. "You're going to be ninety percent dessert before the night's over. Good for you."

She scanned the crowd, briefly catching a glimpse of Tuli. Her breath caught. That was who she wanted to dance with, even after everything. Damn her illogical heart.

Tuli glanced at his phone, raised his brows, then stowed the device in a pocket before striding across the gathering to her. "Hiya, Gordy," he said, fist-bumping her brother, much to his glee. "Lou."

"You clean up well," she said. Just looking at him made her heart feel raw. Achy. Tired.

"We both do." The muscles on his throat worked. "You look beautiful." After a moment, he said in a low voice, "Is cleaning up the same as coming clean?"

Her heart thudded. "Can't say."

Pulling a chair up next to her he, said, "Lou, you know it wasn't me putting up that post."

"I believe you."

"It was Hunter. He got into my phone."

Prickles of irritation skated along the skin of her neck. On the one hand, she could picture exactly this scenario, and a week ago, she had wanted to believe Tuli. On the other hand … "It's clear you don't like my cousin. And I'm not in disagreement. But are you certain? Did he tell you?"

"He hasn't admitted the deed. But it's true."

"Maybe it was a mistake. You take pictures of people all the time, like here. Tonight. You could have posted the wrong thing."

He shook his head. "I post only with permission, or I edit the photos so it's about the scenery and the vibe and the people aren't identifiable."

"It's Yukon Valley. There's not a ton of us. People can figure out who's who."

"I know. Which is why—" He toyed with the white tablecloth. "Forget it. Listen, Lou. I want a second chance. I don't want you mad at me."

Her smile felt unnaturally tight on her face. "I'm not mad at you anymore, Tuli. Regardless of how that picture made it online, I forgive you. But that episode made it clear—we're two different people with two very different sets of goals and priorities in life."

"Seemed like we had the same priority several nights ago."

"That's unfair," she said, dropping her voice. She swallowed against a hard lump in her throat. She would do this for his own sake. His future. "We can continue being friends."

"I don't know if I can go back to how it was."

"Oh."

"I want more."

"You deserve more." She stared at the tablecloth. "That's why I can't be that person for you."

Chapter Thirty-Six

THE SUN HAD gone down, and the tent illumination threw everything outside into deep shadows. Which was exactly where Tuli was hanging out.

For a social guy, he couldn't handle all the laughter and celebration going on in front of him. The chatter and the probing questions from well-meaning people irritated him. It hurt to be this close to Lou, but so far away.

She hugged her brother and headed toward the punch bowl, chatting with friends and elders along the way. Stopping to hold a baby or bend to chat with a child.

Tuli considered—really considered—a future without a child.

A future where he didn't post on social media and connect with hundreds of thousands of fans.

A future where he wasn't the guy who helped put Yukon Valley on the map.

Then he considered a life without Lou in it.

Something shifted inside of him. Not being around her would be the greatest regret of all.

As he took a step toward her, his phone vibrated. He walked away from the gathering as he scrolled.

Damn. He ran through the inbox. A hundred thousand

followers had done their job.

Amplified his request. Reached millions of other people. His followers had Sherlock Holmesed the information.

Now, how to use the gift he had been given?

The answer appeared in the tent, right in front of him. Hunter's and Steve's heads were bent toward one another as they talked, Hunter gesturing with his hands. Whatever he was saying, Lou's dad was buying it, judging from his nods and smiles.

Lou joined them, and Hunter slung an arm around her shoulders. Tuli almost bolted right for the guy. Instead, he strolled toward them, remaining unseen in the shadows.

"We'll have the mine producing by next spring. The corporation and the town will retain all rights," he said. "Just subcontract me to coordinate the permitting and project management."

Steve asked, "Why should you be the one to do this?"

"I'm the perfect bridge. I'm from here, so everyone trusts me, but I also have connections outside of Alaska. I have the mine management training."

"Connections?" Lou asked.

Hunter kept his eyes on her father. "You all are about to have money flowing into this town like you've never seen before. We're all about to become very rich." He pulled out a paper. "With the help of my contacts."

"I need to talk with the committee," Steve said.

"You need to make this decision soon. The company I'm working with books projects years in advance. They're making an exception for you all, but the offer's only good until Monday. I've already put them off as long as I can. If you want this for Yukon Valley, you need to sign. I'll send the paperwork right over to my contacts."

Tuli strolled up. "I bet you do have some contacts."

Lou frowned and tried to move away from Hunter, but his grip tightened around her shoulders.

Tuli rolled his hand into a fist, ready to remove Hunter's arm permanently.

"Tulimak," Steve said.

"Sir."

"We're having a private conversation."

"At a public event." Tuli motioned around him.

Lou gasped.

Hunter glared at him.

"Also, my grandma is part of the committee, as well as a lot of other people here. Don't you think they should be involved in these … pressured negotiations?" He weighted the word with a splash of sarcasm.

Hunter rose to the bait, face reddening. "What's that supposed to mean?"

"For a guy who walked right into town, picked up a job with the fire department he never intended to keep, and then invited himself into the town subcommittee on managing the mining rights, your real goals seem to still be running under the radar. Wonder why that is?"

"What?" Hunter said.

"Tuli, this is not your concern." Steve said. "If you want to come with Ruth to the next meeting, you can bring your questions up then."

"Dad," Lou said, forehead furrowed.

"Oh, I have questions. That's for sure." Tuli turned to Hunter, walked forward a few steps so that he squeezed in between the guy and Lou, making Hunter drop his arm. She stepped away. Good. One problem down. "Ever since you returned to town, I thought your butt-kissing routine was a little too good to be true."

Several other guests milled around nearby, listening to what no longer seemed like a polite conversation.

Damn it, Tuli didn't want to ruin the wedding reception. But words needed to be said.

"So what? I'm a nice guy with skills I can provide to my community. To my *family*." Hunter grinned, but the smile stopped at his mouth.

It didn't escape Tuli's notice that Hunter's dad hadn't attended the wedding. "Only, you haven't been a part of this community for years. Why are you Team Yukon Valley now?"

"I don't have to answer any questions from someone like *you*," he growled.

Lou gasped. "Hunter. You don't have to be rude."

Hunter chopped his hand toward her. "To a guy who can't figure out how to keep his mouth shut, you bet I need to be rude at times. Maybe I came back to reconnect. Get back to my roots."

Tuli said, "You might not need to answer my questions, but you may want to answer the committee's questions—"

"Which I will do at any time."

"No better time than the present."

"Except for now. We have a contract to sign."

"So impatient. Huh." Tuli ignored his protests. "So, earlier this year a vein of gold and provable rare earth deposits were discovered on our village property and local citizens' property. Worth a ton of money. Life-changing money. Town-changing money. Village-changing money."

"We get the idea," Hunter interrupted.

Tuli eased off his right leg as he stood in front of them. "Then Randy Nelson came in and tried to access the minerals—basically attempted to yank it out from under the community. Actually, he'd been trying to get access for years by trying to purchase the Steens's property."

"I don't know anything about that," Hunter said. "Speculators were just doing their job."

"I know all about what happened last winter," Steve replied, a steely expression etched on his face. "We were lucky that the Steens's land didn't get stolen. That would have taken all the self-determination for stewardship and safety out of our hands. The income would have been stolen too."

Tuli dipped his chin. "Stolen. Exactly. The guy who wanted to steal it tried to hurt and threaten people in town to get his way." Tuli rubbed his leg.

Local law enforcement still didn't know who set up the sharpened branches that nearly killed him, but his betting money was that it involved land speculator Randy or his friends.

"When the Steen option got blocked, he even tried to access the minerals by going through Aggie and Bruce's property."

"About killed me too. Literally." Calvin appeared on the edge of the group, Deirdre next to him, and Aggie and Bruce hovering nearby.

"So?" Hunter said. "What's that have to do with me? Move along, man. I was making polite conversation here until you showed up."

"This continues to be a polite conversation. Very polite." Tuli cleared his throat. "So, you said *contacts*. Who are they?"

"I'm not revealing my sources to *you*."

"Then reveal them to me," Steve said.

"Not until we have a deal." Hunter pulled out the paper from his vest and held it out to Steve. Despite the cool autumn air, a few beads of sweat made his forehead shine.

"You don't have a contact. You have a business partner," Tuli said.

"Same thing."

"Oh, but it's not." He pulled out his phone and scrolled. "He's actually not a business partner. You are carrying out a mission *for your boss*."

Lou narrowed her gaze.

Steve crossed his arms over his chest.

"This you?" Tuli asked, pulling up a picture that a follower had DMed. The photo showed a younger Hunter standing in the shallows of a high mountain river with an older guy's arm slung around him. There were a few other men nearby, all in name-brand outdoor gear.

Hunter looked. "Sure. That was back when I was a fishing guide in the Cascades a few years ago. So what?"

"So, this is a fishing trip?" A fishing trip in more ways than one. Tuli's heart thudded as he pressed on.

"Must be."

"You remember this guy?"

"Not particularly."

"You sure about that?"

Hunter made a big show of raising his hands and being socially attacked. "Hey, what's with the twenty questions? This is pretty rude." He took the phone back and studied the picture, as if seeing it for the first time. Tuli would bet good money that was an act. "I guided trips all summer for a few years. Paid for college. I can't remember each of the clients."

Steve piped up. "All right. Enough. What's all this about, Tuli? You're making a scene."

Tuli glanced over at Calvin and Deirdre. "I'm sorry about doing this at your wedding reception. Truth is truth." He turned back to Hunter. "Because this isn't a client, is it? He's a mentor."

Hunter shook his head. "That's a stupid assumption from a picture."

"What about these other pictures?" He held up some more and swiped through them. "You, at the guy's house. You, having dinner with him and friends." He paused, then continued, "You, in a casual snap of the team, featured on this old speculator services website."

"Whoa," Deirdre said, glancing up at Calvin and then over to Mav. "That's compelling information."

"Let me ask again, Hunter. Who is this guy?" Tuli asked.

"That's on a need-to-know basis."

"Well, then. I believe we definitely *need to know*," Steve said. "Sooner rather than later."

Lou had eased toward Tuli. Good. Hunter wouldn't do anything in a crowd, but Tuli still wanted to make sure that Lou was safe and protected.

Most of the several hundred guests now gathered around. Nearly everyone here had a stake in the outcome of this discussion.

"Lou, I'm sorry," Tuli murmured. "I know you don't like scenes." He projected his voice. "Everyone, my apologies. I'm almost done, and then we can get back to this nice celebration." He held up the phone again and brandished it at Hunter. "Tell them, or I will."

Hunter's tan skin turned ashen. Sweat glistened on his forehead. "No idea."

"Last chance," Tuli said. "Who is that guy?"

No one made a sound.

Hunter's Adam's apple bobbed. He mumbled something.

"Sorry, didn't catch that." Tuli made a show of holding his hand to his ear.

"Screw you," Hunter spat. "Randy Nelson."

"And what is he to you?"

"You know."

Tuli batted his eyes at the guy. "I do not."

"My boss."

"And why did he send you here?"

"To get control of the mining rights." His shoulders slumped. "To ruin the town."

Someone gasped.

Hunter pointed. "And to destroy your life, Tuli."

"What?" Lou said, putting her hand on Tuli's arm.

"Yeah, for outing Randy's plans in public, getting him arrested, and costing him most of his savings."

Tuli's head spun. "Wait. This was for *me?*"

"In part. You pissed off a rich dude and made him a lot less rich. If you had kept your nose out of other people's business, it never would have gotten to this point." Hunter shook his head. "My job kept changing. When I first came back last year, I needed to work my way back into town. Then he needed me to step up and help gain access to the mine for his company."

Tuli raised a hand. "Hold up. Did you create the conditions for my snow machine accident last spring?"

"The one that nearly killed him," Mav growled nearby.

"I wouldn't do something like that. Anyone could have gotten hurt, not just you."

Tuli glared at the guy. "That's not a reassuring answer."

"It's the answer you'll get." His angry scowl softened as he looked at Lou, then back around the crowd gathered. "Damn it. I just wanted to be someone my family would be proud of. Someone successful."

Deirdre quipped, "Well, this is definitely the most successful disaster I've seen in a while. Mission accomplished."

Tuli smiled. Good job to her. This was her wedding, and Hunter's actions involved her property. She had every right to be pissed off.

"I still don't understand the rest of it," Tuli said.

Hunter crossed his arms over his chest. "Don't you get it? You ruined Randy's life and, by extension, mine. He wanted me to mess up anything good in your life. Including your relationships with folks in town." He glanced at Lou. "All relationships. Burn every bit of it to the ground." He faced Tuli. "I can't do this anymore." His face twisted. He took a long, hard breath. "Look, I'm sorry. I only wanted to make something of myself. Make my old man proud for once. Become part of a better core family than the one I had growing up. I wanted to be respected, like you were. Recognized for helping the community. I wanted people to think I was successful."

"Rising to success means nothing if it's on the backs of those you push down," Lou's quiet voice cut through the murmurs.

Hunter reared back like she'd slapped him.

"I think you're done here," Steve said.

Hunter turned on his heel, stormed through the crowd, and left.

Chapter Thirty-Seven

L OU PULLED UP to her apartment shortly after the mic drop to end all mic drops.

Her head spun.

To think everyone had believed Hunter's sincerity and that he wanted to help out the community. Dad had bought into the song and dance, even going so far as to encourage her to date Hunter's friend, Zach. Because, somehow, that was more reputable than the alternative.

To think she had given it even a thought.

Tuli had risked his reputation and livelihood to out Hunter's ulterior motives.

He'd leveraged his social media base. Risked his future growth.

Lou knew enough to understand how public opinion and popularity could swing.

Tuli had tried to protect her.

He had accepted her for who she was.

Now it was her turn to return the favor. She climbed the stairs to her apartment, closed the door, and toed off her heels.

Her heart pounded as she sat on her loveseat and picked up her phone, absently petting Frost and cringing as the cat deposited white hair on her dark dress. She opened the social media site she had signed up for. Her account had a generic, fake name and no picture or avatar. She'd created it months ago, mostly to follow along with what Tuli posted.

She scrolled through his pictures of beautiful interior Alaskan scenery, animals, and scenes from town. His pictures of locals brought out each person's inner beauty. She could tell that he made efforts to showcase each personality. His posts also highlighted the community. He had used his platform to help bring awareness to the area. Make things better.

Along the way, he had helped to right wrongs.

Tuli couldn't have foiled Hunter's plans if he hadn't had a public online presence.

Pieces slotted into place. *This* was his job. He was the person behind the account, but he wasn't the account. He only showed people who wanted to be visible. Everyone else? He protected their privacy. He showed the best of everyone. The best of the area.

The whole time, he had been the best of them all.

Sure, Lou had freaked out after her picture had been leaked online. An action that wasn't Tuli's doing.

He hadn't been the one to broadcast anything about their relationship.

Yukon Valley was a small town and a tight-knit community. Relationships came with risks and rewards out here. If she clung to total privacy, she might miss a chance at something amazing.

Did she deserve him?

She hadn't defended him.

But he'd come back to keep fighting for her.

She had revealed her future-altering genetic issue.

He had supported her.

Tuli wasn't Ryan, who had hurt her to the core.

Tuli wasn't her cousin, Hunter, who weaponized family ties.

He was Tuli. He was laughter. He was kisses. He was a joyful warrior. He was toughness in the face of injury.

He was the other half of her life.

For a moment there, he was her future.

Lou leaned back on the loveseat cushions, phone still in hand.

She clicked on the camera app and held the device out in front of her. Looking up into the camera, she tried to stuff every ounce of fear away and channel Tuli's bravery.

She pressed the button.

Scrolling through the burst of photos, she selected the best one. The picture showed her with a small, shy smile, looking toward the camera. Seemed about right.

Then she uploaded it to her account, updated her profile information with her name, wrote a post, and tagged @TheRealAlaska.

Then Lou hit SEND.

THE FIRM FOOTSTEPS on the metal stairs thirty minutes later sent her heart racing.

The knock on the door jolted her.

"Lou, are you in there?"

What was on the other side of that door would change her life, regardless of the outcome.

Slowly, like she was in a dream, she walked over and opened the apartment door.

Tuli's chest heaved, like he had run here. "Can I come in?" He was handsome in his beaded, pale-tan vest and long-sleeved black shirt.

Stepping to the side, she gestured him inside and shut the door, shooing Frost away.

He spun and faced her. "What did you do?"

Rocking back on her heels, she bumped the door as she lifted a hand. "About what?"

He held up his glowing phone. "This. What is this?"

Suddenly, she couldn't speak in front of him. Her shyness swamped her. "I-I ... yeah, maybe that was a bad idea. Making assumptions."

The corner of his mouth quirked up. "I want to know what you mean by it."

Wasn't it obvious? She took a big breath. "I jumped to conclusions earlier." She shook her head. "When that ... picture ... showed up online, all my past baggage showed up. Memories of my last relationship and how Ryan had publicized my personal information."

"I'm sorry that happened. I swear that I didn't—"

"I get it. Truly. I know that it wasn't you. There's nothing to forgive." She heaved in a deep breath.

"For real?"

"Yes. You're all over social media, but you're true blue when it comes to the people you care about. You protect the privacy of folks who don't want their info out there. I get it. I appreciate that you care about my privacy."

His brows drew together as he stood in front of her. "But just now you … put up a post?"

"I wanted to meet you where you were."

"Online?"

"You know what I mean."

He opened his mouth, paused, and asked, "Can we sit for a minute?"

When they walked to the loveseat, she noted his more pronounced limp. He really might have run here from the reception. What had that cost him? Was he injured? His leg okay?

She wanted to ask, but at his core, Tuli was a proud man who had weathered enough from life and from Lou's treatment. She had no right to ask him anything. He'd share about himself when he was ready.

He sat and faced her. "You didn't have to do that."

"The post? I did need to do it."

He frowned. "Why?"

"Partly to prove to myself that a little social exposure isn't going to kill me. Also, to prove to myself that you're not that guy." She took a shuddering breath. Took the leap. "I wanted to show you how I feel in a way that was meaningful to you." Was it too late? Could she still salvage what they had? He might not even want to try.

He gave her a sideways grin and rested his arm on the

back of the loveseat. "I mean, your picture you just now linked to my page got fifty thousand likes and shares in ten minutes and that's pretty impressive. It might be a record for The Real Alaska."

Oh. She took a deep breath and shoved down the raw, exposed feeling. That was a lot of people who had opinions about her. "Well, apparently I'm an influencer." She laughed.

He barked out a laugh. "Well, you certainly influence me, Lou."

"Hopefully, it's a thumbs-up?"

"Way up."

She rubbed her face and sobered. "I'm still not sure if this is fair to you, Tuli. In grade school, when we used to rope other kids into playing house with us, I always wanted to be a mother. You wanted to be a father."

"Yeah."

"I still want that. But I can't have it."

"I can't change the fact that my family background isn't something to be proud of."

"The way you overcame it is."

"Sure, but it's not the same as what you have." He ran a hand through his hair. "It's hard for me to believe that I'll be worthy of anyone. Of you."

"Tuli—"

He held up a hand. "Please hear me. If you worry about social exposure, then being with me means people may judge your choice. You have to know that."

"That's not fair to you."

"Fair got left behind when both of my parents died before I was five. Fair got left in the rearview for you when it was clear your older brother wouldn't have a normal life."

"About that. What if you don't want the future I'm offering?"

"How about you let me decide what I want?" He took her hands and leaned toward her. "Real talk, Lou. I loved playing house with you as a kid. I fantasized for years about being the father I never had. How much better I'd be as a husband. How I would never make the same mistakes he made. I wanted my own family, so that I could do it all better."

Her heart started to crack. "I understand."

"No, you don't. I still want that, but only with you."

"But we can't—"

He shook his head. "You're not hearing me. It's the *you* part that is the most important in this equation. All those years, as kids in school, playing house, my dreams? The most important part was *you*."

How could she be soaring and breaking into pieces at the same time? "What about my DNA?"

"I love whatever makes you who you are. I love that you're a great sister for Gordy. I love how you care for patients in the ambulance, and you're pushing through paramedic training to become even better. You're the truest person I know. Always have been." He took a shuddering breath. "You're it for me, Lou. I would do anything to have you in my life. I would love any child we had together, whether it was biological or adopted or"—Frost jumped up in his lap and Tuli petted him before setting him back down on the floor—"a fur-baby. I will take any of it. As long as it's with you."

"Tuli."

"I want you to be my family. For us to be a family. I want you to be my partner. It's you that I love, Lou. It's you that I want to protect. And I would never let my dreams hurt you—" He bit off the sentence and his Adam's apple bobbed. "Lou, please know that I could never do anything to hurt you." He glanced at his phone and hit a button. "I would rather injure myself than risk your happiness."

The phone screen went blank.

A fear started to grow in her. "What did you do?"

Chapter Thirty-Eight

T ULI TRIED TO ignore the sick feeling in his gut. This was the right decision, and he knew it. Still terrified him.

He'd rather be penniless and unknown with Lou than rich and famous without her at his side. He swallowed. "A while back, you said something that made a lot of sense. *People aren't content.*"

When she rubbed the back of his hand, the connection felt like heaven. He rested his free hand on top of hers.

"That was spoken out of fear and anger in the heat of the moment," she said.

"You're not wrong." Clearing his throat, he said, "You're not content. You're ... well, I don't know what you are, but I know what I want you to be."

"Which is?"

"Mine."

"Like a caveman?"

"Like a partner. Like a lover." He ran his hand up her arm and cupped her face. "Like forever."

Her eyes glinted with unshed tears. His arms burned with the need to pull her into an embrace and never let go. To be the guy she could open up to, cry in front of, express every feeling.

He continued, "It's not a one-way street, though. You are a part of the equation. If being with you means I have to respect your privacy and change how I operate, then so be it."

"What?"

"You're worth it."

"Worth what?"

"This." He showed her the phone. The social media app was up, his profile was selected, but it read, PROFILE NOT FOUND.

"Where did it go?"

His eyes shimmered. "I would do anything for you. I would burn my whole world down, Lou."

"Tuli? No." The impact of what he'd done knocked the air out of her.

"You're it for me, Lou. Nothing else matters."

Her mouth must have hit the floor. "Oh my gosh." She pointed. "That's your life. Your livelihood. Your future."

"I want you to be my life and my future. Anything else is secondary." His chest ached. "I know I come from nothing. My family was not a good one. I don't have a fancy degree or a high-paying job. But I want to be the man you can be proud of."

"You already are." A tear fell.

His chest caved in. He'd never seen her truly cry.

She sniffled. "I've been proud of you since we were in school together. I want you to have everything you want out of life."

"If you're in my life, then I have everything I need right here." He rubbed his thumb over the wet track on her cheek. "I love you, Lou."

The hard lump held back the words for a few seconds. She whispered, "I love you, Tuli. You're my person. Even back on the playground twenty years ago, I knew it, deep down."

"Sure you are okay with a guy who has a bum leg, a part-time deli job, an unlikely future as a firefighter, and now zero followers?"

"You have one follower."

She kissed him until he wished he could hit LIKE over and over again.

Epilogue

5 years later

L OU SMILED AS Tuli stood before a video crew in the town park overlooking the Yukon River on a sunny August afternoon. His handsome face beamed at the camera as he described the newest tourist activity available in Yukon Valley, a crafting retreat where tourists could stay in the Koyukon village and learn from local artists.

He completed the clip and stepped back.

"That should be good," he said to his crew. "Let's head over to the village and get some shots there. We can also use them for our Athabascan Alaska cultural tourism series."

The two-person crew agreed and started packing up their equipment.

"Hi, Lou. Did you get a nice nap?" he asked as he strolled over and gave her a kiss.

She had just finished several night shifts in a row, but had managed to get six hours of sleep this morning. As the town's newest paramedic, Lou still pulled the short straw when it came to which shifts she got assigned. Worth it. She loved using her extra education and new skills to help patients and train EMTs.

All that satisfaction had paled in comparison to when she

woke up and checked her phone an hour ago, though. She had actually jumped out of bed.

The news couldn't wait for Tuli to finish his work.

"How's the project?" she asked, heart pounding.

"Super. Looks like the Athabascan Corporation wants me to train people in other villages to promote their unique locations for tourism and business development as well."

"That's great!" She paused. "Are you going to have time?"

"Between working for Yukon Valley's Chamber of Commerce and the Koyukon village locally and adding the consulting work for the larger Athabascan region, no, I don't have time. I'm about to be very busy."

"Too busy for other things?"

He snagged her around the waist and dropped a quick, hot kiss on her lips. "Hey, Lou," he murmured. "That depends. What did you have in mind?"

Even now, the act made her neck and face heat up like an oven.

"I love making you blush," he said against her mouth.

"I love how you make me blush. But maybe not in public."

He waved his hand. "No witnesses nearby. I checked first."

Kissing him again, she smiled. "I love you."

Tuli pulled back and studied her for several seconds. "You've got a goofy expression on your face. What's going on?"

She swallowed. "Remember how we did all the paperwork and had a home study for adoption?"

"That was two years ago." His brows furrowed.

"There was a baby born in Allakaket. The father passed away last spring, and the mother has significant health issues herself, as well as three other children. She wants the baby adopted. She had hoped for the baby to be raised in Allakaket village, but they didn't have the resources. The Alaska Office of Child Services prioritizes placement with a native couple, and they passed along our information to the Allakaket court."

He gripped her upper arms. "And?"

"They approved us!"

Tuli's mouth dropped open, at a rare loss for words. He blinked and cleared his throat. "We're going to be parents?" His voice still came out hoarse.

"I know we worked on this a few years ago but then gave up." Her eyes stung. "Yes, we can adopt this baby. It would be an open adoption where the child knows their mother and family. But the baby would be our legal child. Are you okay moving forward?"

He whooped and picked her up, swinging her in a circle until her head spun. "Absolutely! When do we pick up our baby? What's the process? We need a car seat. And clothes. Diapers! Toys!" He kissed her full on the lips, then set her down. "I'm so happy for us!"

Her grin matched his. "Me too. Child services needs to do an updated home adoption study in the next week, and if that goes well, we can fly out to Allakaket to pick up our baby."

"Wait. Hold on."

Her heart sank. Maybe this wasn't the best time for him. With his new job and projects, he might not want this right now.

"What?" she asked. "Are you having second thoughts?"

"Huh? No way. This is great news. I just—"

"Yes?"

"Well. What are we having? Not that it matters. I am happy with any child that we are entrusted to raise."

"Oh! We're having a baby girl!"

"That's amazing." He hugged her again and pulled back, a smile plastered on his face. "This is the second happiest day of my entire life."

"Me too. I love you, Tuli."

"I love you, Lou. And I already love our family." His brows shot up as something dawned on him. "Of course, you and I were already a family, but now our family is growing!"

"It's not a done deal. Yet."

He looked around and grabbed at his hair. "Oh man. I want to tell everyone. How am I supposed to do my job while we wait for the visit and approval? I want to see her now!"

Lou laughed out loud. "Use those powers of privacy and discretion."

"You know I'm terrible at keeping secrets."

"You have to. Until we're certain."

His grin grew larger. "What if—and go with me on this one, Lou. What if we made it a surprise baby for our friends and family?"

"Like, keep it a secret until she's actually here, and then be like, 'Surprise'?" Lightness and joy lifted her up.

"Yeah."

"That's a great idea!" She threw her arms around him again.

He eased away from her and started pacing. "Okay. We'll have to work as a team. I need to convert my office to the baby's room. I have the crib in a box in storage, just need to assemble it." He paused and looked at her. "When the baby arrives, we're going to shower her with love."

"And presents. We need to go shopping."

"I can go to Fairbanks on my next day off and pick out a bunch of items."

"I'd like to shop too."

"Of course. Yes." He talked half to himself, ticking off items on his fingers. "Clothes. Diapers. Food." He looked up. "Caribou sausage or not quite yet?"

"Tuli! The baby isn't even a week old!"

"Fine, we'll wait a month." He paused. "Oh. I'm going to set up her first social media account."

"No way!"

He spun on his heel. "You actually believed me? Forget it. I'm protecting this kid's privacy with my life. No pictures of her face until she's old enough to manage her own account. Lots of safeguards and security." He gave her another hug. "Actually, no. I know what's out there. This kid is never getting on the internet. It's decided."

"You're hilarious!"

"Hey, have you told your parents and Gordy? He'll be

excited to hear he's becoming an uncle."

"I haven't told anyone else. You're the first to know."

Tuli puffed out his chest and took a few strutting steps from side to side. He froze. His eyes widened. "I'm going to be a dad?"

"Yep."

"You're going to be a mom?"

"Of course."

"Our dream, in school, so many years ago. Playing house. It's all coming true, isn't it?"

"All of it." She threw her arms around him, and they kissed in the late summer sunshine.

The whole dream had come true.

The End

Acknowledgements

Thank you to Athabascan experts for their insight and time. I always try my best to respectfully depict cultures that are not my own, but inadvertent misrepresentations may still occur. If that happened, I apologize. Those errors are mine alone.

To the entire team at Tule Publishing, thank you for believing in my Alaskan medical romance series and allowing me to share it with readers.

Portions of the subject matter in this book hit very close to home, making it one of the most challenging stories I've written. I am deeply appreciative of editor Julie Sturgeon for her unwavering support and flexibility, providing me the much-needed extra time to sit with this material so that I could nurture and develop it properly.

Gordy #1. For readers who may not be aware, let me share some background. I have had two Gordys in my life— my younger brothers, who both have significant developmental and medical issues. One brother recently passed away, due to complications from his condition. That difficult time informed some of the background of Gordy's character in this book, as well as Lou and Gordy's relationship. That said, it should go without saying that all of the depictions and characters in the Wright family are very much *fiction*.

Gordy #2. One of the towns I used to live in also had a Gordy. He was an amiable chap who had been dealt a difficult hand in life, but it never got him down. Every single day, he walked all over town, covering up to ten miles daily, stopping in stores on Main Street and chatting with locals and visitors alike. If it took him longer to think through the answer to a question or if he got confused at times, no one minded a bit because his big smile and welcoming attitude made talking with him a pleasure. He was known as the town's ambassador. Everyone recognized him, dressed as he was in his worn tennis shoes, weather-appropriate attire, and—as always—his high-visibility orange vest.

All of these Gordys have taught me important lessons. First of all, they showed that each person has value simply by being kind, being who they are, and doing what they can to get through life. Secondly, each Gordy has made it clear that there are lessons in humanity that certain people are especially qualified to teach. And lastly, they taught me that joy and kindness might be free, but they are still gifts. Best we appreciate those gifts and share them with others.

Author Notes

The Athabascan population includes multiple tribes living in the bulk of Alaska's interior and western Canada. Traditionally, their rich culture is kin-based, with semi-nomadic hunting groups. Community is foundational to all Athabascans; however, group-specific language variations and customs have developed over time. My word choices correlate most closely with the Koyukon group, located roughly where I envisioned the fictional town of Yukon Valley.

I learned that the Athabascan culture is also linguistically (due to migration thousands of years ago) related to another group of indigenous peoples. If you're curious about that connection, this Southern Athabascan group includes Navajo, Plains Apache, Western Apache, Chiricahua, Mescalero, Jicarilla, and Lipan populations.

More information regarding Athabascan language and culture can be found in the Alaska Native Language Center through the University of Fairbanks. https://www.uaf.edu/anlc.

One of the many interesting and fun aspects of Athabascan culture was learning about the kuspuk, a traditional garment. These functional and colorful clothes are worn by

Alaskan Native women. According to several experts, it is a source of indigenous pride and cultural respect when non-Native people choose to wear kuspuks. So much so, that during Native American Heritage Month every November, folks throughout Alaska and western Canada participate in #WearItWednesday. Here's a nice article on Alaskan culture that goes into more detail on the kuspuk. https://athabas canwoman.com/?p=3356

The Yukon Valley Salmon Festival was, of course, made up. But there are several Salmon Days and Salmon Festivals to be found in Alaska and the Pacific Northwest. As expected, the celebration dates coincide with the timing of each area's predominant species salmon runs. When we talk about authors taking artistic license and using their imagination, here's my confession: I am a vegetarian! So, if the meat-based recipes I described sound strange, well, that's on me. My research (and creativity) had to do a lot of heavy lifting to come up with those scenes!

Thank you for reading my medical romance series. I hope you enjoyed these stories! If you could take a moment to post a review on the retailer's site or a review site like Goodreads, BookBub, or StoryGraph, that would mean the world to me. Those reviews are so important in helping readers discover authors.

Lastly, I would love for you to virtually hang out with me. If you want all the insider scoop about my doctoring world or writing world, including upcoming appearances, I hope you will sign up for my newsletter HERE.

www.jilliandavid.net/newsletter-signup.html

If you enjoyed *Paging Dr. Breakup*,
you'll love the other books in the…

The Yukon Valley, Alaska Series

Book 1: *Dr. Alaska*

Book 2: *Paging Dr. Breakup*

Book 3: *Five Alarm Love*

Available now at your favorite online retailer!

About the Author

Award-winning and bestselling author Jillian David quickly writes then slowly edits medical romance, paranormal romance, and romantic suspense books. She loves to use medical situations and characters to drive drama in her books. Her favorite cell is the platelet and her least-favorite organ is the pancreas. She fully believes that curse words, when appropriately deployed during surgery, are hemostatic. Which also explains why no book of hers will ever bleed out…

Thank you for reading

Five Alarm Love

If you enjoyed this book, you can find more from all our great authors at TulePublishing.com, or from your favorite online retailer.

TULE